THE GREAT SEATTLE EARTHQUAKE

THOMAS P. HOPP

THE GREAT SEATTLE EARTHQUAKE
Book Two of the NORTHWEST TALES series

ISBN: 9781093530476

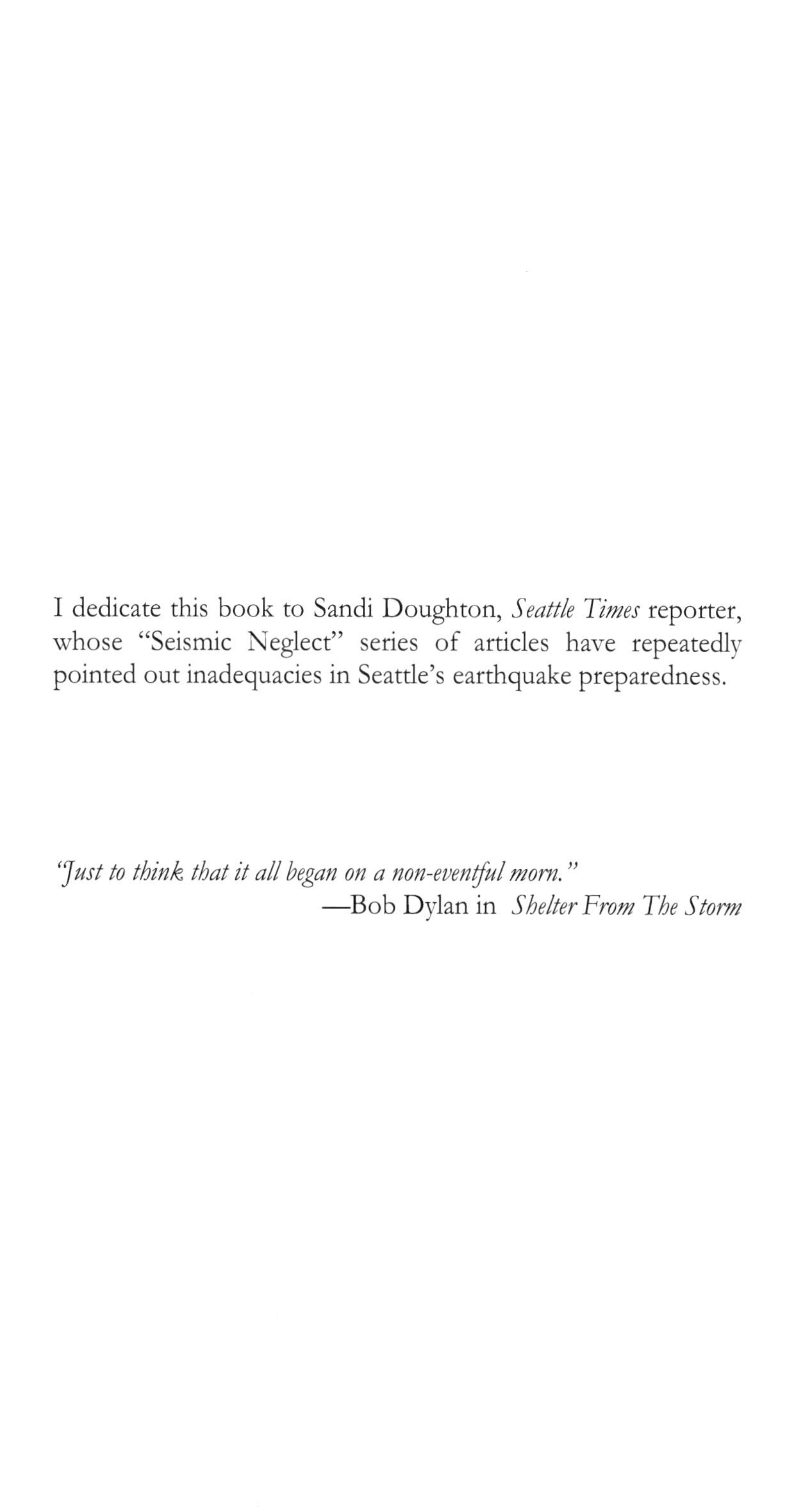

I dedicate this book to Sandi Doughton, *Seattle Times* reporter, whose "Seismic Neglect" series of articles have repeatedly pointed out inadequacies in Seattle's earthquake preparedness.

"Just to think that it all began on a non-eventful morn."

—Bob Dylan in *Shelter From The Storm*

Praise for Thomas P. Hopp's Writing

"Solid science and pacing that never quits."

—Kay Kenyon, Philip K. Dick Award nominated author of *Maximum Ice*

"A gripping mix of science and Native American culture. Compelling."

—Curt Colbert, Shamus Award nominated author and editor of *Seattle Noir*

"Thomas P. Hopp's expertise in Seattle's tectonics and cultural history infuse his new thriller, THE GREAT SEATTLE EARTHQUAKE, *with non-stop action reminiscent of Michael Crichton at his best, and characters as compelling as those found in a John le Carré novel. Fast paced, tense and surprisingly humorous, I couldn't put it down."*

—Dr. Pamela Goodfellow, author, editor

"One shock leads to another."

—Carmel Valley News

SEATTLE AREA MAPS

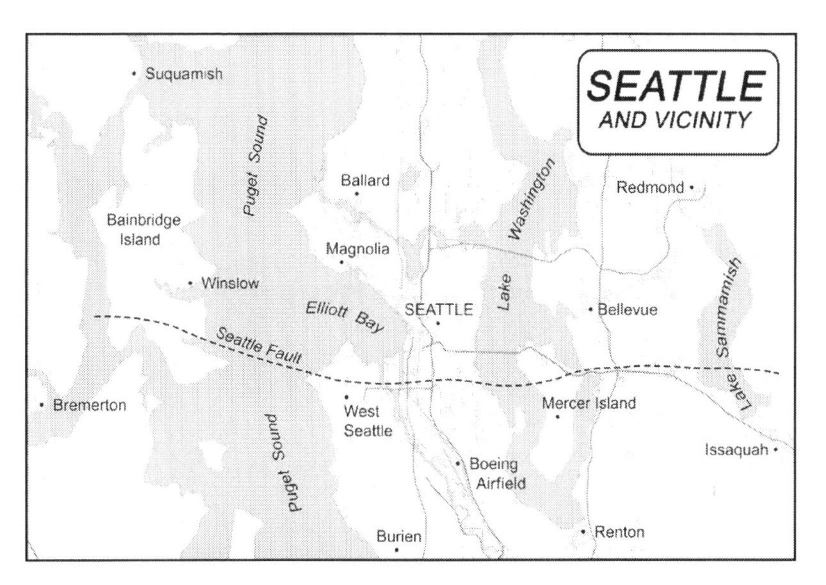

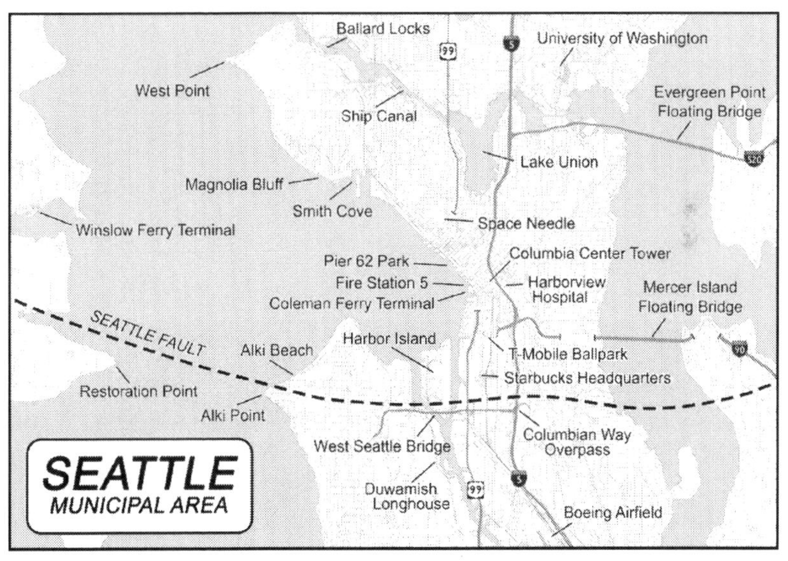

PART ONE: FORESHOCKS

Chapter 1

In April 2015, Grace Toscano, a 16-year-old high school student, was experiencing the greatest adventure of her life. An exchange student program had taken her from Tillamook, Oregon to Kathmandu, Nepal, where she was participating in a medical assistant program, helping doctors dispensing medicines and carrying out procedures in one of the poorest parts of the city.

On the morning of the twenty-fifth, she took some time off for sightseeing. With her guides Sanjeev and Puja, she left the Hotel Lion for a walking tour of the old city, a place of narrow cobblestone streets, overhanging brick buildings strung with clotheslines, and endless crowds of people. Many of the women were dressed in colorful saris and some men wore traditional tunics and baggy suruwal pants, although as many were dressed in Western attire. Poor, barefoot kids scampered through the crowds or played ballgames on street corners.

On their way to visit a Buddhist temple, the three paused in a square to watch women drawing water from a trickling fountain. A sudden shudder passed underfoot, eliciting shouts and screams from the crowd in the square. An instant later, the earth pitched madly upward and sideways, throwing Grace and her guides to the ground. Most of the crowd fell too, their screams melding with new and horrifying sounds—the shattering of window glass, the clatter of bricks tumbling from buildings, and the subterranean rumble of an earthquake.

As she and her companions struggled to their feet on heaving ground, horrors confronted Grace on all sides. The façade of an older four-story building tore away and dropped a thunderous cascade of masonry onto the people below, crushing and burying them in seconds. On the other side of the square a five-story building buckled and collapsed on itself, crushing everything and everyone inside.

Down both side streets, similar scenes of death and destruction were obscured by vast gray billows of dust, though the screams of injured and panic-stricken people rivaled the roar of the quake. Grace and Puja clutched each other and screamed repeatedly, united by mutual terror, while Sanjeev stood by, his mouth agape in shock.

Then, almost as suddenly as it had come, the earthquake subsided. Its noise died down to a murmur and the screams quieted as everyone caught their collective breath.

"Oh my gosh!" Puja cried in her deeply accented English. "Are you all right, Grace?"

"Yeah, I'm okay." Grace realized she was clutching Puja in a vise-like embrace and let her go. The three huddled silently for a moment, gazing at a cityscape transformed. Brick rubble was piled on the pavement several feet deep in places. Dangerous-looking black tangles of power and TV cables snaked through the rubble. Building fronts were cracked, crumbled, or fully collapsed. Dust thickened the air, stinging nostrils and blotting out the view of anything beyond the nearest buildings—or what was left of them.

As the last noises of the quake faded, stunned people began moving amid the ruins. Some tottered slowly, in shock. Others raced one way or another on urgent quests to get help or seek loved ones. Many were bloodied. Some hobbled on injured or broken legs. Others lay motionless, their bodies twisted and their limbs intermingled with fallen brickwork. Grace gasped and gasped again, taking it in with her heart pounding like it might burst.

A white sacred cow appeared, its halter woven with flowers and its forehead running with blood. Lowing in pain and favoring an injured foreleg, it limped around a corner and vanished into the dusty pall.

Grace, Puja, and Sanjeev stared at one another, uncertain what to do, until a nearby sound caught their attention.

"Madat!" A young man called for help in an agonized voice. "Madat!" He lay on his back on the pavement in front of what had been a spice market, his lower body buried by several feet of brick rubble. The three hurried to him and were quickly flanked by several men who began frantically tossing bricks aside in an effort to free him. Grace thought he looked about the same age as her. His large dark eyes peered at her pleadingly under a brow wrinkled with pain.

"Madat!" he moaned as the men bent to their task. The pile of rubble was prodigious and as the rescuers—now including Sanjeev—threw bricks away, more bricks tumbled into the gap they made in the pile.

"Madat!" The strength drained from the youth's voice.

"He may have internal injuries," Sanjeev said as he continued removing bricks.

"Madat," the youth's voice faded to a feeble exhalation. As the men finished pulling bricks off his feet, his plea faded away completely. "Mad-da..."

"No!" Grace shouted. Seeing his lips turning blue, she forced herself between the men and knelt to put an index finger on his carotid pulse point. She felt nothing. She put her lips near his, to sense the faintest exhalation. There was none. Acting on instinct and training she had received at the hospital, she started CPR while the men stepped back to watch.

She placed the heels of her hands on the boy's chest and gave several dozen sharp compressions, then she tilted his head back and gave him two mouth-to-mouth breaths of air. She repeated the sequence of compressions and breaths several times, and then checked his pulse and breathing. Still nothing. She went on for many minutes with her own heart pounding and tears streaking her dusty cheeks. The men stepped in again and pulled the youth out onto open pavement. Grace followed and hurriedly resumed the resuscitation.

After a few more minutes without effect, Sanjeev gently touched her shoulder. "You should stop."

"No!" she cried between breaths to the victim's mouth. "I won't stop."

"He is gone," Puja said.

"No he's not!" She kept at it until Sanjeev and Puja pulled her away and lifted her to her feet. "No!" she shouted again, looking down at the youth's face with tears blurring her vision. The face no longer showed pain. Instead, it was fixed in death, eyes staring blankly, jaw open and slack, skin as pale as milk. "No-o-o-o!" Grace screamed, letting her own agony out.

Puja put her arms around Grace and held her close. Then, with Sanjeev's assistance, she guided her away toward the hotel, as the would-be rescuers left the body where it lay and hurried off to help others.

Now, five years later, Grace was on another adventurous journey, and its many wonders and sheer beauty had helped her leave those painful memories behind. She was one of four people in an SUV moving westbound across Lake Washington on the I-90 floating bridge.

"Seattle, dead ahead!" Earl Adams III called out as he piloted his sleek BMW X5 through light traffic. He and his passengers were enjoying views of glittering skyscrapers ahead and rugged mountains to the east and west.

"It's a perfect day for sightseeing," Carrie Parsons rejoiced, sitting beside Earl in the front passenger seat. "Sunny. Just a few white clouds. And—Oh! My! God! Look at that!" She pointed across the shimmering lake waters.

"Mount Rainier!" Grace exclaimed from her place in the back seat as she took in the sight of the great rounded mountain, still snow-capped in late summer. "Isn't that it, Matt?"

"That's Rainier all right." Matt Balen was seated behind Earl. "You're lucky to get such a good view. Lots of times, she's got her head in the clouds."

"You would know," Earl said. "You're the Seattle native. We're all East Coasters."

"No, we're not," Carrie corrected him. "Grace is from Tillamook."

"What I meant was, we're all Yale students." Earl sounded slightly miffed. "And Matt is a Stanford—"

"Dropout," Matt concluded.

"Who knows everything there is to know about every place we've been since we picked him up in Yellowstone Park," Carrie interjected with a note of defensiveness on Matt's behalf. "Every town, every river—"

"Every star in the night sky," Grace added dreamily.

"And Mount Rainier looks just like you described it," Carrie said to him. "Gorgeous. Don't you agree, Grace?"

"Yeah." Grace wasn't only gazing at Rainier but at Matt too. Carrie's word choice struck her as a fair assessment of the man as well as the mountain. A lanky fellow with long dark hair pulled back man-bun style, his handsome bearded face rivaled the splendor of Rainier. "Beautiful!" she murmured as she watched him watch the mountain.

"Too bad we'll be losing our guide in a few minutes," Earl interjected with what Grace thought was a less-than-sincere tone. "GPS says two miles to West Seattle and that's where you get off, Matt." This wasn't the first time Grace had noted a hint of disdain for their hitchhiking acquaintance from Earl.

There was a lull in the conversation as they finished crossing the mile-long span, ample time to gaze at Rainier's imposing white form gliding along the horizon. Carrie turned and lightly tapped Matt on a knee. "We're going to miss having you around. I wish you could stick with us and show us your home town."

"We've been over this before." Earl's tone was acerbic. "Rooms at the Four Seasons are all taken. We're lucky we made reservations months ago. Otherwise, we wouldn't have a booking there, let alone a suite with a separate room for Grace. Are you suggesting Grace and Matt should double up?"

Carrie clucked her tongue. "Earl! Cut it out!"

There was another long silence in which Grace felt herself blushing and Matt avoided eye contact by staring steadfastly at Mount Rainier. Seeing this, Carrie changed the subject.

"You know, Matt, it's been more than a week and I hardly know anything about you. Tell us at least a little something to remember you by."

"There's nothing much to tell." He stared hard at the mountain.

"Oh, come on, now. Are you hiding a dark secret? Tell us about your parents. We're taking you to their house, right?"

"I don't want to talk about them." Matt focused on the mountain until the SUV entered a tunnel on the Seattle side of the lake.

"Please," Carrie needled. "There has to be something you can tell us about yourself. Everybody's got a story."

"Well, I don't."

"Why not?"

"Never mind."

Grace had heard this one-sided conversation several times and had even tried to engage Matt herself once or twice. She sighed, allowing a melancholy smile. It seemed her encounter with this intriguing man would end in a few minutes when he was dropped off at home.

On the city side of the tunnel, traffic thickened. Earl said, "Okay, Matt. Give me some directions. Which lane do I get in to take you to West Seattle?"

Grace and her two friends were on a pre-senior-year vacation tour that had started in the Northeast and would make a counterclockwise circuit of the United States. The three travelers had met Matt on a ranger-guided walk-and-talk about the volcanic landscape of Yellowstone. Grace had been impressed that he seemed to already know every fact the ranger shared. Furthermore, he had made the tour more interesting by asking questions about calderas, hydrothermal vents, fissures, and fumaroles that livened the discussion and offered insights to the group of several dozen tourists.

The trio had happened to meet him again the next day on a boardwalk that meandered among boiling fountains in Norris Geyser Basin. They had learned he was camped near their hotel, and for several days he had become their personal guide to the wonders of the park. He had excelled in describing the ways of wildlife, the behavior of geysers, and even the volcanic heat sources that lay beneath their feet.

Several years older than Grace, Matt seemed quiet by disposition, but any question about nature or wildlife tapped within him an extroverted wisdom that seemed beyond his years and education. When the time came for the travelers to continue their continent-spanning tour, Carrie had casually asked if he'd like a lift back to Seattle. Worry lines had furrowed his forehead for a moment, but then he'd said, "Sure. Why not?" The next morning he had loaded his backpack in the rear of the SUV, and they were on their way.

In conversations on the long drive, Matt had learned that Earl was the son of a wealthy Yale-educated lawyer and businessman, and that he intended to follow in his father's footsteps. Carrie, he learned, was the daughter of a New York City stockbroker with ambitions to go into politics. Grace had explained that she was a dairyman's daughter who had managed to win a Medical Sciences scholarship to Yale. Earl and Carrie had confided that they planned to marry after graduation. The four of them had discussed shared interests in hiking, kayaking, and mountain climbing.

But every time the conversation turned to Matt's past, the others had learned nothing. That mystery remained firmly guarded, although most everything else about the man was an open book.

A mile north of the travelers, in an office at the University of Washington's Geophysics Department, Professor Ronald Rutledge was revising a manuscript on his desktop computer. Titled, "Interconnectedness of Earthquake Faults in the Puget Sound Basin," the paper described findings he and his colleagues had recently uncovered regarding the system of faults underlying Seattle and Puget Sound.

While editing the manuscript, he had drifted into a reminiscence of his personal earthquake experience decades earlier. In 1965, he had been an eighth-grader at James Madison Middle School, which sat directly on the Seattle Fault. When an earthquake of magnitude 6.5 stuck, he had managed to come out unscathed while other students were seriously injured and several people in the Seattle area were killed. That brush with disaster had inspired him to study geology in college and go on to earn a PhD in geophysics. His job now was managing the

Pacific Northwest Seismic Network, which monitored that very same Seattle Fault, among others.

"Professor Rutledge?" Ron's reminiscence was interrupted by his graduate student, Lori McMillan, who stood in the hallway outside his office door. "I think you should come see this."

He shook off chill memories of screaming classmates, violently pitching floors, and tumbling brickwork, and glanced up at her. "What is it, Lori? Another local quake?"

"Yep. Under Bainbridge Island."

"Let's have a look." Rutledge rose from his desk and followed Lori down the hall to the Seismology Lab. There, she and postdoc Kyle Stevens had been watching a wall-spanning bank of video monitor screens showing traces of seismic activity in the region.

"That was a pretty good jolt," Kyle said by way of greeting.

"Or, a pretty bad one," Lori said as the three of them looked over scribbled traces on the monitors.

"You're right, Lori." Kyle smirked. "Good, if you want to study seismic events, hella bad if you're afraid The Big One is about to hit."

Lori looked concerned. "The Big One isn't about to hit, is it?"

Kyle shrugged.

Rutledge eyed the monitors with a thoughtful scowl.

The laboratory of the Pacific Northwest Seismic Network was on the ground floor of the Geophysics Building on the University of Washington campus. It was a large room filled with multiple desks and wide-screen computers used by staff to create maps and models of earthquake shaking forces. On one side of the room a floor-to-ceiling wooden cabinet housed a dozen wide video monitors showing real-time seismometer data from around the region.

The seismographic traces looked like row upon row of shaky horizontal black lines, drawn from left to right and top to bottom on white screens. They were the computerized equivalents of the old-style technique of wrapping sheets of white paper around slowly rotating drums and tracing lines with black-ink needles that laid down jittery squiggles with every vibration of the earth. Each of the eight monitors showed jiggles here and there, where the seismometer stations that were the sources of their data had detected small vibrations scattered around the Northwest.

Even in times with no significant earth movements, these horizontal traces recorded little bursts of vertical scribbles several times an hour, registering relatively insignificant events or perhaps the passing of a heavy truck or train. Normally, such minor tremors, which might read out as 1.0 or less on the 10-point Moment Magnitude Scale, were of little interest.

Today was different. The two young researchers had spotted a pattern playing out on the screens. One monitor in particular, the one whose screen code, BABE EHZ UW, indicated its source was a seismic station across Puget Sound on Bainbridge Island, showed four much larger scribbles laid down in the last several hours. Although the amplitude of these shakes was nowhere near the size that would record a major earthquake, it was the nearness of the tremors to each other in time that was attention-getting.

"What magnitude is the latest one?" Rutledge asked.

"The computers are still crunching the numbers," Kyle said. "But the previous three have all been right around 2.0."

The Bainbridge Island trace had scarcely settled down when it registered another spasm of scribbled spikes and valleys.

"Wow!" Kyle's mouth hung open. "That's the fifth quake in two hours! We've got a quake storm going on for sure."

"I can't believe I'm getting to see a quake storm so soon," Lori told Rutledge as he continued to scowl at the screen. "You just lectured about these last week. There goes another!"

Kyle glanced at a wall clock. "Six quakes in two hours and… three minutes. Totally a major storm."

Rutledge nodded. "Add that to three other storms we've had in the past month, and we've got a really significant phenomenon going on—maybe even a full-blown slow-slip event."

"Slow-slip? What's that?" Lori asked.

"Something you'll get in next week's lectures. It's the idea that lots of little quakes allow the fault to move smoothly without a major event."

"And that's a good thing, right?"

"Possibly, but there are two things that can happen next. The little quakes may let off underground pressure, avoiding a major quake. Or, they may transfer pressure from one fault and build it up in another."

"And that means The Big One might come sooner, not later," Kyle said.

Lori shuddered involuntarily. "Couldn't they… just stop?"

"Good question." Rutledge thought a moment. "Quake storms do tend to come and go. But when the storms reach a fever pitch, then the likelihood of a major earthquake goes way up."

"There goes another spike!" Kyle pointed at the Bainbridge monitor. "Seven of 'em now, now. This is epic!"

"Have you pinpointed exactly where they're coming from?"

"I've got the mainframe crunching seismometer data and triangulating the location." He indicated several other monitor screens. "We're picking up decent signals in Tacoma, on Whidbey Island—"

"But they're all later and smaller than the Bainbridge signal," Lori said. "So, the source has got to be pretty close to Bainbridge Island."

"Good eye," Rutledge said. "Once Kyle's calculations are done, I'm sure it will be darned close. Maybe on the west end of the Seattle Fault."

"The Seattle Fault?" Lori said. "But that's practically right under us! Now you're scaring me."

"I'm scaring myself."

On the opposite side of Seattle from the seismology lab, Alki Beach was a two-mile-long arc of sand stretching from Alki Point in the west to the north tip of the West Seattle Peninsula. The center of the arc was flat and ideal for sunbathing, volleyball, swimming, or picnicking on takeout food from restaurants along the landward side of Alki Avenue. On this warm Indian summer morning, the beach had yet to accumulate many strollers, waders, dog-walkers, or joggers.

North of the volleyball courts, the beach had been disrupted dramatically. A roughly circular depression about twenty feet wide and six feet deep had been shoveled out and marked off with yellow warning tape. On hands and knees inside the excavation were two archaeologists, Professor Leon Curtis of the University of Washington and his coworker and doctoral trainee, Ann Butterfield. They worked carefully with hand-trowels and soft brushes to remove sand from ancient objects that had lured them from the corridors of academia to the sunny beach.

Until a few days ago, Ann's PhD thesis studies had involved little more than library research. But the discovery of this place had given her the opportunity to expand her skills in archeological field work. A tall, thin young woman, Ann was dressed in a white cotton blouse, blue shorts, and hiking boots. A straw sun hat shaded her lightly freckled face.

The pair had excavated much of a huge cedar log that had lain under the sand for centuries. A ten-foot length had been exposed, although the log likely continued much farther under the sand. Blackened by wood rot and punky, it bore markings diagnostic of an upright post from a Native American long-house. Totemic faces were carved around its circumference—although on the upper surface they had been partially eroded by pile worms. The bottom surface that had been buried more deeply in sand was preserved in better detail.

As intriguing as the house post was, Leon and Ann were busy uncovering what lay just beneath it: a set of human bones, stained orange by organic material seeping from the log.

"The more we uncover," Curtis said as he removed small bits of sand from the skull, "the more certain I am that something tragic happened here."

"You think the house post fell on him?" Ann asked.

"It seems likely."

"There's one thing I don't understand. Why didn't his

people pull him out and give him a decent burial?"

"That's a mystery." Leon, a big, tawny-bearded, bearlike man wearing khaki shirt and shorts and canvas hat, sat back on his haunches and stared at the skull through his wire-rimmed glasses. "I wish you could tell us what happened," he murmured.

A tall thin man in an olive-green field coat and safari hat crossed the tape line and sat down on the slope of the dig. "Good morning," he said.

Leon greeted the newcomer with a smile. "Peyton McKean! Glad to see you could make it. Your bosses at ImCo gave you some time off, did they?"

"Nope. I'm playing hooky."

Leon laughed, and then made introductions. "Ann Butterfield, meet Dr. Peyton McKean, a molecular biologist with Immune Corporation, Seattle's biggest genetic engineering company."

"Nice to meet you." Ann rose briefly to shake his hand.

"So, what have we got here?" McKean surveyed the site.

"I think we're inside a collapsed portion of a longhouse," Leon explained. "Looks like a house post fell on this man and crushed his chest."

"Man," McKean keyed on Leon's word choice. "You've already figured out this skeleton has a Y chromosome—without a DNA test?"

"There are other ways to tell a skeleton's gender," Ann remarked. "We think it's a man based on the relatively narrow pelvis compared to what we'd expect for a woman."

"Yes, of course, but you'll allow me to confirm your gender diagnosis with a genetic test?"

"That's why we called you here," Leon said. "To confirm his gender and his Native American origins—and to get us a tribal affiliation."

"Native-American-or-not will be easy. As to tribal affiliation, the genetic databases on Native DNA are still pretty limited. But I'll do what I can."

"Notice anything interesting about the skull?" Ann challenged McKean.

"Answer: yes. It's peculiarly shaped. A very flat forehead. I suppose that could be deformation due to the weight of sand covering him. He's at least two meters below the surface of the beach."

"*Could* be the weight of sand. But I suspect there's another reason. He might be royalty."

"Ah. Yes." McKean eyed the skull carefully. "Compressed and flattened frontal bone. The children of chiefs and other high-ranking natives had cedar planks bound to their foreheads as infants, which flattened the cranium in front and heightened it behind."

"Not a bad guess, for a molecular biologist." Ann smiled.

"Guess?" McKean paused to mull the concept.

"Even Chief Seattle had a flattened forehead," she said, "according to some old reports and a few surviving photos."

McKean leaned near and pondered the skull. "His high status couldn't save him when his house collapsed."

"We've been puzzling over why no one pulled him out and buried him according to tribal practices," Leon said.

"And—?"

"No answers yet. The custom was to put the body in a dugout canoe and leave it on an elevated platform on a mortuary island, so birds could pick the bones clean. But this is just... wrong." Leon continued his careful scraping. "We'll keep digging. Maybe we'll turn up a clue. Or maybe you will, Peyton. Did you bring your test kit?"

"Two of them," McKean patted two bulging pockets of his field coat. "One kit for C-14 analysis on that log, and one kit for DNA analysis on a chip of bone. We can certainly narrow down his date of death and his race, if not his social status."

"Do you think you can get a reliable carbon-14 date from that wood? It's been in the ground a long time."

"Centuries, from the looks of it."

"Or millennia."

McKean took a freezer bag from one pocket of his coat. It contained a collection of gadgets and a pair of blue plastic examination gloves, which he put on, and knelt near Leon. He pushed an index finger into the surface of the log, squeezing moisture from its spongy matrix. "I've never heard any mention of a village on this beach," he murmured as he closely inspected the log.

"You're right," said Ann. "There are no published accounts of anyone living here before the pioneers arrived."

"Ann would know that fact, if anyone would," Leon told McKean. "She's been sorting through every anthropological and historical archive she can find, preparing her PhD thesis on Salish Indian oral traditions."

McKean stood up to gain perspective on the site and the beach around it. "The elevation seems significant. The old ground level where the skeleton lies, is much deeper than the current sand surface."

"Right again," said Leon. "It's just shy of two meters lower, according to our surveys."

"That's one mystery we're trying to solve," Ann added. "High tides here rise above the old ground level. Of course, the tribe would never have built below high-tide level, or they'd have been swimming to and from their beds. So, one possibility is that this house existed in a time long before the global sea-level rose due to polar ice melting at the end of the last Ice Age. The entire ocean was several meters lower, then."

McKean cocked an eyebrow. "That suggests this site could be several thousand years old, at least."

"That's what we've been thinking," Leon agreed. "If Puget Sound was lower when this house was inhabited, then we've got a truly ancient site here. Maybe the oldest on the continent!"

"That might explain the lack of Native traditions telling of a village here," Ann suggested.

"I see," said McKean. "You think it may have been abandoned so long ago that memory of the village has entirely faded from Duwamish tribal lore?"

"Exactly. And that lore goes back several thousand years, at least."

"Anyway, Peyton," said Leon. "You're just the man to give us some answers. You and your DNA and carbon-14 tests.

Where would you like to take your samples?"

"For the house-post sample, the deeper the better. I want to avoid contamination by carbon from modern microbes rotting the wood."

"I hope you won't need to harm the carvings," Ann said.

"Answer: no. I won't have to do that. Here's a spot where someone has accidentally dug into the side of the log with a shovel." He glanced meaningfully at her.

"That's not our doing. We've been super careful every step of the way, but the teenagers who first dug up the log weren't. They were digging a huge pit for 'mega-bonfire,' as they put it. When they hit the buried log, they thought they would add it to the fire, until they spotted the carvings. Then they called the police."

"And the cops called the Duwamish Tribe," Leon said, "when they realized the importance of what was here. And the tribe called me. Now I've called you, Peyton."

"All very logical." McKean took a large pair of forceps from his bag, and a purple-capped plastic test tube, which he unscrewed with the fingers and thumb of one hand. "This shovel scrape will allow me to get beneath the rot and into solid wood." He gingerly reached the tips of the forceps into the gash, tugged, and drew out at a tan-colored stick of harder wood. "That nice tawny color says this wood has not been subjected to rot." He dropped the piece into the tube, resealed the cap, put the tube back in the plastic bag, and stowed it all his coat pocket. Then he pulled the second kit bag out of his other pocket and repeated the process to take a small bone chip from one of the skeleton's crushed ribs.

"There!" he said when he finished stowing the second kit and removed his blue gloves. "We'll have a genetic test and C-14 date accurate to plus-minus fifty years."

"How long until we see the results?" Leon asked.

"A day or two. Maybe a few days longer if the testing facilities are tied up with other projects."

"We'll be waiting on pins and needles," Ann said.

"Sounds painful," McKean remarked absentmindedly.

"Slivers of wood and bone?"

His task finished, McKean moved along the length of the house post, inspecting the sculpted faces. "Look at the fine preservation of details!"

"Those sculptures will all crack and dry if we don't get preservative on them—" Leon stopped in mid-sentence when a strong tremor shook the ground. The earth motion subsided as quickly as it came, but not before all three scientists were on their feet, glancing around in surprise.

Ann's cheeks flushed a bright pink. "Was that an earthquake?"

"Not a big one, thankfully," said McKean.

"It felt pretty strong to me!"

Up and down the beach, people had stopped in their tracks and were glancing concernedly in every direction. However, nothing seemed amiss. The waters of Puget Sound were placid, and the Olympic Mountains loomed serenely in the distance.

"Over almost before it began," Leon said.

Chapter 2

The same temblor that jostled the archeologists was felt, seconds later, two miles away in downtown Seattle. Skyscrapers rattled from base to tip, especially Seattle's tallest building, the Columbia Center Tower. There, the shaking was amplified by the building's 76-story height. In the exclusive top-story restaurant, the Columbia Tower Club, well-dressed women screamed, and well-heeled men cried out as tables rattled across the polished hardwood floors.

Nevertheless, no noticeable damage was done to the grand glass-enclosed spaces. Despite a seasick rocking motion that persisted for nearly a minute, conversations in the restaurant returned to normal as the swaying subsided. The tower's designers had made their tall edifice as earthquake-resistant as possible, producing a steel-and-glass structure of three units, each with an outward-opening C-shaped cross section. The lower two interlocked with and supported the uppermost to a height that could penetrate cloud layers drifting over Seattle. On this fine cloudless day however, the diners had been gazing at horizons nearly a hundred miles distant when the shaking started.

Although no building in Washington state stood taller than the Columbia Center Tower, that was about to change. Two blocks to the southwest, in a building that was tall but whose top stories were still under construction, two men stood on a mid-level floor that was made of bare concrete and steel. They paused, lost for words, as streamers of dust filtered down from the unfinished ceiling.

"This is exactly what I'm here about," building inspector Daniel Federly said. "Earthquakes, and this building's earthquake reinforcement—or the lack of it."

"Lack?" the other man, Eldon Devine, sounded annoyed.

"You just saw how well it took that shake."

Eldon Devine was among the world's richest and most powerful men, heir to a real estate fortune and a billionaire many times over. Although the building had yet to attain its full height, Devine often came to stand on its dusty concrete floors and stare out from its windowless steel-girder-framed walls. He and Federly had been doing this when the quake struck. Now he turned to look Federly squarely in the eyes.

"Who sent you here to pay me this unexpected—and unwanted—visit?"

"I'm here at the request of the City Council."

"You mean, that witch Mariah Rey, don't you?"

The two men were a study in contrasts. Federly was dressed in slacks and shirtsleeves and wore a yellow hardhat. He was of medium height and solidly built. He had a pleasant face, although today his brows were furrowed, and his eyes squinted with an inner sense of strife. Devine's habitually downturned mouth—the product of years of sneering at subordinates—was accentuated by deep creases running from the sides of his nose to his jawline. His designer charcoal pinstripe suit scarcely disguised his slumping shoulders and protruding belly.

"Grand view isn't it?" He turned from Federly and opened his arms as if to embrace the whole of Puget Sound and the Olympic Mountains—and to deflect the conversation the inspector was intent on having. "I always take the best for my share." Devine wore a broad self-congratulatory smirk that repelled Federly. "They say it's a view to kill or die for." A gust of wind lifted his combed-over hair, exposing white roots. He smoothed it back in place with thick fingers.

"It's a grand view, all right," Federly admitted.

Devine pointed overhead. "The top ten floors aren't even built yet. My penthouse office will have unobstructed views in every direction. When I build a tower—and I have twenty-five Emerald Towers in cities around the world—I make damn sure it looks down on everything else in town. This one will be eighty-one stories tall when it's done."

"I'm aware of that, and your reputation for the grandiose."

"Grandiose? Grandiose? What's that supposed to mean? That I'm a show-off? An egotist? That's fine with me. People can think whatever they want, as long as they look up to me and say, 'Yessir, Mr. Devine.' That's one reason my towers are covered in emeralds—well, chrome-green glass, but don't tell the peasantry that." He chuckled at his own little joke.

Federly folded his arms across his chest. He let out a long low exhale and paused to cool his temper while watching a ferry approach Colman Dock. The huge boat looked like a toy from this perspective. He turned and started the conversation he had come to have with Devine. "I was talking with Deb Garland yesterday, the city's Director of Emergency Preparedness."

"Another one of my favorite people," Devine muttered.

"Her office is only a couple of blocks from here."

"Is it?" Devine made a point of sounding disinterested.

"Yes. Well, Deb and Mariah Rey have both expressed some concerns about this building."

"Have they?" Devine said this with even less interest. He yawned without covering his mouth.

"Yes, they have. And to be frank, Mr. Devine, they have watched this building go up and are aware of certain things."

"Things?" Devine huffed. "Things like what?"

"They say it looks like you have nowhere near enough X-shaped cross-braces to protect against side-to-side shaking in an earthquake."

"Phoo! Side-to-side? This building is all about up!"

"I can see that. But I also see what they're talking about. They think you may have multiple violations of earthquake codes."

Devine's face reddened. "Well, why don't you tell them they can mind their own business?"

"Well sir, you see, that *is* their business. And mine."

"The plans for this building passed every kind of review with flying colors."

"I wouldn't know about that, but I can see with my own eyes. Furthermore, I have been reading the serial numbers on some of your steel beams and girders."

"So?"

"So, I think maybe they are not what they're supposed to be."

"How's that?"

"They are of a lower grade of steel, or too lightweight, or both. I won't be sure until I get to my main computer and run the numbers."

"If you find anything amiss, talk to me first."

"I don't think so."

"This structure's plans," Devine growled, "passed earthquake preparedness review twice."

"If you say so…"

"I do say so. A person only has to know the right people and have the means to convince them." He smiled smugly.

Federly returned Devine's smirk with a scowl. "Bribe them? Is that what you mean?"

"I didn't say that. There are other ways of making people see things your way. Soft spots. Mistakes they've made in their past."

"Blackmail?"

"I didn't say that."

"Then how?"

Devine smiled vindictively. "By whatever means suit me and my legal people at the time."

Federly caught himself clenching his teeth. "There's nothing you can do to keep me from reporting any violations I see to the proper authorities."

Devine broke into a pugnacious grin. "You go ahead and do that. Then we'll see whose side the proper authorities are on. Meanwhile," he turned from Federly and looked out the window opening, "in a very short time, this will be the tallest building in Seattle. Columbia Center will forever be second-best. They'll be looking up at me, and I'll be looking down on them."

"Forgive me for saying this, Madam Governor, but this has to be the umpteenth earthquake preparedness report commissioned by a governor of this state." *Seattle Times* reporter Laura

Stern lay the thick document on the fine cherry-wood desk between them. "I've read it cover-to-cover, like most of the others. What I want to know is, will you take action this time on some of the outstanding issues?"

Governor Sheila Long paused thoughtfully before answering. She glanced around at the old oil paintings and portraits covering the wood-paneled walls of her office as though she were trying to think of some way of sidestepping the question.

"We've made great progress in retrofitting major bridges and freeways, as well as many of the old brick school buildings. And we've bankrolled low-cost loans for owners of old buildings to bring them up to compliance with the guidelines. Over seventy percent of older brick buildings within the City of Seattle are now reinforced with steel cross-braces."

"I know. I've been following those programs for years with great satisfaction."

"Yes, I can imagine so, given that your 'Seismic Neglect' articles are what brought the need to the public eye."

"But I'm here today specifically to discuss skyscrapers."

"Yes, I know that."

"More specifically, Devine's Emerald Tower."

"I know that too."

"My sources tell me the earthquake preparedness design for that tower is inadequate."

"I've heard that as well."

"There are allegations of—if not outright bribery—then favors done or promised by Devine to certain members of the Urban Planning Commission."

"I've heard the allegations, but I've never seen proof."

"And you don't yourself have any knowledge of improprieties?"

"If I did, the persons involved would already be under investigation or in jail. You're not suggesting I'm party to any—"

"I know your reputation for personal integrity, Madam Governor, and I have no reason to doubt it. Please consider these questions just a part of my effort to dig for the truth—"

"I understand."

"—and a duty I bear as a reporter committed to public safety and the public interest."

"I understand that as well."

"So why, then, have certain city engineers who will go nameless, and certain individuals with the Fire Department, informed me that the design and construction of Devine's Emerald Tower do not seem to remotely meet our current codes?"

The Governor hesitated a long time before answering. "I'm no expert on building design. So I have to rely on others to tell me whether a particular building is up to codes."

"And are you satisfied Devine's tower is up to codes?"

"That's what my experts tell me."

"Do you believe them?"

"I have no reason not to."

"Have you gone there yourself and looked the building over during construction?"

"I'm very busy."

"Yes. Of course." Laura paused thoughtfully. "So, do you trust your advisors to be scrupulous and honest in this matter?"

"I think so. What else can I do?"

"Perhaps we could turn to the specific question of the height of Devine's Emerald Tower. It's about to set a record for the region. Isn't that a problem right there? I mean, how tall is too tall in a seismically active town like Seattle?"

The Governor shrugged. "You tell me."

"I can't. But there has got to be a limit. Otherwise, I can imagine a scenario where a quake makes the tallest building topple into the next building, and then another and another until the whole city falls down like a line of dominoes."

"Thanks for the nightmare scenario, Laura," the Governor said uncomfortably. "I'm going to lose some sleep over that one, let me assure you."

"Nothing about the current situation assures me of anything. Why not put an upper limit on building height in the center of downtown?"

"We have people actively pursuing this, but there is no precedent for how-tall-is-too-tall. At the same time, there has been vehement resistance among real estate developers to any limits at all."

"Developers like Eldon Devine?"

"Eldon Devine and quite a few others."

"I've been told Devine's eighty-one stories are a violation of even the current building codes."

"He got a variance."

"How did he do that?"

"I'm still trying to figure that one out."

"Can't you firm up the rules and enforce them?"

"Some in the State Legislature say our rules are too strict already. It's a free country. And lately, as you know, the U.S. government has been dead set against regulating much of anything."

"But what's right is right, Madam Governor. I have repeatedly published warnings about the potential for hundreds of thousands of casualties. Don't you care?"

Governor Long sighed wearily. "Oh, yes I do care, very much. But caring is one thing, and enforcement is another. There are powerful forces working against me on this. Very well-financed forces."

"Forces that could keep you from getting re-elected?"

"If I'm not re-elected, then I can't try to make the situation better, can I? And, in case you hadn't noticed, wealthy people and corporations rule American politics these days. I have to be pragmatic, or they'll have one of their hand-picked men sitting in this office next term."

"I suppose you're right. But meanwhile, it seems like a new and taller building springs up in Seattle every few months. Then they fill up with apartment tenants or thousands of workers. Doesn't your conscience bother you about that?"

"It does very much. If I could overcome the powers that be and put things right, I would do so in a heartbeat. However, the grim reality is that rich financiers want tall buildings on their downtown properties."

"Rich like Eldon Devine?"

The Governor took a deep breath. "Don't get me started on

him. Not only does he have the deep pockets to thwart any regulation we try to throw at him, but he's prone to suing those who get in his way."

"I heard via the grapevine that he threatened to sue both the city and the state if he didn't get his building approved. Is that true?"

"It is."

"So, when the day comes that a big quake strikes, how are you going to feel?"

"I will feel terrible if there is any loss of innocent life."

"And about the capitalists who thwarted you?"

"Off the record?"

"Okay. Off the record."

"I'll hope they burn in hell."

Peyton McKean lingered at Alki Beach, chatting with the two archeologists as they worked.

"I've been thinking," Ann Butterfield said as she removed sand from the wrist bones of the skeleton. "Maybe the reason no one buried this man is that there was no one around to do it. What if the longhouse was flattened by a tidal wave? The rest of the tribe might have been drowned or driven from the area. Tsunamis aren't unheard of around here."

"Like the sunken campsite uncovered at West Point in Discovery Park in 1992," said Leon Curtis. "It's pretty clear that was the result of a tsunami."

"So, not only was this man crushed," McKean observed, "but he was immediately buried in washed-up sand."

"Exactly," Ann replied.

"Sounds like the work of A'yahos." A gravelly voice suddenly joined the conversation, startling the three scientists.

"Ah-Yah Who?" Leon looked up at an old, weathered, Native American man who peered down at him across the warning tape.

"A'yahos," the old one repeated. "The earthquake serpent spirit."

Another Native American man stood just beyond the old

man, smiling at his remark and their reaction to it. His grin widened when he got a look at one particular person in the excavation. “Peyton McKean! What are *you* doing here?”

McKean smiled in recognition. “It’s been a long time, Franky Squalco.”

“Yeah. I haven’t seen you since our days in art class at West Seattle High School. Remember that? Maybe twenty years ago? What you been doing all that time?”

“PhD in biochemistry. Medical research. How about you?”

“Fishin’.”

“For a living, you mean?”

“Yeah. Gill nets on the Duwamish River. It’s not much of a living when the salmon aren’t running. But I get by.”

“It’s good to see you again, after so long.”

“Good to see you too. You always were the smart one. What business you got with these bone diggers?”

“DNA testing and carbon dating on our friend here.” He gestured at the skeleton.

“Probably an ancestor of mine,” Squalco said.

“Would you be willing to give me a DNA sample, so I can cross-check? I’d love to—”

“No, I wouldn’t. White man’s already taken enough from my people. You don’t need our genes, too.” He said this congenially, but there was a hint of an edge on his voice.

While they chatted, the old man circled the dig, moving slowly with the aid of a tall walking staff carved with totem animals. He stopped on the other side of the log from where Leon and Ann were cleaning the forearm. “See! That’s A’yahos, right there.” The skeleton’s hips and legs had been uncovered and were lying across a large, rectangular, blackened cedar plank, three feet wide by six feet long. On its surface was an ornate totemic carving of a snake with heads at both ends. Between the heads, a serpentine body rippled the length of the plank like a series of waves.

“He slithers this way”—the old man made wave-like motions with his free hand—“then he slithers that way.” He made a wave motion in the other direction. "Like the tide running in and out of the Duwamish River channel. Or, like it used to, before pahstuds came and straightened the river out."

The old man's piercing dark eyes, deeply lined, brown-skinned face, wild head of coarse gray-black hair, and sparse scraggly beard seemed to place him in another era—an older, more primitive time. His attire was peculiar too. Worn blue jeans and an orange plaid flannel shirt were nothing special, but his shoulders were covered by a cape of woven cedar-bark fibers with woven animal silhouettes on it. Nothing at all covered his feet, which were thick, brown, and weathered, as was the hand that clasped the carved walking stick.

Ann stood and looked at the serpent carved on the plank. "I've read about A'yahos. What else do you know about him?"

"He was one of my family's totem animals, a long time ago. My grandfather taught me about him. In my family tradition he's got two heads so's he can see whichever way he's going."

Leon stood, as well. He eyed the man for a long moment while Ann spoke with him. "Do I know you?" he asked. "You're not one of the Duwamish tribal folks I usually work with."

"I'm not part of the tribe, officially. Leastways not any one tribe. I've got Muckleshoot, Duwamish, Suquamish, and a couple other tribes in me," he chuckled. "Name's Henry George." He smiled, revealing a tooth missing up front. "I'd shake your hand, but it's too hard to climb down in that sand pit."

"If you're not a member of the Duwamish Tribe, then you're not allowed down here anyway."

"Suits me fine. Only having a look-see. I wouldn't know which tribe to enroll in anyways. But I've got ancestors from around here just the same."

Leon knelt to continue his work.

"So, tell us some more about A'yahos," Ann asked.

"Sure." George squatted in the sand on the edge of the pit. "When he wasn't mad, he was like a peaceful tide, winding in and out of the river channel. But when you got him riled up, watch out. He could slither right into the ground and make the land shake, you know? He could make earthquakes. Made the land ripple just like his body." George made his slithering hand gesture again. "After that he'd make the tide go out all at once. Then he'd bring it back in as a tidal wave. Seems to me, that's what happened here."

"Seems that way to us, too," Ann replied. "But it's nice to have it confirmed by someone with knowledge of tribal lore."

"He's full of it," Squalco interjected. Then he laughed at his own gaff. "I mean, tribal lore. I'm taking him to Suquamish." He pointed across the Sound. "We just stopped by on our way over there. He'll be an honored elder in this year's Paddle to Seattle. He's gonna speak and drum and sing tonight for the young people who'll paddle their canoes across to Seattle tomorrow for the Salmon Homecoming ceremony."

"That's right," George said. "Salmon runs is always bigger when you sing them a welcome-home song. Then the nets get really full and everybody eats well."

Chapter 3

Sixty miles away to the Northwest, in their home west of the town of Port Angeles on the Olympic Peninsula, the Hewitt family sat around their kitchen table. Breakfast was later than usual because a faculty day had excused the kids from school.

Ten-year-old Emily, the eldest of the two Hewitt daughters, spoke up peevishly. "I wish you didn't have to fly tomorrow, Mom."

"Sorry." Jane Hewitt paused with her last bite of omelet on her fork. "But you'll have plenty to do with Daddy at the beach in West Seattle. Then you can watch me fly my helicopter over the Seattle Mariners' baseball game at T-Mobile Park. We're doing a Coast Guard preparedness demonstration for The Big One."

"I wish we were going to the game instead," eight-year-old Caylie complained.

The Hewitts' Victorian three-story house was set near the top of a bluff overlooking the Strait of Juan de Fuca. Ryan Hewitt glanced out the bay window of the kitchen nook, taking in the miles-long sweep of the Strait and the mountains of Vancouver Island across the twelve-mile wide waterway. It was a grand view, but he wasn't neglecting the conversation. He turned to his daughters with an enthusiastic smile. "Come on, girls. We'll have fun! I know a place where there are dozens of tide pools filled with little sea creatures. Hermit crabs, little shrimps, sea anemones—all kinds of things to see while we're waiting for Mommy's fly-over."

Emily was unpersuaded. "I'd rather be at the game and watch Mom fly over."

"I'm sorry, honey, but I already told you why not. The Mariners will go to the playoffs if they win one of their next two games, so the stadium is sold out. We couldn't get tickets if we tried."

Caylie sighed. "I like when we all go to the game. And I 'specially like riding to my seat on my Daddy's shoulders."

"Sorry, Sugar Plum." He caressed her hair. "There'll be another time."

"What's The Big One?" Emily asked her mother. "A fire?"

"No, Kiddo. It's an earthquake. A really major earthquake."

"Sounds scary."

"It would be."

"Would you rescue people?" Caylie asked.

"If people needed me, I'd rescue them."

"Would you rescue me?"

"Of course, I would. But let's hope it never comes to that. On Saturday, it really won't be anything special. I'm just supposed to fly to Seattle in time to hover over T-Mobile Park right after the seventh inning. Just demonstrating how the Coast Guard's emergency evacuation capabilities are always available."

"In your bright red-orange helicopter?" Emily asked.

"That's right. I'll be flying Dolphin 224, honey."

Caylie said, "It's a pretty helicopter. I wish we could all fly in it with you."

"You know I can't take kids along. This is strictly professional flying. It's not for fun."

"Besides," Ryan said. "I think you'd be bored after a while, Caylie."

"No, I wouldn't."

"Yes, you would," Jane affirmed. "It will be a long day without much excitement. First, I have to fly to Seattle and land at Boeing Field. Then I have to wait on the ground for hours until it's the seventh inning. Then I'll take off and go hover over the stadium for just a few minutes. Then I'll be free to fly home to the base here at Port Angeles. It's going to be a long boring day with a lot of waiting around and only a little fun flying over the stadium. You'll have a lot more fun with your dad."

"That's right," Ryan agreed. "We'll start with a ferry ride to Seattle in the morning."

"Yay!" Caylie cried. "I love riding the ferry!"

"Then we'll spend a long time at the beach. And then, when

it's time, we'll go watch Mom hover over the stadium. I know a great spot where we can see the whole Seattle skyline as well as the stadium. We'll bring binoculars, so we can see her close-up. Does that sound okay?"

"Well, I guess so," Emily replied.

"That's the spirit. Now help me clear up these dishes before we watch TV."

Dr. Rutledge had spent the last several hours at his office desk, writing. He wasn't working on his scientific paper, but rather a much shorter and equally important document—a TV script. Months previously, Seattle City Councilwoman Mariah Rey had acted as go-between to connect Rutledge with the Mariners' top management so he could present what was a new idea to them—adding tidal-wave preparedness to their already-in-place earthquake preparedness plan. They had been reluctant, but Mariah Rey tirelessly harangued them for weeks. At one point, when discussions seemed to be bogging down, she even threatened legal proceedings to force the change.

In the end, Rey's pressure and Rutledge's scientific arguments won the day. The Mariners and T-Mobile management had agreed to undertake the lengthy process of revising their emergency plan. They also agreed to allow Rutledge—at Rey's insistence—to broach the subject of a tsunami threat to a crowd at the stadium. Management ultimately decided it was preferable to assign the task to an outsider like Rutledge rather than associate the idea with any personality linked to the team, like well-known announcers or players. Hence, today's writing effort, putting together a scripted speech for Saturday's sold-out game. He was nearly finished when Lori McMillan appeared at his door.

"Dr. Rutledge?"

He was about to deflect whatever question she had, so he could finish his work, but he hesitated when he saw how concerned she looked. "What is it?"

"There's been a big shift in the quake storm."

"A shift? What sort of shift?" He got up and followed her

to the lab.

Kyle Stevens sat at a computer workstation, his face lit by the ghostly white glow from the banks of seismic monitor screens and showing the same concern as Lori's. He gestured at the monitors, where Rutledge could see many new small tremors on several of the seismic traces. "The whole storm has shifted from Bainbridge Island to Issaquah." On his workstation screen was a map of the Puget Sound Basin with land areas in green and water in blue. Scattered red and yellow dots pinpointed computer-calculated epicenters of the small earthquakes. "The yellow dots are yesterday's quakes. They're all west of Seattle, mostly under Bainbridge Island."

"But look at the red dots," Lori said. "Those are this morning's quakes. Every one of them is on the east side of Seattle, under Issaquah."

"I don't like the look of that." Rutledge frowned. "You're saying they've bracketed the city on both ends of the Seattle Fault line."

"I just know something bad is about to happen."

Rutledge shook his head. "No one has ever come up with a way to be sure about such things—and I don't have a crystal ball."

Although they shared a common interest in earth sciences, Rutledge's two young proteges were a study in contrasts. Kyle Stevens didn't fit the image of what people might expect a Postdoctoral Fellow at the Pacific Northwest Seismic Network to look like. He wore his straight black hair in a short shock-top with shaved temples. Large hollow black spools perforated his earlobes. A two-pronged silver ornament hung from his nose. A multicolored dragon's head tattoo adorned the side of his neck, its serpentine body disappearing under the collar of his black T-shirt. Lori McMillan—the department's newest graduate student, with a bachelor's degree in Geological Sciences from Montana State University—was dressed conservatively in a plain plaid dress, a white blouse, and a pale pink sweater.

Kyle suggested, "At least you can use this seismic shift to

create a little excitement at your tsunami pep talk."

Rutledge swallowed hard. "I'm not sure I'll even mention it. I don't want to be an alarmist. Quake storms come and go. This may amount to nothing in the end."

"Or something major could happen," Lori said.

"That's always possible. But T-Mobile management won't be too thrilled if I frighten people. They're underwhelmed by the whole idea of a university professor lecturing a sports crowd. They're worried I might scare fans away from future games."

"Maybe you *should be* an alarmist," Kyle said. "Have you ever seen their IN CASE OF EMERGENCY announcement on the big Center Field screen? It's like, just a video with a map of the stadium and some arrows showing how to get out, depending on where you're seated. It doesn't mention earthquakes or tsunamis—even though T-Mobile Park is basically right at sea level."

"I'm aware of that," Rutledge replied. "It's only sixteen feet above the median tide line. It was built on what used to be Duwamish River mud flats. If people follow those evacuation routes, they'll run straight into a major tsunami threat."

Lori sat at another computer workstation and googled up a document. "Here's the Ballpark Emergency Response Plan." She scrolled down through page after page of information intended to guide stadium staff through any emergency situation.

"It's got a terrorism section, a fire section, and an earthquake section. But all the announcer is supposed to say is, '*Please be patient while we look into this.*' That's a direct quote."

"By the time they announce that," Kyle said, "people will be running for the exits."

"Here's more. After security people check out the stadium, the announcer is either supposed to say, '*Today's game has been canceled, please exit the stadium,*' or, '*Today's game will continue shortly.*' And there's one more last bit at the bottom of the page. It says, '*Shelter in place message.*'"

"That sounds good. What's the message?"

Lori shrugged. "It doesn't actually say what the message is supposed to be. It just says, '*Shelter in place message.*'"

"That's pretty sketchy."

"And pretty scary. All they've got is just general stuff. Nothing earthquake-specific. There are no drop-and-cover instructtions. There's no stay-where-you-are instruction. And no mention at all of a tsunami."

"I'm going to try to change that," Rutledge asserted.

"How long are they going to let you talk?" Kyle asked.

"It's supposed to be a two-minute spot."

"Two minutes? Wouldn't you need, like, two hours?"

"I've been having trouble writing my speech for exactly that reason."

"Here's more." Lori scrolled farther down the screen. "It says the announcer should tell people to follow the public-address system announcements and any instructions on the scoreboard."

"A scoreboard is useless if it goes black," Kyle said. "Do they have emergency power? Will it work after a major quake?"

Lori brought up another page. "Here's a section on power. '*The electrical design of T-Mobile Park consists of five 4000-Amp and one 1200-Amp switchboards feeding the main facility and one 2500-Amp switchboard feeding the Central Plant and Parking Garage. Emergency power is provided by an 800-kilowatt generator feeding a 1600-Amp emergency switchboard.*'"

"Sweet. So, they should still have power."

"But no one will know what to announce."

"That's exactly what my speech will address," Rutledge said. "What would you tell the crowd, if you were me?"

"Tell them everything," Lori said. "Give them a reason to care."

"In two minutes?"

Kyle grinned. "Just tell them to bend over and kiss their asses goodbye!"

"Very funny," Rutledge grumbled.

There was a long pause while they watched a new series of spikes appear on the monitors, followed shortly by a new red dot on Kyle's map. Again, the epicenter was just east of Seattle.

"This is crazy-making," Lori murmured.

"But is it really such a big deal?" Kyle asked Rutledge. "I mean, the Seattle Fault already fired off an epic quake in the year 900, right? So, it isn't too likely to rip again in our lifetimes—is it?"

Rutledge shrugged. "The models say smaller quakes come every three hundred years or so. And there have been several of about 6.0 magnitude. But the possibility still exists we could see something bigger."

"Okay, but the Seattle Fault is relatively small compared to say, the San Andreas Fault in California. So, no worries of a really bad-ass quake, right?"

Rutledge's brows knit. "From time to time even small faults let go with something much worse than average—quakes that are both strong and shallow. That's what worries me about the Seattle Fault. It may be nowhere near as big as the San Andreas Fault or the Cascadia Subduction Zone off our coast, but it's right under us. Proximity is the key. A huge full-rip 9.0 quake that's fifty miles off the coast or fifty miles down, is a lot less dangerous than 6.7 right under your feet. There's no time or distance to weaken the impact."

"So, the full force hits you?" Lori asked uneasily.

"Unfortunately, that's right. And the full force of 6.7 at zero miles is tremendously stronger than 9.0 at fifty miles, as I know only too well. The 1965 quake caused major damage to buildings, roads, and bridges—and a few deaths. Luckily, not mine."

Kyle tapped his computer screen between the clusters of red and yellow dots. "Hopefully, the center of the Seattle Fault will start having slow-slip quakes, too. That way, nobody gets hurt."

"That would be the best outcome," Rutledge agreed.

"And the worst?" Lori asked.

"I'd better get back to my speechwriting."

Blazes Cannabis Emporium had a prime location in the center of the Alki Beach community. The sandy shores attracted hundreds or occasionally thousands of people partaking of fresh air, clean salt water, sun-baked sand, and several dozen eateries, bars, and other establishments across the street from the beach.

Today's crowd was growing, and a fair number of beachgoers were affirmatively answering the question GOING TO BLAZES? asked by a banner hung in the front window of the Emporium on the upper floor of an old two-story brick building.

The morning's brisk business contributed to wide smiles worn by the proprietors, Moe Zinkernagel and Zoey Laffite. The former was a tall, bearded, big man in a Bob Marley T-shirt and blue jeans, and the latter was a petite female dressed in a retro tie-dyed shift. They managed a long glass display case at the back of the sales parlor, reminiscent of a candy-store counter. Inside it were dozens of glass jars filled with green buds. Customers, queued up in two lines, could probably tell by the faint glazing of the proprietors' eyes that their morning had included a wake-and-bake session with some of their own goods.

The customers were an amiable bunch. They calmly underwent mandatory ID checks before Moe and Zoey could assist them, ring up their transactions, and send them on their way with small white paper bags. These might contain a few ounces of marijuana buds, or an electronic cigarette vape with a cartridge of cannabis oil, or a small blown-glass pipe with a carburetor hole, or a larger glass water-pipe bong. Or they might contain any of dozens of medibles—marijuana brownies, cookies, sodas, lollipops, or cannabis tinctures found in glass cases and coolers lining the sides of the parlor.

Moe and Zoey's dog, Rex, was a smallish curly-haired piebald mutt. A mellow animal with a red-white-and-blue paisley bandana around his neck, he sniffed the ankles of customers and acknowledged pats on the head with lazy tail wags as folks theorized what mix of breeds he might be.

In the last little while, Rex had met an interesting mix of humans. He'd sniffed the polished shoes of a straight-laced guy who came in to buy a new vape as a birthday present for his girlfriend. He'd gotten a scratch behind the ears from a customer whose magenta-dyed hair was fashioned into a bale of dreadlocks hanging behind him halfway to the floor. The Rastaman had left with medible macaroons to soothe his grandmother's arthritis. Now, as the lines dwindled away, Rex received one last head pat from a middle-aged man in a business suit before he stepped to the counter.

"Help… we… can you?" Moe mumbled.

"What?" The man didn't catch Moe's garbled greeting.

Zoey giggled and pointed at Moe. "A little too much wacky weed, you know?"

"I know." The businessman grinned. "You guys sell good stuff." He looked at each of them carefully. "Do you guys… smoke on the job?"

They glanced at each other, trying to maintain poker-faces but breaking into paroxysmal guffaws. "This isn't a job!" Moe gasped after a moment, squeezing tears from the corners of his eyes. "It's a way of life!"

The man nodded and smiled. "It's nice to know you sample the stuff you sell. Anyway—" He peered through the glass countertop at dozens of lidded glass jars containing bunches of marijuana buds ranging from green to brown to purple and frosted with silvery highlights of drug resin on fuzz-covered leaves. "I'd like to buy an eighth."

"Can do, man." Moe slid the glass door on his side of the counter open. "Which one?"

"That's just it," the fellow shrugged. "I don't remember the name of what I got last time. You sell so many varieties."

"Sixty-six," Zoey concurred. "Last time I checked. And we've got a semi-truck coming in from Methow Valley to-morrow with a half dozen more. They've had perfect grow weather east of the mountains. Record crops."

"And record wowee!" Moe chuckled. "—if you know what I'm saying. Chronic!"

"Anyway," the customer said. "I thought if I looked them over, I might remember."

"Be our guest."

"Hmmm." The man stared at jars labeled PURPLE KUSH, CHOCOLATE GODDESS, and PINEAPPLE SKUNK-WEED with uncertainty. "I just don't know."

"Was it pure indica? Or pure sativa?" Zoey offered. "That

would narrow it down a bit. Or was it a hybrid?"

"I'm not sure."

"Did it give you a quick rush? Sativa's got a lot more THC than cannabidiol, so it hits harder. Gets you baked, pronto."

He shook his head. "That doesn't sound right."

"Okay, then. Maybe indica. A lot more cannabidiol. Smoother body rush. Not so much head-rush. A mellower buzz for your 420 pleasure."

"Mmmm. Maybe. Or somewhere in between."

"That could be almost any of the hybrids. And we've got a lot of them. What color was it? A straight up green color—like your eyes?"

"No."

"Brownish?"

"Yeah, I think so."

"Or purple? When it gets a lot of sun, it goes purple."

"I don't think it was purple. More of a brownish-green with a lot of white frost on it."

"That'd be the tetrahydrocannabinol resin coating the leaf hairs," Moe said.

"Trichomes," Zoey corrected.

The customer sighed. "Maybe you guys should just recommend something. Somewhere right in between chilled and baked."

"Got just the thing." Moe fetched a jar labeled ROSEBUD out of the cabinet and set it on top. He unscrewed the wide lid and held the jar up under the man's nose, so he could inspect the buds closely. "Take a whiff."

"Mmmm. Interesting. Spicy!"

"Smells kinda like rose petals, right?"

"I guess. But I don't think that's what I had before."

"Okay." Moe screwed the lid back on, replaced the jar, and pulled out another labeled BROWN GONE-JA. "Maybe this was the one. We sell a lot of this. Just about a fifty-fifty indica-sativa hybrid. It's from one of our most reliable growers over in Twisp. He's a real genius at making hybrids."

After a sniff, the man said, "Yeah, that might be it. It had that frankincense smell."

"We've got a special on it today," said Zoey. "Buy two eighth-ounces and the third eighth is half price."

"Three eighths? That would probably last me a year."

Moe cracked a smile. "Not me."

"Not me," Zoey giggled. "Maybe a couple of days."

"Well, it's a lot for me," the man said. "But okay. Three eights of BROWN GONE-JA."

"You won't regret it, my friend." Zoey used a large, lime-green plastic forceps to transfer some of the silvery brown buds onto an electronic balance. "Just the right blend of mellow and woo-hoo. I like to smoke it before watching a movie."

"And I like to smoke it before lunch," Moe said. "It gives me an appetite."

"As if you needed one." Zoey added an extra bud for good measure, then transferred the buds to a small zip-lock bag and sealed it. She put the merchandise into a paper bag and rang up the sale. "That'll be seventy-five bucks. Two times thirty plus fifteen."

The man handed over four twenties. "Keep the change."

"Thank you muchly." Moe put the twenties in the register and dropped a fiver in a half-filled tip jar.

As he was leaving, the man paused at the door. "Have you heard the new drug czar in Washington DC said he's telling the DEA to crack down on legal weed places like this?"

Moe shrugged his shoulders. "We heard, but nothing's come of it yet."

"Besides," Zoey added, "why would they want to crack down on decent hardworking people like us? This job has strict qualification requirements, you know."

Moe looked at her, mystified. "It does?"

"Yeah. Like you've gotta be able to work a cash register and make change when you're wrecked."

The businessman smiled. "Just thought I'd mention it." He turned with a wave and left.

Moe nudged Zoey with an elbow, shooting her a paranoid glance. "You think he's right?"

"Hey, honey. We've been threatened before."

"We have?"

"Yeah. Like that little shakeup this morning. Who knew this place was on an earthquake fault?"

"But a DEA agent on our case is worse than being on an earthquake fault."

"It is, huh? Whose fault is that?"

"It's our fault, I guess. I mean, we must own it, if it's right under us."

"Let's don't make any faults assumptions."

"Oh. There you go again, finding fault."

"It's not my fault. Maybe your fault but it's not my fault."

"That's faulty logic."

"We should get some insurance on this place."

"What kind? No fault?"

"No. Fault."

"Who's gonna get it? Me? With all my faults?"

"It's only partly your fault. The rest is my fault."

"No, it isn't."

"Yes, it is."

"No. It isn't."

"Is."

"Isn't."

"Is too."

"Is not."

The bell on the front door jingled as a new customer walked in. He was a muscular fellow in a black T-shirt with brightly tattooed arms who looked like he might get the munchies after a solid bong rip and empty half a refrigerator. As he approached them, Moe and Zoey murmured back and forth between themselves.

"Zip it, Zoey. Here comes a customer."

"No, Moe. You shut up."

"You first."

"No. You."

"If he doesn't buy anything," Moe said, "it'll be your fault." They both broke into gut-rattling guffaws as the man came to the counter. He calmly watched them shriek with laughter while Rex claimed his ankle-sniff and head-pat.

"Ca— can we— help you?" Zoey gasped between giggles, tears streaming down her face.

"Yeah," the tattooed man said. "I'll have whatever you've been smoking."

Chapter 4

City Councilwoman Mariah Rey's office in Seattle City Hall was a modest one, but brightly lit by tall windows that brought in a great amount of daylight—enough to grow some potted peace lilies and an avocado plant. They also brought in an inescapable sight. Across the street was Eldon Devine's growing tower, which rose to seemingly impossible heights.

Rey grumbled, "I have to watch that monstrosity get taller every day."

Inspector Dan Federly, seated opposite her at her desk, turned and glanced at the tower. "What did the City Engineering Department have to say about that place?"

"It passed their review."

"Hard to believe. Unless somebody…"

"Was on the take?"

"The thought had crossed my mind."

"We have no proof of anything like that. Nor even a hint of impropriety." Her eye was caught by the movement of an orange construction crane atop the tower as it lifted a load of steel I-beams that would raise the building even higher. "I have been frustrated in every attempt to make that man accountable," she muttered. "He's too rich and too powerful for anyone to rein in."

"Well, somebody's got to nail him, and I may be your man."

"What have you got?"

"I ran the serial numbers on some of the beams and girders. Like I thought, they are inferior quality—cheap stuff."

"I wonder," Rey said. "Do you think we can get a stop-work order based on just that alone?"

Federly shrugged. "I think maybe so, though he's bound to fight it. And he's already got a subcontractor covering it all with interior finish work on the lower stories."

"Believe me, more than one of us on the Council have tried

to corner him, but he always finds a loophole to wriggle through. He's got darn good lawyers. They scare me. He's even threatened to sue Council members personally."

"Can he do that?"

"I'm not sure."

High above them, on the thirty-first floor of the tower, Devine squared off combatively with Bill Torgelson, president of Ballard Construction Company. The contractor was dressed in dusty work clothes and a hardhat, which contrasted strongly with Devine's immaculate pinstriped suit. Torgelson's firm had been hired to finish interior spaces of the building even as construction of the framework continued high above them. His teams of carpenters, masons, electricians, glaziers, plumbers, and painters had worked their way up to the thirty-fifth floor, roughing in the office spaces and installing windows. In the area where the two men stood, they had completed their task to the last detail, providing Devine an oasis of finely finished work-and-living space where he could oversee the building's completion in posh surroundings suited to his tastes.

Torgelson spoke urgently to Devine. "I've got more than a hundred and fifty BCC employees working on this building. I've never hired such a large crew in all my time in the business."

"That's a good thing, right?" Devine replied in patronizing tones.

"True. At least it *was* a good thing. But your payments are now two and a half months in arrears. I'm bleeding money. I can't make ends meet."

"You should have thought of that before you signed the contract. *I* can't be held responsible for *your* lack of planning."

"Lack of planning? I planned to do honest work and receive honest pay for it. Don't you understand that? My finances are in a crisis and you're to blame."

"Welcome to the big time."

"It has nothing to do with the big time. I've had large contracts before. And big organizations—honest ones, I mean. They pay their bills on time."

Devine glared at Torgelson. "Are you calling me a crook?"

Torgelson hesitated as if nothing would suit him better than to affirm what Devine had just said. But after a moment he said in measured words, "No. But I need you to pay what you owe me."

"And I need you to get out of my sight!" Devine yelled.

"All right." Torgelson's voice trembled with suppressed rage. "I'll go. In fact, I'll be only too happy to quit looking at your fat face and your weak hands that never did an honest day's work. But on the way out I'll tell my foremen that nobody reports to work after today. We're on strike, starting immediately. Let's see how you like that!" He turned and walked toward the elevator.

"Hey!" Devine called after him. "Don't walk away. I haven't finished talking to you!"

Torgelson turned and glared at Devine. "What?"

"What was your name, again?" Devine asked with regal disdain and a haughty smirk.

"Bill Torgelson."

"Well, Bill Torgelson, I've got news for you." Devine's thin lips stretched into a vindictive smile. "You're not on strike. You're fired! You and all your people! How do you like that?"

Torgelson's eyes widened. His mental wheels spun at the staggering implications of those two words—*you're fired*—and the finality with which they had been spoken. "You can't do that—!" He choked on a mix of horror and rage.

"I just did." Devine watched Torgelson squirm with undisguised delight.

"We still have a contract." Torgelson changed his tone to a plea. "My people need their jobs. They've got families. They need their pay—"

Devine grinned triumphantly. "Oh! You're breaking my heart."

"As if you had one!" Torgelson switched in a heartbeat from contrition to anger.

"You can tell all your little people who need their little paychecks that they won't be getting any more from me."

"At least you will pay what we are owed!"

"Don't count on it." Devine's vindictive thin-lipped smile stretched across his face almost from ear to ear.

"I'll—" Torgelson seemed on the verge of having a stroke. "I'll see you in court."

"Go ahead and sue!" Devine flushed with the excitement of the mismatched battle. "I *own* the courts. And I'll sue you right back. I'll take everything you've got, including your home."

"You're not a capitalist!" Torgelson shouted. "You're a gangster!"

Devine smiled more smugly than ever. "Gangsters are the purest form of capitalism. They know it's all about money. And they'll crush you if you disagree. Now get outta here!"

Torgelson hesitated as if he were about to say more, his mouth half open.

"How much are you worth?" Devine demanded.

"I— What do you mean?"

"If you add up everything you've got."

Torgelson shrugged. "I don't know, exactly."

"I'd say you're worth five million, including your penny-ante little business, your little home, and everything else you've got. Ten million, tops. Am I right?"

"I'm not going to answer that."

"Well, let me. You're not worth even a thousandth of what I'm worth. You're an ant, with your little hive of worker ants, and I am a giant. You could work all your penny-ante little lives and never amount to a tiny fraction of what I'm worth."

"You're not a giant!" Torgelson screamed. "You're a monster! An ugly monster made out of money. And you've got no heart!"

Devine grinned wickedly. "Heart? What good is a heart? What I've got is a big foot to crush little ants like you."

"You think it's fun, don't you?" Torgelson shouted. "Crushing little guys like me."

Devine tilted his head back, the better to stare down his nose at Torgelson. He thought for a long moment while Torgelson stewed. "Yeah," he allowed at last. "I do think it's fun. In fact, I love it. It's what gets me out of bed in the morning."

Torgelson sputtered and choked on a mixture of rage and disgust. He glared at Devine but had lost the ability to summon words.

"Out!" Devine backhandedly flipped his fingers as if shooing away a fly. "Get out of here!"

"You'll hear from my lawyer," Torgelson growled.

"And you'll hear from mine. I've got teams of lawyers that would like nothing more than to ruin you. Some of the best in the business. And some of the meanest. I'll pay them with the money I save by not paying you!"

"My crews will be out of here by tomorrow," Torgelson turned to go. "Then you can have your goddamn building all to yourself." His shoulders had slumped further with each exchange. Now, as he walked to the elevator, he shuffled across the polished black granite floor like he had aged fifty years in thirty seconds.

Devine watched in haughty silence with his arms folded across his wide belly until the elevator doors closed. Then the vindictive smile spread across his face again. His thin lips remained tense, however, as though even this moment of triumph was stirring deeper needs for more dominance and control.

"You were pretty tough on him," a female voice came from a doorway behind him.

Devine turned and smiled at the woman. "Yeah," he said smugly. "I was, wasn't I? But you should see me when I'm *really* mad."

The woman, tall and trim and blond and dressed in a black business skirt-suit, was Kelly Anton, the newly appointed head of his legal department. She asked, "Were you referring to me when you said your lawyers would take delight in ruining him?"

"Sure. Was I wrong?"

"No."

The two of them shared a long, conspiratorial laugh.

Chapter 5

Just offshore of the town of Suquamish, on the Olympic Peninsula side of Puget Sound, twenty-seven dugout canoes floated on the placid waters of Agate Passage. Each of the canoes, carved from a single giant Northwest cedar log, carried up to twelve paddlers and passengers on cedar-plank seats within its wide hull. People sat two-abreast in the large watercraft, some of which were thirty feet or more in length.

Each canoe was carved with Northwest Native images of animal-human spirits who, according to legend, were the ancestors of those who paddled the canoes. There were bears, eagles, wolves, killer whales, and seals, all depicted in bas relief and painted with natural colors of berry red, charcoal black, shell white, and copper green. The paddlers, or pullers, as they preferred to be called, were lightly dressed or bare-chested and shiny with sweat from their exertions on a hot afternoon, making the long haul down from Tulalip on the Snohomish Reservation.

In some of the bow seats were elders dressed in fine native costumes. Some wore headbands of cedar bark fibers, or basket-woven conical hats with topknots signifying rank and ancestry. Some wore shawls of cedar, willow, and dark spruce-root yarns with intricately woven illustrations of animals on them. Others wore red-and-black felt dancing shawls with totemic figures outlined in iridescent abalone-shell buttons. Some wore Western pants, dresses, and shoes under these, while more traditionally minded folks wore cedar-fiber skirts or breechclouts and no footwear at all.

The expressions on the faces of these grandmothers, grandfathers, hereditary chiefs, princesses, matrons, and patrons were jovial and positively expectant. It had been a long day on the Salish Sea, and all knew hospitality, joyous reunions, song, dance, and merriment awaited. The canoe journey would pause here overnight and then start for Seattle with the morning tide.

As they rested on the smooth waters, the canoe visitors gazed at a crowd of more than a thousand people waiting to greet them in front of a huge longhouse. The House of Awakened Culture's seven tree-like uprights underpinned immense horizontal log beams that in turn supported a back-slanted roof.

The front of the longhouse was constructed of cedar planks, and wooden interior walls were visible through large open doors. The building stretched a city block in length and a tenth of that in width. Though of modern construction, it recaptured the form of longhouses that had lined the low bluff at Suquamish for millennia before American pioneers had brought calamity to these shores. The building's wide-open interior was designed to host great intertribal gatherings and feasts, rain or shine.

Today's greeting ceremonies were being held outside on a wide lawn to take advantage of fine weather. On that lawn was an outdoor kitchen under a pavilion roof. In a firepit within the kitchen, scores of salmon fillets were grilling over a great bed of glowing wood coals. Native chefs and servers tended the fillets or dished up cooked salmon at serving counters near the pavilion. Long lines of guests received paper plates brimming with salmon, corn on the cob, new potatoes, and trimmings. Then they moved along to join a crowd standing on the high bank above the beach or sitting on bleachers facing the shore.

One young woman with Indian braids and a deerskin vest and dress with tasseled hemlines took a plate to a group of elders seated at a long table under a big-top tent roof and gave it to Henry George. "Thanks!" He grinned at her. "I'll just have time to shovel in a few quick bites before the show starts."

He ate quickly, sticking a plastic fork into steaming salmon and taking large mouthfuls. "Mm-mm!" he said between bites. "The best salmon ever!"

She smiled. "It's always the best salmon ever!"

Before George was quite finished, a voice called from one of the canoes in slow, strong, oratorical tones that echoed off the surface of the water. "People of Suquamish! Us Makahs in this canoe come from Neah Bay! We request your permission to come ashore!"

"Oops," George took a final bite, then rose. "Gotta go."

The canoe orator, an old man with long white braids and a beaded vest, raised an eagle-feather fan in one hand as he stood at the stern of one of the larger canoes. "We have journeyed far. We are tired. We are hungry. And we have heard of the Suquamish People's legendary generosity, and their friendliness to strangers. We ask that you share your hospitality, your food, and your shelter with us tonight. We are poor, and we have not brought great riches with us. But we bring the songs of our Makah tradition. And we bring drums. And we bring beautiful costumes. And we bring our dances. We ask only that you give us permission to come ashore and share your home."

Henry George hurried down a ramp to the beach where a group of greeters had gathered overlooking the canoes. Joining them, he took up a tambourine-shaped buckskin hand drum, which he pounded with a beater stick. Other greeters shook carved wooden rattles, clacked sticks together, and voiced whoops and ululating cheers. The large crowd lining the shore joined in, then all grew quiet again to listen to the reply.

"Makah people!" the leader of the drummers, Tribal Chairman Mike Raven, called out in a loud, clear voice. "I welcome you to the home of the Suquamish People. We see you are tired. And we know you must be hungry, because you have traveled far today. We are happy to offer our hospitality. Come ashore. Join us. Share our food. Share your songs and dances. We are glad you have come."

As the sound of another salute of drums and shouts died down, the Makah pullers steered their canoe to the cobble beach where young men and women drew it to shore and helped them debark. A team of twenty strong young men lifted the massive canoe to their shoulders, then marched it up the ramp and set it on the lawn with other canoes already there. Henry George and the greeters moved along the beach to a position in front of the next canoe, and the ritual of request and response was repeated.

Again, the canoe skipper made his plea for hospitality—this time for a group who had paddled more than six hundred miles from Bella Coola, British Columbia. Again, Raven accepted on behalf of the Suquamish People and granted permission to come ashore. Then the greeters moved on to the next canoe and the next until the welcomes were done and the canoers were all debarked. George returned to his table and resumed his feast among friends. The newly arrived crews made their way to the kitchen and got their own servings of potlatch food. Added to the menu were bounteous quantities of clams, oysters, and Dungeness crab, all steamed in the traditional way, on large mounds of beach cobblestones made red-hot under bonfires, onto which the shellfish were heaped by the ton.

After dinner, the Native singing and dancing at the Awakened Culture Center went far into the evening. Inside the great hall Makah dancers in painted cedar eagle masks and brightly feathered capes performed a barefoot twirling dance with arms outstretched, commemorating Thunderbird's soaring hunt for the Great Whale. S'Klallam dancers pantomimed how Raven, the Trickster, stole daylight from Ogre's Longhouse. Samish dancers demonstrated how the Changeling, Dokwebalth, transformed from animal to human and back again. All these choreographed stories were accompanied by massed voices and thundering drums that made the huge log beams of the longhouse vibrate with living energy.

As the evening went on, Henry George stepped outside and took a seat on one of many folding chairs. He was taking the cool air and watching twilight colors paint the sky, when the young woman in buckskins approached him again, this time accompanied by three people.

"Henry George," she said by way of introduction, "I want you to meet some special guests of ours, Ginny and Arnie Musselshell and their nephew Johnny Steele." The three shook his hand and took seats around him. "They're celebrating Johnny getting straight A's at Neah Bay High School this year."

"Straight A's?" George said. "That's a heck of a lot better

than I ever did. And you're a sharp dancer too. I saw you in that Thunderbird dance a while ago."

"Thanks."

"And I saw you in the Eel Dance, too. Was that your girlfriend you were holding hands with? Or no one special?"

"No one special." Johnny looked a little embarrassed at the attention he was getting.

"Enjoying our little get-together?" George asked Ginny Musselshell.

"It's wonderful." She gestured out over the water. "The view from Suquamish is spectacular. Mount Rainier is gorgeous."

They turned to gaze at the snow-capped volcano, bathed in sunset pinks and purples, looming above the glittering waters of Agate Passage and the dark, tree-covered silhouette of Bainbridge Island. The mountain seemed to glow with its own inner light.

Johnny pointed to another part of the skyline. "What are those towers over there? Seattle?" The upper stories of a dozen skyscrapers were visible over the top of a headland. They glittered brightly enough to rival Mount Rainier's eminence.

George said, "Didn't use to be anything to see over that way when I was a kid. The buildings in Seattle were shorter then, so they didn't rise over the hilltop. Now, they got a bunch of skyscrapers so tall you can see them all the way over here on the other side of Puget Sound. And there's one with a crane on top, still getting taller. See it?"

"That's progress," Arnie Musselshell said. "I guess."

"When I was a kid, I used to think Seattle was far away. Now, I guess one of them pahstuds could be looking at us right now, if he had a telescope."

"Pahstud?" Johnny puzzled. "What's that?"

"It means Boston, in our language. The first American pioneers came here in sailing ships from Boston Harbor. So, we called them pahstuds. That's as close as you can come to saying Boston in the Lushootseed language."

Johnny nodded. "That's like in the Makah language. We call

them babalthuds. I think it means the same thing."

"Let 'em watch us if they want to," Arnie said. "We'll stick to our traditions."

"And our songs and dances," Ginny added.

"Gives me shivers to see you young people dancing," George told Johnny. "That's a tradition that's thousands and thousands of years old."

Ginny said, "Johnny's Thunderbird dance is one of our oldest traditions. It's been handed down from grandmas and grandpas to younger generations since forever."

George nodded. "Traditions is what brings people together, just like this Canoe Journey. Nowadays, canoe families are the pillars of our culture." He gestured toward the front wall of the building. "Like the seven posts that hold the roof up on this place." The posts featured elegantly carved totem statues of ancestral figures.

"I wish they had something like that in modern society," Johnny said. "Nowadays it seems like everybody is just out for themselves—or for money."

George grunted in disdain. "Money's the root of all evil, they say. But you know the way of our old chiefs, don't you? Not like them rich pahstuds in Seattle." He nodded toward the glittering towers. "Those fellows want to keep it all to themselves. They just get richer and richer, and they don't care about nobody else. Seems to me, pahstuds are trying to be like that old Led Zeppelin song, the one about buying a stairway to heaven. But nobody can do that. No matter how high you build your skyscraper, the sky will look down on you. So will the S'kelle-laitu, the sky spirits, and Shuq Siab."

"Shuq Siab," Johnny repeated. "Who's that?"

"That's our word for God. It means Honored Man Above. Nowadays, they got men in those towers who think they're above us all. They look down on us. But they ain't no Shuq Siab."

"Men like Eldon Devine?"

"So you've heard of him all the way out in Neah Bay?"

"Sure. What? Do you think we don't have TV and the

internet? I heard he's gonna have the tallest building in Seattle pretty soon. That one with a crane on top must be it."

"A man like Eldon Devine," George grumbled, "he likes to look down on everybody. King of the Pahstuds. Top of the pig pile. For him it's just money, money, and more money, piling up as tall as those buildings. But it still ain't no stairway to heaven."

"Never will be," Arnie agreed.

"In the old times, you know how tall our tallest buildings were?"

"One story?" Johnny ventured.

"That's right. We built 'em long, not tall. That's because this is earthquake country and it's a lot harder to knock down a one-story building than an eighty-one-story building. That's a big difference between our culture and pahstud culture. We've always been humble and close to the earth. So, when A'yahos shook the ground, our buildings didn't fall over. Or if they did, it wasn't too hard to patch them up again."

Johnny sighed. "What can I tell you? We live in Twenty-First Century America. Sketchy guys like Eldon Devine call the shots, like it or not."

"I like it not," George said. "Things has gotten out of hand. Out of the people's hands."

"Hasn't it been that way since the beginning of time?" asked Ginny. "The rich get richer and the poor ones fade, so the Bible says."

"So the pahstud Bible says. But it didn't used to be that way 'round these parts. Before pahstuds came, we didn't use no money at all."

"That's right," said Arnie. "We'd just trade one thing for another, like a hide for some fish, maybe."

"You know what was so good about that? There was no rich people."

"Not even our chiefs?" Johnny asked.

"They didn't have no money, so how could they be rich? There wasn't anybody like Eldon Devine, way up there in his humongous tower. Regular people can't get near him. He's so high up, we look like ants to him. He's high and mighty because of his money. In the old times, he wouldn't be up in that tower. He'd be right here along with everybody else in this longhouse. Back in our times, there was nothing to separate chiefs from people. So, chiefs had to rule with something Eldon Devine doesn't know anything about."

"What's that?"

"Sharing. Back in those days, if anyone was starving, it was because everyone was starving. The chief didn't get no special privileges. And if there was good fishing, or a good hunt, then everybody ate, because the chief's main job was to see that everyone got their share. And everybody had a place to sleep. And everybody was as happy as they could be."

"Sharing!" Johnny exclaimed. "That's exactly what's missing these days."

"That's right. And it was money that put an end to it. Once money came, people were either rich or poor. They lived in separate houses. Big ones for the rich. Little ones for the poor. It wasn't the same anymore, and it was money that did it."

"Was life really so great back in the old days? There must have been some greedy chiefs who robbed the people."

"Nope."

"How can you be so sure?"

"Remember, we all lived together back then."

"So?"

"So, s'pose a bad chief went to the latrine late one night." George chuckled.

"I don't know. What?"

"Then one of the regular folks might follow him out and stick a knife in his ribs while he's peeing. Because they didn't live separately. They used the same latrine. No executive washrooms."

"I get it! If a chief treated the people bad, he got killed! So, there really weren't any Eldon Devines back in those times!"

"Not a one. They'da got stabbed while they're doing their business. And nobody woulda cried much when they found 'em next day face-down in the latrine. Not if they was as greedy as Eldon Devine. Everybody woulda lined up to pee on his corpse."

Johnny laughed. "You know, I can see your point. It's like, the physical separation made by money allows rich men and kings to take over and make life miserable for common folk. It's the actual *distance* between rich and poor. The tall buildings, the huge mansions and estates. That's what allows them to be so greedy and mean-spirited without anyone being able to stop them."

"That's right. They use money like a wall between them and the common people."

"And it seems to me," Ginny interjected, "the more money some folks get, the worse they treat other people."

"Not every rich person is bad, though," Arnie said. "Bill and Melinda Gates."

"Sure," George shrugged. "There are some good rich people too. But think of this. All the rich people—every one of them—would be forced to be good if their money couldn't keep them apart from regular people. They'd either be good, or they'd be dead. Politicians too. Money is what makes 'em able to choose whether they want to be good or bad. And a hell of a lot of 'em choose bad, seems to me. Way too many. Most of 'em don't even try to be fair, because nobody can touch 'em. They're too high up for anyone to see 'em in their towers. But they're still miles below Shuq Siab and the S'kellelaitu."

"I wish I could have seen our culture before babalthuds came," Johnny said. "I like the way people rolled."

"Oh, I don't know," George said. "Our culture's not so far gone. You see it here, tonight. Look over there. There's a mom with her baby nursing in her arms, breathing in time to the drums. Tomorrow, when you go out in them canoes, you look at that Seattle skyline. Look at Devine's half-finished Stairway to Heaven and decide. Who's more real? The pahstuds in their towers, or that mother right there. Then you'll be sure our culture's still here."

While they talked, the dance troupe from Quileute finished its performance. Nisqually singers, drummers, and dancers were gathering around a large floor tom-tom preparing for their own show. As George had waxed philosophical, a crowd of young people and a few elders had gathered around, transfixed by the wisdom they were hearing. George glanced at the faces, including some small children with wide and adoring eyes.

He smiled and held up an index finger. "I just remembered something. Before I come over here from the Seattle today, I seen something over there that brought back memories of a long time ago when I was a little kid—like you!" He pointed the oratorical finger at some children who had come close to him. They retreated a step, bursting into giggles.

"There was this man and woman over there, from the University of Washington. They was digging up an old longhouse on Alki Beach. They say it's from an old village that was sunk by an earthquake and a tidal wave. So that got me thinking. People should know what my grandfathers taught me about tidal waves. Especially you little kids."

Some of the children settled on the grass to listen as more people, young and old, gathered around. "Have you ever seen the tide go out all at once?" George leaned near the row of children seated in front of him, making the smallest ones snicker nervously at his intensity. "Has anyone here felt the earth shake and seen the tide go out all at once?" he asked louder, glancing at the adults. They shook their heads no.

"Well, neither have I!" He let out a loud, rasping laugh. "But there are legends about when the tide went out all at once. They're part of our tradition. And people knew what to do when they felt the earth shake or saw the tide go out fast. Do you?" His finger jabbed this way and that, singling out audience members, and finally stopped on Johnny Steele. "Do you?"

"Nope." Steele played along. "What do I do?"

"Run!" George shouted. "Run for the hills! 'Cause A'yahos is mad, and a tidal wave is coming!"

The children squealed with delight and fear.

"A tidal wave is so big it can wash away a whole longhouse!" George proclaimed. "Or wash away the people in it. So, you better run! Go uphill as fast as you can. Don't stop to take nothing with you—except kids, and old people, and maybe a dog or two. But don't wait too long because that old wave is coming! And if you're out in your canoe, then you better paddle away from shore, not toward it. The wave will pass right under you with barely a ripple. But if you're in close to shore, it will tip you over."

He put both hands on his knees and glanced around at the transfixed faces. Then he bowed slightly and ended his story with a smile and a traditional line: "And that is all."

A cheer went up. Children clapped their hands. Some of the elders made the traditional Salish thank-you gesture, raising upturned, cupped hands in front of them to pantomime receiving a gift.

Inside, the Nisqually drummers started pounding a rhythm on the big tom-tom and their dancers took to the floor. George told Johnny, "Those guys and gals are great. I heard them at their casino. But I see my ride is here—Franky Squalco. We gotta go and hop a ferry. I'm needed on the Seattle side of the Salish Sea bright and early tomorrow. I've been asked to greet your canoes again on the waterfront. I guess they can't get enough of me."

"I can totally see why."

George laughed good-naturedly. "I'm part Suquamish and part Duwamish too, so on the Seattle side, the Duwamish part of me will greet you. I hope I won't bore you."

"The crowd over there is gonna love you, Boss, just like this one."

Chapter 6

Saturday morning dawned clear and pleasantly cool, another fine Indian summer day. On such days, people tended to start slowly. Not so Leon Curtis and Ann Butterfield. They arrived at the excavation just after daybreak with a sense of urgency. Not only was most of the site still unexplored, but they feared that curious beachgoers might disturb the bones and artifacts despite the warning tape. Beyond that—and most significantly—they knew ancient wooden objects crumbled to dust soon after they were exposed to air. Archeology was often a race against time, and the two scientists felt this acutely.

They peeled away brown plastic tarps covering the site and set to work on the day's most critical mission: removing the chief's skeleton from the wet ground and carting it off to safety at the Burke Museum. They began the hours-long process of carefully lifting fragile bones, placing them in numbered and labeled specimen boxes, and loading them in the back of Ann's red Chevy Blazer SUV. She had claimed the angle-in parking place nearest the dig site, and that was convenient—but their work would consume the entire morning, nonetheless.

"It would be nice to have some help with this." Ann used a small trowel to tease bits of sand away from the skull in preparation for the delicate, four-handed task of transferring it into a box with a cushioning bed of white plastic fiber wool.

"I wouldn't trust this critical work to volunteers." Leon knelt opposite her, removing bits of sand from the other side of the skull with a small brush. "Maybe I'll put out a call for help once the skeleton is out, and we start working our way along the house post. Meanwhile, let's just keep moving as fast as we can."

His cell phone rang, and he sat back on his haunches to answer. "Hello? Peyton McKean! How are you? Yes? You got the carbon-dating results? That was fast. Eleven hundred years, plus-minus one hundred years? That's fantastic!"

Ann stopped digging and sat up as he thanked McKean and clicked off the phone. "So, it *is* from the 900 AD earthquake!"

"Apparently so." Leon stood and scowled thoughtfully at Puget Sound.

She stood up beside him. "What are you thinking?"

"The tide is low now, but it's coming in. High tide will be about noon. I'd like to get our survey kit out and measure the exact difference between high tide and this level. I'm sure high tide would inundate this site by at least two feet if there weren't a sand barrier in the way. It would have done the same back in 900 AD."

"I get your point. If the site isn't ancient, then the low sea level of Ice Age times can't explain how they were able to live here. Eleven hundred years ago the sea had already risen. They would have been underwater at high tide."

"Exactly. So, that suggests this site must have sunk during the 900 AD earthquake."

"That jibes with something Henry George told me yesterday before he left for Suquamish. He said he knew the story of this place. He said it was called the 'Outside Village' because it faced the Sound, but there was a sister village on the other side of West Seattle in the Duwamish River Valley. The people there called themselves the 'People of the Inside.' That's what the word Duwamish means. So, this place, according to Henry George, is where the 'People of the Outside' once lived. And now we know what happened to them. They were flooded out after the earthquake."

The Makah canoe *Tatoosh* was a work of art in addition to a means of travel. With room for eighteen people fully loaded, she was among the largest canoes in the flotilla. She was among the most elaborately carved as well, with painted faces and bodies of animals on both sides from stem to stern. In keeping with her name, which meant *Thunderbird*, her bow was graced with a scowling eagle's head reminiscent of the Seahawks' team logo but done in tones of black, red, and tan—colors of much more ancient origins.

Along with several dozen other canoes, the *Tatoosh* had been carried to the shore and was ready for launch once she was loaded with people and supplies. Nine a.m. was the departure hour for a three-to-four-hour paddle to Seattle in time for an early-afternoon greeting ceremony at Pier 62, followed by another evening of feasting and dancing.

Arnie and Ginny Musselshell were helped aboard at the bow, accompanied by Johnny Steele, who took to a plank seat just behind them with his ornately carved paddle in hand.

Alki Point juts westward into Puget Sound from the mainland of West Seattle. Across the waterway, Bainbridge Island's Restoration Point juts eastward, aimed directly at Alki. The two-mile channel between the points obscures the fact that they are geological evidence of the Seattle Fault that created them. A huge container cargo ship chugging down the middle of the channel crossed the submerged portion of the fault and continued southward, bound for a terminal in Tacoma. Simultaneously, a white-and-green Washington State ferry crossed the fault northbound at a brisk clip on a run from Bremerton to Seattle.

Ryan Hewitt and his girls had ridden an earlier ferry from Winslow to Seattle. He had driven his station wagon from downtown Colman Dock to West Seattle, eventually reaching a favored spot on the south shore of Alki Point. There, he parked on Beach Drive Southwest beside a long sidewalk that edged a fifteen-foot bulkhead that rose up from the beach.

As he turned off the engine, Emily cried, "Look at all the tide pools!"

"Let's go see!" Caylie exclaimed.

"That's the plan! Come on, girls. We've got the rest of the morning to play at the beach, then lunch at Spud Fish and Chips, then we'll go to the viewpoint at Don Armeni Park and watch Mommy fly over the stadium. And then we'll catch a ferry and go home. Mommy will already be there waiting for us."

"Cause Dolphin 224 flies really fast!" Caylie asserted.

The girls threw their doors open and scampered down a

concrete ramp to the beach while Ryan put on a wide-brimmed hat and sunglasses and gathered an armload of colorful plastic buckets and shovels. He and the girls all wore shorts and T-shirts and canvas tennis shoes that could go into the washing machine after the inevitable dunking one or more would take on slippery seaweed-coated beach rocks ponded with salt water. It was a glorious, warm day. The girls quickly found a large tide pool and crouched on either side, oohing and aahing at green anemones and purple snails covering its bottom.

Ryan smiled at their enthusiasm, and then glanced along the half-mile length of beach. The tide was coming in. Within a few hours the rocks and tide pools would be covered. By then, he judged, they all would have worked up an appetite for lunch. For now, it seemed an ideal morning at this lesser-used beach. The rocky shoreline was nearly devoid of other beachcombers. Small waves lapped placidly at green-seaweed-strewn boulders and rock ledges. Sunlight glinted off blue-green ripples with dazzling, golden-hued charm. On the point, the classic white stucco lighthouse with salmon-colored tile roof looked idyllic. The thrumming engines of the mile-distant container ship and ferry added low, resonating rhythms to the otherwise still air. Ryan inhaled its fresh salt smell and smiled. He could feel the life of the Salish Sea vibrating all around him. Things were going just as planned.

Chapter 7

Earl Adams III, Carolyn Parsons, and Grace Toscano had left Earl's BMW in a parking garage and crossed the green spaces of the Seattle Center campus to the Space Needle. They were standing in a short line to buy elevator tickets when Grace cried out in surprise. "It's you! Where did you come from?" She smiled excitedly as Matt Balen approached them.

Grinning at her, Matt shrugged. "I heard you guys talking yesterday about coming here. I thought it would be nice to see you again." He spoke to all of them, but his eyes lingered on Grace's.

"It's nice to see you, too!" Grace bubbled as if they hadn't seen each other in years.

When Earl's turn came at the ticket window he said, "Three."

"Four," Carrie quickly amended, nudging Earl with an elbow.

"Four." Earl put a credit card in the window tray.

Moments later they boarded one of the multi-windowed exterior elevators and it lifted off quickly with a dozen passengers aboard. As the car vaulted skyward, the attendant gave a rehearsed speech. "Traveling at almost sixty miles an hour straight up, the elevator will reach the 520-foot observation level in less than half-a-minute. Enjoy the views as we go. They're even better at the top."

"We're surprised to see you," Earl told Matt. "I'd have invited you, but I thought you wanted to spend some time with your folks."

Matt's smile faded. "It probably was a dumb idea to even go there."

A long pause ensued until the elevator doors opened onto the observation deck level.

"Anyway," Matt said as they got off, "I thought I could

point out some of the sights."

"That's a great idea," Grace replied.

"But right now," Carrie said, "we're late for our lunch reservation. Maybe you can show us the sights afterwards."

"Oh, yeah, lunch." Matt grew uncomfortable as they walked toward the restaurant entrance.

"Come on and join us," Earl offered good-naturedly. "I'm buying."

"I… don't mean to impose."

"Not a problem," Earl laughed. "I think I can afford it. Especially for such interesting company—a native Northwesterner, and a man with no past."

Carrie clucked her tongue. "Earl!"

Grace put a hand through the crook of Matt's elbow as they walked. "They say the view from the restaurant is as good as from the observation deck."

It was the Washington State ferry *Issaquah* that had crossed the Seattle Fault as Ryan Hewitt looked on. She was heading for Seattle with a few tardy baseball-game commuters among her passengers. These included David McGee and his grown son Zack. Dressed in team jerseys and ball caps, they had been last-minute walk-ons—or rather, run-ons—at Bremerton on the west side of the Sound. The pair stood at the green-enameled metal railing on the upper passenger deck, watching Alki Point lighthouse glide past as they moved swiftly north. Below the more-than-solid steel decks, the *Issaquah's* engines thrummed powerfully.

"Sorry we're late." David leaned his elbows on the railing with the wind off the bow buffeting his gray goatee. "Your stepmom needed the car, and she was running late. So, here we are, one ferry after the one we wanted to be on. But we won't miss much of the game."

"Are you sure?" The wind jostled the twin braids of Zack's black goatee.

"We'll miss an inning or two, but we'll be there for the real excitement."

As Professor Rutledge's noon-time appearance at T-Mobile Park approached, Lori McMillan and Kyle Stevens were in the seismology lab watching data roll in on the monitor screens. An expression of wonderment grew on both their faces.

"Another slow-slip event?" Lori wondered.

"I don't know," Kyle replied. "There are an awful lot of small jolts registering all over the place."

"Where are they centered?"

Kyle shrugged. "I couldn't guess. Not without some computer triangulations."

"But they're blanketing all the closest stations." Lori indicated one plot that had just registered a substantially larger jolt. "That's a West Seattle station, and it's getting the spikes before the others, isn't it?"

"Yeah."

"I think I'll call Dr. Rutledge. He'll want to know about this." She punched a number on her cell phone and a moment later was talking to Rutledge, who was on the sidelines at T-Mobile Park. She explained what they were seeing while Kyle sat at a computer station processing the triangulation data.

"I wish I could see for myself," Rutledge said.

"I've got the epicenter!" Kyle called out loudly enough for Rutledge to hear. "It's right under Alki Point! And it's real shallow!"

"That means we've seen activity on both sides of the Seattle Fault and now in the middle," Rutledge said. "I wish I could talk some more but I'm just about to go onto the field."

"Big crowd?" Lori asked.

"Huge."

"Got stage fright?"

"Yeah. I guess so."

"Are you worried about these small shocks?"

"Uh, no. Uh, yeah. Uh, I'm not sure. I've got to go now. Wish me luck."

"Break a leg!"

PART TWO: FRACTURE

Chapter 8

It was straight-up noon when the fireboat *Leschi* pulled away from her dock at Fire Station 5 on the Seattle waterfront just south of Pier 54. In the wheelhouse, Fire Chief Dale Klimchak commanded a crew of four including himself, Pilot Chip Sandoval, Engineer Richard Lester, and Deck Hand Rita O'Rourke. Today the *Leschi's* assignment was to display the power and majesty of a fireboat with all her deck guns jetting rainbow arcs of water while greeting the canoe flotilla from Suquamish.

The 108-foot *Leschi* was the pride of Seattle Fire Department's Marine Division. She was a state-of-the-art beauty gleaming in red, white, and black, powered by twin 1,550-horsepower diesel engines turning twin 72-inch propellers. She was capable of a flank speed of 14 knots, although today she moved much more slowly to avoid trouble in crowded waters.

Klimchak stood at his station at the center of the wheelhouse. "We've got a triple pass about to happen," he advised Sandoval.

"I see it," the pilot, seated on his right near the rudder wheel, acknowledged. A huge cruise ship, the *Alaskan Queen*, was pulling away from Pier 66 aided by two tugs, while the ferry *Issaquah* approached Colman Dock and the *Leschi* herself moved out toward the group of several dozen canoes that had just rounded Magnolia Bluff.

"I don't like all this complex maneuvering," said Klimchak.

"We'll find our way through okay," Sandoval replied.

"Are you ready with the pump engines, Rick?" Klimchak asked the engineer. Lester, a 40-year veteran of the department, manned a touchscreen display on the port side of the bridge that gave him a visual representation of a maze of on-board control systems. On his screen, he could see and control each pump, valve, and "monitor," as the ship's four, cabin-mounted water cannon were called, as well as a 55-foot telescoping crane with a ladder and its own monitor.

"I'll have them at full power by the time we're on station," he said of the ship's two pump engines, each of which could put out 5,000 gallons of water per minute.

Klimchak turned to his own radar, sonar, and radio station, feeling a little uneasy using ship-to-ship and ship-to-shore communications to orchestrate *Leschi's* maneuvers among vessels large and small. "Sometimes I wish the Port would organize things just a bit better," he grumbled.

"The ferry is running late," Sandoval said. "And the canoes are early. The cruise ship is right on time. And we're—"

"Right in the middle of it."

"I'm sure our Chippendale Boys can handle it," Rita O'Rourke quipped, referring to the Chief Officer's and Pilot's names as well as their physiques. It was a given that all crew members' fitness training included carrying an adult over their shoulder during rescue practices—and Rita was no exception.

It was to be an early game for the Seattle Mariners, starting at 12:40 p.m. They were hosting their perennial division rivals, the Oakland Athletics, with both teams' playoff hopes on the line. A win would advance the Mariners to the playoffs as a wild card. A loss would retire them for the season. The significance of the game had brought out a record crowd. There were few empty seats in a stadium with a maximum capacity of nearly 50,000 people.

The two teams had occupied their dugouts and both bullpens were busy. The Mariners were on the field, warming up by tossing balls around the bases or doing stretches to prepare for fast acceleration if a hit came their way. The pitcher was loosening up his arm with a series of fastballs, knuckleballs, curveballs or straight pitches, high-and-inside or fading out of the strike zone.

The hugger-mugger of tens of thousands of voices echoed within the stadium. The retractable roof was rolled away to the east on giant railroad-car wheels. Sunlight flooded the field, and the grass was fresh, green, and crisscrossed with mowing patterns.

Ronald Rutledge felt as small as an ant in the Mariners' dugout with such a stupendous crowd surrounding him. He would have preferred a much more low-stakes game, but events had conspired to make this the inevitable date for his appearance. Unthinkable though it might be to fans and management alike, a loss today would end the season. That would postpone the tsunami talk for another year. As he chatted aimlessly with catcher Aron Carter, who would take his First Pitch, Rutledge began to overheat. He took off his sport coat and laid it on a bench. He rolled up the sleeves of his light blue shirt and loosened his red necktie, but still felt sweat moistening his brow.

"The Seattle Mariners would like to remind everyone," announcer Brett Stertzel said over the booming PA system, "that today's admission fee brings you an extra benefit. That's right folks, not only will you be treated to the thrilling conclusion of regular-season play and the Mariners' advance to the playoffs..." Stertzel paused to wait out the predictable roar of affirmation from the crowd. "...but we will have an added attraction—an earthqua-a-a-ake dri-i-i-i-ill!" Though Stertzel tried his best to make the news sound thrilling by drawing out the last two words, the crowd was not keen on the idea. The stadium hushed and boos broke out here and there. More boos followed, and then laughter from ten thousand throats made it clear game-goers had little interest in the drill.

Stertzel resumed. "But first, ladies and gentlemen, boys and girls, will you all please stand or kneel for our national anthem. Today's singer is a surprise guest, Ed-d-d-d-dy Shred-d-d-d-der! The murmur of anticipation rose again as a color guard brought the flag onto the field and stood at attention beyond the pitcher's mound. The crowd roared its approval as Shredder walked onto the field with his guitar strapped on and strummed an opening chord. Thousands of hands were placed over hearts as he sang, "O-oh say can you see..."

Tim Carrington stood on the outdoor second-floor landing of a shake-roofed condominium building in West Seattle's Delridge

District. He rang the doorbell, and after a moment, Valerie Styles opened the door and graced him with a pretty smile and a smooch on the mouth. Then she went to her couch on one bare foot and one purple-and-pink running shoe.

He leaned on the doorjamb. "I thought you'd be ready. We're gonna be late."

"I'm almost ready!" She finished putting on the other shoe, went to a closet, and took out a white hoody sweatshirt. "Last-minute wardrobe change. I decided it might get cold on the pier later." She tied the sleeves of the sweatshirt around her waist and picked up a large leather-and-black-canvas purse. "Ready!" she smiled, heading out the door. He followed her down to a carport where his emerald green Explorer waited in a stall marked VISITOR. They were a study in contrasts, she in form-fitting purples, blacks, white, and pink, and he in a baggy T-shirt and vest in hunter's camouflage with cargo shorts to match. A camo kepi on his head lent him a paramilitary look. He opened her door for her and then got in and fired the ignition. In seconds, they were racing along Delridge Way northbound.

"You don't need to go so fast," she complained when he floored it to make a yellow light. "We can miss a few minutes of the canoe ceremony. Was traffic bad coming here?"

"Traffic is always horrendous on I-90 through town from Everett to West Seattle."

"You should have given yourself more time."

"Not really. I'm getting to know your habits after—how many dates? Five?"

"I think it's six, counting this one."

"You're a slow dresser. You're obsessed with the weather and wearing just the right thing."

"At least I care how I dress. You're so predictable. Camos. And a field coat in the back seat." She turned and there it was, piled in a corner.

He shrugged. "Ready for anything, including the apocalypse."

She clucked her tongue. "Sometimes I wonder how Merge.com ever connected us. I like to shoot wildlife with a camera. You, on the other hand—well, you'll never get me to go hunting with you."

"I wouldn't want to. But it's obvious why Merge connected us," he chuckled. "We're both wildlife enthusiasts."

"In completely different ways! I've got pictures of animals hanging on my walls, and you've got that—*ugh*—stuffed head!"

"It's only a deer—and a four-point buck, mind you. That's not exactly one of your precious endangered species."

"Our relationship is endangered every time I see that thing. It's gross."

He glanced at her. She didn't look as testy as she sounded. He said conciliatorily, "So, we have a few differences."

"A few! The stupid computer matched us for both loving to ski. But I like cross-country and you're addicted to downhill."

"Adrenaline, man!"

"And we both love road trips. But I drive an eco-friendly hybrid and you drive a gas-guzzling environmental disaster!"

"And I'm Mr. Punctuality, and you're Ms. Chronically Late. I wonder what keeps us together?"

She thought a moment and then smiled naughtily. "Some weird nocturnal attraction?"

He grinned. "That's a *whole* 'nother matter. And it's not weird at all."

"Normal boy-girl stuff," she agreed.

"Anyway. If I had tickets to the baseball game, we'd be late already."

"Oh, no, we wouldn't. You'd have made a point of getting here sooner and bugging me to finish dressing."

"Or start undressing."

She chuckled. "It won't hurt you to miss a game and get some culture today. And at the rate you're driving, we'll get to the canoe ceremony early—if we don't get killed first. Slow down!"

"Yes ma'am." He eased off on the gas pedal. "Better?"

"Much better!"

"You young people are really pulling your weight!" Arnie Musselshell called to Johnny and the others paddling the *Tatoosh*. They plunged in their paddles and took solid strokes in time with a Native chant called out from the stern by skipper Kenny Helm.

"I bet we'll make the crossing in record time," Ginny added.

With *Tatoosh* in the lead, Kenny was navigating for the entire flotilla. He eyed the huge cruise ship to port and the ferry overtaking them to starboard, and used his paddle blade like a rudder to adjust *Tatoosh's* heading.

The cruise ship steamed on northbound and the ferry approached Colman Dock, leaving the canoes plenty of room just as another ship drew near. Oohs and aahs burst from people aboard *Tatoosh* and other canoes as the fireboat *Leschi* sent out wide, arching jets of water in their honor. Glinting sunlight painted rainbow colors on mist descending from the streams as the *Leschi* moved nearer. Filled with delight and pride, Kenny voiced his call-and-response song loudly and the crew answered in a rhythm that kept their paddle strokes perfectly synchronized.

In the stadium, Ron Rutledge's moment had come. High above him in the broadcast center, Brett Stertzel announced, "And now, ladies and gentlemen, the Mariners proudly present a very special guest to throw today's First Pitch. From the Seismology Department at the University of Washington, Professor Ronald Rutledge!"

Although Stertzel's voice carried the enthusiasm he usually reserved for all-star players or pop stars, the crowd remained quiet as Rutledge and Carter emerged from the dugout and walked toward the pitcher's mound. Stertzel tried again. "Taking the field now accompanied by our own Aron Carter, let's welcome Doc-tor Rut-le-e-e-e-edge!" The smattering of applause seemed more in appreciation of Carter than Rutledge. Stertzel continued. "The Professor will make a brief statement before he throws the First Pitch."

There was a microphone on a stand near the pitcher's mound. When they reached it, Carter handed a baseball to Rutledge. "Keep it short and sweet. People want to get this game started."

The crowd was restless, murmuring.

"Dr. Rutledge has just a few words to say now," Stertzel said. "And then he will appear again during the Seventh-Inning Stretch. After we sing Take Me Out to the Ball Game and before we play Louie Louie, he will join us in the broadcast booth to give a brief—he promises to be very brief—lecture on tidal-wave preparedness. Won't that be fun?"

A murmured chorus of groans and boos arose in the stands. As Carter jogged to take his place behind home plate, Rutledge stood at the microphone, baseball in hand. He began uncertainly. "I promise not to bore you with a long speech today—"

"You already are!" someone shouted from the seats behind home plate.

"Just throw the ball!" someone else hollered.

Up in the stands, about midway on the first level of the right-field side, real-estate salesman Craig Palmer sat with his young son Willy and Willy's friend Liam Beasley. "C'mon buddy," he grumbled at Rutledge. "Get on with it."

The boys were excited. "We know how to duck and cover in an earthquake!" Liam said.

"We learned it in school," Willy added. "Watch!"

They demonstrated, giggling. Dropping on elbows and knees on the concrete floor between the rows of seats, they covered the backs of their heads with both hands, fingers knit tightly.

"Watch out you don't get any chewing gum stuck on you," Craig cautioned. Down on the mound the professor was going on about earthquakes and tidal waves, but Palmer ignored most of it, being more amused by the boys' giggling antics.

"Come on, girls," Ryan Hewitt called to Emma and Caylie. "It's time to go." The girls, having roamed the rocky beach all morning, squatted beside what might be the last tide pool not yet inundated by the incoming tide.

"No!" Caylie cried. "I wanna stay!"

"Just a few more minutes, please!" Emma cajoled. "We found the most darling baby eel!"

"Sorry girls. We need time to get lunch at Spud's before we go and watch Mommy."

"Okay." Emma reluctantly stood up.

"No!" Caylie moaned, staying put.

Ryan chuckled forbearingly. "Caylie, I thought you were the one who didn't want to come here at all."

"Well, I wanna be here now!"

"Look, honey. The tide is almost high. It's going to fill up that tide pool and that little guy is going to swim away."

"Well, I wanna see him do that."

"Okay, then. Just a few more minutes."

Jane Hewitt's Dolphin 224 had lifted off from Port Angeles a few minutes earlier. She and her three-man crew were seat-belted in and wearing their helmet visors down to shield their eyes from sunlight glinting off the waters of Puget Sound. Moving at a comfortable cruising speed of 120 knots with their twin Lycoming turbine engines humming, they were on a bee-line course for Seattle, on what promised to be a gorgeous day for their cameo role at the game.

In the Space Needle restaurant, the Adams party was finishing lunch. While they ate, the circular restaurant had completed an hour-long rotation on its giant platform. Starting with a south-facing vista of Mount Rainier, the view had imperceptibly shifted to Elliott Bay and the Olympic Mountains in the west, then Smith Cove, Shilshole Bay, and the San Juan Islands to the north. Lake Washington and the skyline of Bellevue with the Cascade Mountains in the east had followed, with Matt providing detailed commentary. Finally, Seattle's downtown skyscraper district loomed to the southeast and Rainier took center-stage again.

The waiter approached. He was a tall, fine-looking young Creole whose faint accent suggested he might have family origins in Jamaica or New Orleans. His nametag read DeWAYNE.

He recited the dessert menu in a precise, almost Britannic lisp that gave the impression he may have studied acting.

"Anybody interested?" he asked when finished.

"Just give us a couple of minutes," Earl said.

"Certainly, sir," DeWayne hurried off, his thin frame moving with poise and elegance that could only have looked more refined if he had carried a swagger stick.

The table conversation turned to what to do next. Earl favored the Seattle Art Museum, but Matt counter-proposed the Burke Museum on the University of Washington campus. Grace noted Earl's look of irritation as she and Carrie were swayed by Matt's contention that the Northwest Native American and natural history collections at Burke were not to be missed. She watched Earl's expression darken as she and Carrie laughed at Matt's smart-aleck quips and absorbed his deep knowledge of local attractions.

When Earl felt the one-man show had gone on long enough, he leaned across the table and said tersely, "So, Matt, I'd like to hear some more about *you!*"

The humorous light faded from Matt's eyes. "No. You don't."

"Yes. I do. If I'm paying for your lunch, and you're tagging along with us to the museum, then I'm afraid I'll have to insist."

After a sudden drawing-in of breath, Carrie protested. "Earl! Don't you think you're being a little harsh?"

Earl was undeterred. "So, Matt? Let's have it." He sat back in his chair and folded his arms across his chest.

After a long pause, Matt said almost inaudibly, "All right."

Grace didn't like the way the two men locked eyes across the table. She touched Matt's hand and whispered, "You don't have to."

"Yes, I do." Matt drew in a deep breath. "Where to begin?" He lowered his gaze and stared at the white tablecloth. "I've had a run of bad luck. Just a couple years ago, you'd have said I had it all going my way. Ex-Marine, two tours in Iraq, honorable discharge, military scholarship to Stanford University. High-Tech Engineering major, Dean's List. How's that for starters?"

He glanced sharply at Earl whose eyebrows involuntarily went high.

"I'm impressed," Earl replied. "Go on."

"I got a little cocky, I guess you could say. Me and another guy, Gary Hobart, came up with a plan for a tech company startup we called Solaris Corporation. I was working on a minor in Chemistry, and he was in Electrical Engineering. We designed a small solar power generator so efficient it will work in rainy climates or sunny, in a jungle or a desert."

"Solar power on a rainy day?" Grace quipped. "Sounds like a good idea for a solar-power company from Seattle."

"It's a super-efficient system. One small unit can make enough power to run a health clinic in the field, or a food distribution facility with cold storage, or provide lighting for a refugee camp."

"It sounds so humanitarian!" Carrie remarked.

Matt shrugged diffidently. "That was our big idea. Bring power to people wherever they needed it. It could be on an emergency basis, or permanently if a small community didn't have an alternative. Economically priced too, we thought."

"Thought," Earl repeated.

"Thought. Ever hear of Eldon Devine?"

"The real-estate billionaire?"

"That's the guy. He liked our idea when we pitched it at a Stanford student-investor conference. He said he'd bankroll the whole startup, from early development through manufacturing of prototypes. But he insisted on being our only shareholder. Said he wanted to own the majority of the stock when the idea went over big. We didn't particularly like giving him a major share, but he stuck on that point, so we agreed."

"So, what happened?"

"Gary and I both dropped out of Stanford and moved to Seattle. That's where Devine wanted us—under his watchful gaze. And it was fine with me because I grew up here. We created the first prototypes in a small building in the SoDo district just south of the stadiums. It took us about a year to work the bugs out and start making them. We rigged up the first unit on the rooftop and it worked beautifully. We ran an electrical line down into the shop and actually started using its power to manufacture the next units. It worked like a charm, even on rainy days."

"Keep going."

Matt shrugged. "One day Eldon Devine showed up at the shop. He said, 'You're both fired.'"

Grace and Carrie gasped.

"No explanation given?"

"Oh, he explained. He'd just bought an Arctic oil company because the government opened the nature reserves to drilling and oil companies were striking it rich. So, he pulled the investment rug out from under us and put the money into oil exploration"—Matt snapped his fingers—"just like that."

"What a jerk," Carrie said.

"Jerk?" Matt laughed wryly. "That's an understatement. We were pleading. 'You can't do this! We've got the first prototype finished! Give us a couple months to prove it's reliable. Please!' But he grinned like he thought it was funny."

"What a monster!" Grace cried.

Matt nodded. "All our time and effort wasted, and he's laughing. We were almost crying. In fact, later, I did. I'll admit it."

"You should cry," Grace said. "I would. In fact, I'm about to start now." She was red-in-the-face and dewy-eyed.

"With a prototype, you could have found other investors," Earl suggested.

"We tried. But we had to tell them about Devine, who still held our stock. When they checked with him, he told them we were lying when we said it worked. I think he wanted to block solar power as long as he was in the oil game."

"That's horrible!" Grace wiped a tear from the corner of her eye, as did Carrie.

"Anyway," Matt concluded. "It got me pretty down."

"I guess it would." Earl's face registered sympathy too.

Matt shrugged. "What else can I say? I got depressed. I developed a drinking problem. I decided I'd just get out of town and go somewhere I could forget about it all. I was short on money and my folks couldn't help, so I snapped. I cancelled the lease on my apartment, got a backpack and some camping gear, and I bounced outta town. No plans. No goals. No expectations."

"Whew!" Earl said when Matt finished. "That was an earful. Well, I guess I asked for it."

Matt stood, now red-faced himself. "I think I'll go outside get some fresh air." He turned and started for the door to the Observation Deck.

"Wait!" Grace jumped up to follow him. "I'm coming with you."

He didn't look back, but she hurried after him as he went out the door.

After a moment, Carrie chided softly, "You were a little hard on him, Earl."

"I guess I was."

DeWayne reappeared. "Any desserts, here?"

"I'll have coffee," Earl said.

"So will I," said Carrie.

"Anything else?"

"Have you got any humble pie?" Earl asked.

Grace caught up to Matt as he stopped near the glassed–in edge of the observation deck. He touched a tall pane with his fingertips. Noticing her beside him, he mumbled, "I thought there'd be a railing I could jump over."

"Matt!" Her eyes widened. "Don't talk like that!"

He thought a moment and then chuckled softly. "I guess I can get a little melodramatic. Now you know why."

"But you shouldn't feel that way. You've still got a lot to live for. I can see that, even if you can't!"

She put a hand through the crook of his elbow and hugged his arm. "You didn't really mean you'd jump?"

"Not really."

"And at the Emerald Fountain in Yellowstone? Carrie said you told her you'd been thinking about jumping in when we came along."

"The thought had crossed my mind. But no. If I'd really wanted to, you'd have found me floating there."

Grace shuddered but continued hugging his arm. After a moment she suggested, "You could show me some more sights."

Morosely, he pointed out a low warehouse in the SoDo district. "That's where Solaris is… was, I mean."

Grace wrapped her arms around him and hugged him, shaking him a little. "Cheer up. I have confidence in you. You're the kind of guy who can make things happen if you keep a positive attitude."

He smiled. "You're probably right. I just haven't figured out what to do yet."

"I have my own problems," she confided.

"You do? Like what?"

She described the disaster in Kathmandu and her failed effort to save the young man. "I developed a full-blown case of PTSD."

"I can see how you would."

"I was so haunted by the memory of that boy's eyes, and the sound of his pleas. It wrecked my sleep. I'd burst into tears without warning. I saw a psychiatrist in New Haven for years. I still have nightmares. But I'm learning to cope."

She pressed her cheek to his chest and hugged him more tightly.

"I'm sorry you went through all that." He put his arms around her and kissed the top of her head. She let out a deep sigh. They stared out at the view without seeing it.

Chapter 9

The morning's efforts at Alki Beach had gone well. Leon Curtis and Ann Butterfield had recovered the entire skeleton. They had arranged the bones in museum storage boxes and loaded them into the back of the Blazer. Below where the skeleton had lain, they had uncovered more traces of waterlogged, partially decomposed, but ornately-carved planks. Leon knelt beside one of these and inspected it closely. "We're going to need more help from the museum. A bigger excavating team and a new grant to pay for it. If we keep finding artifacts at this rate, it'll take *years* to collect everything."

Ann didn't reply. Standing for a moment to stretch her legs, she was looking to the south. Now, she suddenly gasped.

"What is it?" Leon rose and followed Ann's gaze, and then he gasped too.

At the far end of the beach the surface of the sand was moving in serpentine undulations that came toward them rapidly. In shocked disbelief, Anne murmured, "It— It looks like Henry George's A'yahos! It's…"

"—an earthquake!" Leon finished in a shout.

The earth-waves emanated from Alki Point, which lurched upward, impossibly, as they watched. Apartment buildings on the point shook and shattered. Trees and street-lamp poles danced crazily. The Alki Lighthouse was uplifted *en masse* along with the ground under it. Off the tip of Alki Point, the sea bottom itself thrust upward out of the water.

It took scant seconds for the sand ripples to reach Leon and Ann, while they stood paralyzed by fear. When the earth-impulse struck, it pitched them both off their feet. They scrambled to rise but continuous violent shaking kept them on their hands and knees. Ann screamed again. Leon cried out as a wall shored up with plywood burst, spilling tons of sand onto his legs and pinning him to the bottom of the pit.

When the main quake impulse rolled on to the north, the earth continued moving with smaller jarring vibrations. Ann managed to clutch her way up one side of the pit and look south again. A whole new hillside stood where Alki Point had lain, and a new spit of land extended a quarter mile beyond what had once been the tip of the point. Beyond that, Ann could see where the fracture continued under Puget Sound to Restoration Point on Bainbridge Island. Above the unseen portion of the fault, the surface of the Sound had risen by perhaps fifty feet on a line between the two headlands. The fault had thrust, not just upward, but northward as well, imparting a strong northbound push to the huge wave.

Ann turned to Leon and cried, "There's a tsunami coming!"

Leon was digging desperately at the sand pinning his legs. More sand was slumping into the pit, spilled by fresh tremors. "Help me!" he begged.

"Oh my God, Leon!" Anne resisted a panicky impulse to run for her own life, dropping to her knees and tearing at the sand covering his legs.

Just three miles northeast of the rupturing fault, the ground had yet to move. Visitors at the Space Needle had no inkling of the catastrophe about to hit. As stupendous shock waves within the earth raced toward them, Earl and Carrie lingered over coffee.

"I've still got my doubts about the wisdom of those two getting together," Earl said.

"I think they make a darling pair," Carrie countered. "It's love, in bloom."

Earl shrugged and took another sip. "I'm surprised she's so eager to get involved with a guy with a history like that."

"But it's not your decision to make, is it?"

Out on the observation deck, Matt and Grace were wrapped in each other's arms. Although the breeze was cool, their bodies were warm where they pressed together. She raised her face to gaze into his eyes, and he bent and kissed her lightly on the lips. She flung her arms around his neck and drew him to her. As passion suddenly sparked between them, he kissed her more firmly. And then, just as suddenly, he stepped away from her.

"What?" She was surprised by the abruptness of his move.

He wasn't looking at her. He was looking past her, his eyes wide with disbelief.

She followed his gaze and her heart leapt with fear. The entire landscape to the southwest looked like a living thing. Tall trees and buildings in West Seattle moved in metronomic motion, tottering from side to side or falling amid billows of dust. Nearer, the gray concrete arch of the West Seattle high-rise bridge rippled and lurched like a bucking animal. Its roadway made rolling, twisting contortions that tossed cars and trucks from one lane to another—or off the bridge entirely. Puffs of gray dust erupted from every joint in the structure.

"What's going on?" Matt puzzled, unable to accept the witness of his eyes.

"An earthquake!" Grace gasped.

Leon Curtis's legs were buried deeply but with four hands digging frantically, he was able to pull them free in seconds. He and Ann scrambled out of the pit. On the main beach level, the ground was still heaving under their feet, but they knew they faced a much greater threat.

"The rest of the legend!" Ann cried. "A'yahos sent the tide out all at once. Look!"

As Henry George had suggested, there were now bare tide flats where the Sound had stood high moments before. Stranded fish flopped on the sand. The wave had already covered much of the distance from Alki Point, drawing down the water ahead of it as it rose into a towering wall of glinting, blue-green death.

"And it's coming back—fast!" Leon finished the legend as they turned and sprinted away at a dead run. "We'll never outrun it!"

"Get into my car!" Ann hollered without slackening her sprint. "I'll drive us up the hill."

The close-by location of their parking spot was now a godsend. They rushed to the SUV and jumped in. Ann fired the ignition and roared away from the curb with tires screeching. Other beachgoers were rushing to their cars as well, but chance favored Ann with a spot directly across Alki Avenue from hill-climbing Bonair Drive. Ann narrowly beat other cars racing for the intersection and floored it up Bonair.

"Ah-hah!" she cheered, but her exultation was short-lived. Almost immediately, she came upon a jam of cars converging at the Halleck Avenue intersection. "Oh no," she groaned, entering a stop-and-go tragi-comedy in which each driver waited for his or her turn to proceed uphill. People were astonishingly polite given the stakes. The pause gave Ann and Leon time to glance out the rear window and watch the wall of water rise to thirty feet high, then forty. At fifty feet its crest curled and broke, roaring louder than a 747 jetliner.

When her turn came at the intersection, Ann floored the accelerator and continued up Bonair, steering white-knuckled in a single-file line of cars. Though the cars made quick progress up the gently rising, partially forested road, the wave moved faster. She and Leon cast terrified glances back as it swallowed the beach, the dig site, and the sidewalk in seconds. Then it inundated Alki Avenue, engulfing dozens of jammed cars, and roared uphill as a wall of froth that towered above them and came on at horrific speed.

A quarter-mile southwest, all was chaos inside Blazes Emporium. Glass display shelves lay toppled and shattered. Vapes and marijuana jars littered the floor. Coolers had tipped and spilled their medibles. But at least the two-story building still stood, thanks to its quake retrofitting. Zoey rose from where she had been tossed to the floor and hurried to the shop's shattered front window.

"Whoa!" she cried to Moe, who took longer to get to his feet. "Have a look at this!"

He joined her to observe an Alki Beach community shaken to its foundations. Along Alki Avenue several buildings had collapsed completely. Others were partially destroyed. Parked cars had been crushed by falling brickwork. Dazed people staggered on the still trembling sidewalks or dashed from stricken buildings in states of panic.

"Look!" Moe pointed to the beach itself. "The tide is like, totally out!"

"And what's that, farther out?" Zoey puzzled.

"It's"—Moe stammered—"a tidal wave!"

A mountainous ridge of water stretched from Alki Beach entirely across the Sound to Bainbridge Island, rising taller than the building they were in. As the pair stood open-mouthed, speechless, and frozen in place, a saving grace was that the water wasn't coming directly at them. The monstrous wave had already rushed past them northbound, and they were viewing its rear slope, spared for the time being from its all-consuming force.

"What do we do? What do we do?" Zoey cried.

"I don't know! I don't know!" Moe hollered back.

"Mmmph!" Rex shook his head in doggie perplexation.

Chapter 10

On the Space Needle deck, Matt and Grace stood transfixed by what they were seeing. The West Seattle bridge had rocked and swayed until it seemed on the brink of crumbling altogether. Dust fell along its length, billowing around the structure's concrete pillars. Then the central arch spanning the Duwamish River tore free and collapsed to the choppy waters below, dragging with it a pall of dust and a few unfortunate vehicles.

"Oh my God!" Grace cried, trembling in Matt's arms. "The people!"

"Why don't I hear anything?" Matt wondered as the debris impacted the river and sent out vast white jets of spray on all sides, some nearly as tall as the span itself. "I guess the sound hasn't reached us yet."

"I don't want to hear it!" Grace shuddered.

On top of what remained of the bridge, Tim Carrington and Valerie Styles were the most terrified onlookers of all. Moments before, they had been hurrying to the canoe event. As Tim's Explorer had approached the center of the span, the huge ripple of earthquake energy caught them from behind, rolling under their car and throwing it high into the air. Other vehicles had also been lifted off the pavement, falling back to the surface in crazy orientations. Some had tipped on their sides. Some were upright but cocked at odd angles across several lanes. Some had skidded, some had scraped on bare metal, some had gone over the abutments and fallen, but most had halted with their occupants in states of panic.

Tim's Explorer came down relatively straight, bucking like a bronco but still moving forward at about fifty miles an hour. Tim slammed on the brakes and with tires screeching, slowed as quickly as he dared without losing control of his steering. He gritted his teeth as the center span ahead of them crumpled and dropped away.

Valerie screamed as the Explorer slid toward a new, huge void nearly sixty feet across.

Although their speed decreased to only a few miles an hour, they neared the edge of the gap with dismaying certainty. The Explorer's momentum brought them to—*and then over*—the brink. Valerie wailed as the pavement went out from under the front end and the tires dropped into space. Death seemed certain, but the undercarriage scraped noisily on the pavement and their forward motion abruptly ceased. Somehow, the rear tires gripped the road even though it heaved back-and-forth, side-to-side, up-and-down.

When the most violent shaking subsided, Valerie tamed her screams. Tim sat with his hands gripping the wheel, his foot jammed on the brake pedal, and his teeth clenched so tightly they were in danger of shattering. They both stared out, wide-eyed, at the jagged edges of pavement sixty feet away across the gap. On the waterway, a hundred feet below, white mist from the fallen section was still dissipating.

Valerie struggled with her door latch, but it was jammed. "We've gotta get out!"

"Wait! Wait!" Tim cautioned. "Look how far over the edge we are!" He used his left foot to engage the emergency-brake pedal, locking the car to the pavement as much as he could, given the energy still reverberating through the bridge. "It's a long way down if you open that door."

She stopped tugging on the handle and glanced out her side window. "My God!" she murmured. "We're halfway off the bridge! What are we going to do?"

"Just hold very still. Let me think." His greatest fear with the Explorer in such a precarious position was that any shift of their weight might topple them over the brink. Beyond that, thinking was hard to do. The bridge rippled with earthquake energy and each shudder or scrape of the Explorer's undercarriage brought them closer to death.

"One wrong move—" He couldn't complete the thought. Instead, he glanced over the sloping engine compartment and saw the river roiling below. Vehicles that had gone down with the center section had already sunk.

On the Space Needle deck, Matt gestured at a new disturbing sight. "Look at that!" While the bridge continued to crumble, other parts of the landscape began to transform in alarming ways. As the roar from the bridge collapse finally reached the Space Needle and grew in volume, dozens of tall cranes on Port of Seattle container terminals appeared to come to life. One by one, the orange behemoths began moving like long-necked dinosaurs in a crazy galloping dance.

"It's coming toward us!" Grace gasped as one crane after another joined the dance, each crane nearer than the last. One dropped a freight container onto the decks of a ship it was unloading. "We need to go warn Earl and Carrie!"

"No!" Matt kept her in his embrace. "We can't reach them before it hits, anyway. I'd rather stay here and see what's coming."

"Okay." She held her trembling body tightly against his.

They watched in horrified fascination as the quake impulse continued north, rippling through the low structures of the SoDo District and raising palls of dust from buildings as they swayed or fell. Streetlight posts wagged from side to side. Some larger buildings partially crumpled or collapsed completely. The largest building in the area was the Starbucks Corporate Center, a twelve-story boxy brick structure with a central clock tower adorned on all sides with green-and-white Starbucks Mermaid logos. The main portion of the building, long ago reinforced with cross beams, held firm. But one of the mermaids shattered and fell in pieces to the street below. The building shed tons of brickwork, followed down by streamers of red dust.

Although the Starbucks building withstood its ordeal, other non-retrofitted SoDo buildings of brick or wood cracked and tumbled down in a succession of disasters, each following rapidly on the heels of the disaster preceding it.

Matt watched the wave of destruction sweep northward with his cheek pressed against Grace's head. "It'll hit the stadiums next."

In the as-yet unaffected baseball stadium, Professor Rutledge had given the crowd a brief outline of the drill to come. "I'll give you the full details at the seventh-inning stretch," he concluded. "I'll walk you through it then, and you can try it for yourselves. Okay?"

The crowd remained quiet.

"Now then," Rutledge said to himself as a field crewman removed the microphone and stand. He stepped onto the mound, hefted the baseball, wound up his arm and delivered the best pitch he could manage. It was a decent throw, heading true to the strike zone and Aron Carter's waiting glove. An odd rumbling arose as it sped through the air.

Suddenly Carter was thrown down on his face and the ball skimmed over his back, bouncing away crazily on the ground. Crazy, too, was the way the stands behind Carter moved in a giant rippling motion as if the crowd had spontaneously decided to do The Wave. The energy of the motion was powerful enough to toss people entirely out of their seats and propel them several feet in the air. They came back down screaming and tumbling over one another, spilling drinks and popcorn everywhere.

A split instant later Rutledge himself was tossed off his feet. He cried "Earthquake!" as he fell. Flat on his back, he heard tremendous rumbling noises in the stands high and low, cheap seats and expensive, as the stadium flexed and rocked in chaotic motion. Massed shouts and screams of thousands of men, women, and children added chilling high notes to the deep subterranean roar reverberating like thunder through the stadium.

Rutledge got to his hands and knees, gaping at the wildly gyrating stands as a bolt of raw terror coursed through him. Dust billowed everywhere. Shattered window glass fell from executive suites onto people in the stands below. Here and there, execs fell too.

In the stands, Craig Palmer also shouted "Earthquake!" as waves of chaotic motion swept past. Willy and Liam shrilled, "Duck-

and-cover! Duck-and-cover!" Dropping onto the concrete, they covered their heads as they had done playfully minutes before.

"Dad!" Willy called when his father hesitated. "Come on! Duck-and-cover!"

Following the boys' example, Craig dropped into the aisle and covered his head with his hands. An instant later, a heavy sign placard, twenty feet wide, crashed down on their seats and the seats of the fans around them. The sign, which read ALL-STAR CLUB, had been dislodged from the front of the over-hanging balcony section above them.

Both boys screamed as the placard thundered down and dust billowed around them. Palmer added his shout of shock as he crawled nearer the boys, offering his shoulders to the placard, which had been stopped by crumpled seatbacks just inches above them. Glancing to one side, he saw the bloodied, twitching arms and legs of some unlucky souls who had remained in their seats just a split second too long.

Chapter 11

Moments before, Lieutenant Jane Hewitt and her helicopter crew had been taking in the sights of Seattle, gawking like tourists as Dolphin 224 cruised along the placid waterfront. Coming in from Port Angeles on a vector to Boeing Field, they were on track to land and wait for a seventh-inning call from the stadium. As they passed the Space Needle, Jane spoke through her helmet microphone, "I never get tired of this view."

"Look at that fireboat with all its jets going!" Copilot Ramon Valenzuela replied. "And the big Ferris wheel on Pier 57. I'll bet they've got a great view!"

"Not as good as we've got," Jason Chow, the flight mechanic, chimed in from his seat on the flight deck.

As they overflew the *Leschi*, the canoes it was saluting, an incoming ferry, an outgoing cruise ship, and tour boats and dozens of other watercraft coming and going, Jane said, "It looks like a busy day in the Port of Seattle."

"Roger that," Rescue Swimmer Tyrell Collins replied over the intercom. "Crazy busy."

They had been neglecting the view to the south, but suddenly, all that changed. From her high perspective, Hewitt's eye was caught by the crumbling West Seattle bridge and the contortions of the nearer landscape. As the impulse of quake energy rippled through the waterfront district under them and billows of gray dust rose from dozens of damaged and falling buildings, she reflexively steered off her course and made a wide circle, viewing events that were still unfolding. She exclaimed into her microphone, "This is no earthquake drill folks. This is the real thing!"

"Madre de Dios!" Ramon Valenzuela responded.

"I can't believe what I'm seeing," Jason Chow said.

"Believe it," Hewitt shot back. "The fun and games are over on this mission. We're in for some real-life rescue work."

"I thought we were just logging some flight hours," Tyrell Collins said. "Lucky I brought my diving gear in case an emergency call comes in."

"I think we'll be getting that call real quick," Hewitt said.

"And then a lot more," Valenzuela agreed.

"Look at the stadiums!" Chow cried out. Both T-Mobile Park and CenturyLink Stadium billowed clouds of dust as they rocked to their foundations.

"Let's go check that out," Hewitt pushed the helicopter's nose down and accelerated toward the stadiums. "T-Mobile was our destination anyway. Ramon, get in touch with Boeing Field and tell them we'll be late."

"No can do," Valenzuela came back after a moment. "Their radio signal is dead."

In the still-calm center of downtown, few people had an inkling of what was coming. Office towers were largely deserted on a Saturday and only a few people working near south-facing windows were even aware of anything out of the ordinary.

Inside Devine's tower, Kelly Anton stepped off the elevator into the softly lit entry of the thirty-first floor executive office complex. She was there to meet him for what he had unabashedly proclaimed would be a nooner rendezvous with luncheon laid out by a chef who had already left the building. Devine was waiting at the landing, where the black granite floors and cedar walls complemented his stiff-looking black pinstriped three-piece suit, pink shirt, and gold necktie. He made no effort to conceal how he eyed her up and down as she got off the elevator. She was dressed provocatively in a red, hip-hugging skirt suit with a low-cut, chest-revealing white silk blouse—risqué for business attire but well-suited to this occasion.

Other than his brief once-over inspection, Devine seemed distracted. He scowled. "Who does he think he is, that inspector? I've got a hundred thousand times as much money as he'll see in a lifetime."

"Federly?"

"Yeah, Federly. I want you to get a restraining order on that pipsqueak and keep him out of this building. Or find out who he reports to and apply pressure there. I want him to hear the words, 'You're fired!' sometime soon."

"Even pipsqueaks can be dangerous, Eldon. Especially when they're armed with the truth. Remember, he's been here. He's got the witness of his own eyes."

"So what? If he makes allegations, I'll just spin lies faster than he can find the truth. If he says it's not X-braced, I'll say it's Z-braced. If he says it's too lightly built, I'll explain just how massively it's constructed."

"Even if that's not true?"

"Truth? Lies? That's not the issue. It's how *fast* you spin lies. The truthers have never been able to keep up with me."

"But there are a lot more truthers in this world than liars. They'll win by sheer numbers."

"Not as long as I can lie faster than they can find the truth."

"Can you?"

"I'm sure of it."

"I wish I were."

"Trust me."

"Trust you? You're the most untrustworthy man I've ever met."

They glanced into each other's eyes, and for a moment there was complete silence. Then they both burst into laughter. They laughed for some time, but abruptly stopped when a deep thundering rumble arose within the building.

"What the—?" Devine never finished the sentence. The floor and walls heaved sideways, throwing them off their feet. As they struggled to rise, cracks appeared in the floor, inches wide. Interior window glass shattered. Vases and picture frames dropped and disintegrated. Cedar wall panels splintered. The black granite reception desk toppled and fractured into shards that skidded across the floor.

Kelly screamed and Devine bellowed a curse as they foundered on a floor that seemed to have come alive under them. It was impossible to rise to their knees, let alone stand on the slick polished tiles.

Two blocks away, Dan Federly and his wife Alisha were at the Fourth Avenue entry of the Columbia Center Tower. Dressed nicely for a planned luncheon in the rooftop restaurant, they were just entering the building when the first jolt all but knocked them to the ground. Within seconds, a stream of hysterical people began rushing past them to get out. Dan's first impulse was to join them, but his building-inspector instincts froze him in place.

"No, people!" he shouted at those stampeding by, "don't go outside! It's more dangerous out there than it is in here." He took Alisha by an arm and drew her to a large pillar. They pressed themselves tightly to it as people streamed from the lobby, nearly sweeping them along in their panicked flow.

As a man in a light-blue sport coat brushed past him, Dan threw out an arm and stopped the fellow. "Wait! It's dangerous—" he began, but the man doubled a fist and punched him hard on the jaw, nearly dropping him.

"Wait yourself, jerk!" the man growled, then resumed his sprint outside.

The floor tossed again with a colossal jolt, forcing Dan and Alisha to hug the pillar to keep their feet. Then a new sound manifested itself. Almost lost in the thunder of the earthquake and screams of fleeing people was the tinkle of falling window glass. At first the *tinks* and *tangs* were barely audible. But they swelled as fragments of heavy glazing dropped from the building façade onto the pavement in the midst of the crowd racing for safety. In that hope, they were sorely mistaken.

"Oh my God," Alisha cried as clinking, clanking, shattering sounds increased to a roar. Greater and greater volumes of glass streamed down, peeling away from higher floors and combining with torrents of glass falling from lower stories. As blade-like shards slashed or impaled one victim after another, cries of agony competed with the roar of tons of glass shattering on the street and sidewalks. Only those who had heeded Dan's pleas to stay under the protective cover of the entryway were spared.

The glittering torrent took on the proportions of a lethal

Niagara Falls. The thunder of thousands of shattering panes was punctuated by the cries of mortally stricken victims. Heavier thuds came from floor-to-ceiling glazing, which had dropped intact from tens of stories above, and now cleanly cut some hapless souls in two. Other victims were knocked down and submerged in layers of glass stripped from the building's once-gleaming exterior.

Then, as the earth motion passed on to the north, the fearsome cascade ceased almost as quickly as it had begun. Alisha sagged against Dan. He caught her in his arms as she fainted dead away in the face of the grisly carnage. He cradled her in his arms until she revived enough to get her feet under her. She pressed her face against his shoulder and wept. He stayed silent. His attention was gripped by a new and riveting sight. High above, the unfinished top of Devine's tower was shedding steel girders and beams. Its construction crane tilted alarmingly.

"Let's go inside," he said.

"Where to?"

"As far from that Emerald Tower as we can get."

Matt and Grace had stared, dumbstruck, as the stadiums rocked with the force of the ground movement under them. They had watched the earth impulse propagate northward among the downtown skyscrapers. Buildings tottered and flexed visibly. Showers of window glass peeled away. Palls of dust billowed from each stricken building. None toppled completely, but all swayed and twisted like trees in a windstorm. The crazy gyrations of each skyscraper in succession emphasized the stupendous power of the shockwave racing toward them.

"It's almost here!" Grace's voice grew thin.

"A matter of seconds," Matt acknowledged grimly.

They looked into each other's faces.

"Do you think it will knock this place down?" she asked.

"Let's hope not."

Grace glanced down at the Seattle Center grounds, vertiginously far below. "Oh God!" she prayed. "Please don't let us fall all the way down there!" As the rippling earth movement reached the Center and propagated across the lawns to the base of the Space Needle, her heart palpitated. She threw her arms around Matt's neck to keep from fainting and barely whispered the words, "Hold me!"

He pulled her close with one arm while grabbing a guardrail with his free hand to steady them. "Here it comes!"

Chapter 12

When it hit, the quake pitched every part of the Space Needle upwards and sideways at the same time. Matt's grip on the railing helped them keep their feet through the first immense jolt. Then as suddenly as they had been pitched one way, the Space Needle reversed direction and swung back like a giant metronome. Again, Matt's desperate grip kept them on their feet.

"Hold on!" he shouted over the roar coursing through the building.

"I am!" she shouted back. "I'm holding onto you!"

Inside, Earl and Carrie were caught unaware. Their view had rotated until they were looking northwest. Consequently, they saw no hint of the oncoming threat. When the quake's force struck, they were cast out of their chairs to the floor. They had considered themselves lucky when the *maître d'* had shown them to a table next to the windows. Now, they felt much less lucky as the glass shattered out beside them, falling away into space.

The restaurant rocked so heavily that the landscape seemed to gyrate in response. Mountains and clouds, waterways and headlands appeared to rise *en masse* and then drop dizzily as the Space Needle lurched north and then swung south. A circular motion developed as well, imparting a rolling stress that shattered windows one after another starting with theirs and repeating like The Wave propagating around a football stadium. Each window did not so much shatter as explode into thousands of glass splinters that flew out and then dropped away. At several tables, unfortunate patrons were pitched out as well, plunging with screams that diminished with distance.

Windows were not the only structures stricken by the power of the quake. Ceiling tiles tumbled down around Earl and Carrie, trailing choking dust clouds. As shock after shock rippled through the building, something heavy tore loose above Earl's head. Issuing metallic groaning, whining, and snapping sounds, a massive air-conditioning unit crashed onto their table, shattering it. They scrambled to get out of the way but only Carrie succeeded. With a heavy crunching thud, the unit came down on one of Earl's legs, pinning him to the floor and forcing a scream of agony from him.

As the rocking motion of the Space Needle subsided, Carrie scrambled to Earl on hands and knees. Horrified by his contorted face she cried, "Are you hurt bad?"

"Yeah!" he moaned through gritted teeth. "Real bad!"

Not knowing what else to do, she heaved her shoulder against the four-foot-long, box-shaped machine. It didn't budge. Her eyes widened when she spotted blood oozing from underneath. "Can you pull your leg out, Earl?"

Wincing with pain, he shook his head. "No."

Inside T-Mobile Park, Ronald Rutledge stood up and looked around in bewilderment. From his central viewpoint on the pitcher's mound the entire stadium, although it still stood, was a scene of extreme chaos and terror.

Everywhere he looked, dust billowed. Frightened people seemed to be of two minds. Some individuals or groups rushed toward the nearest exits while others stayed put as if waiting for a providential voice to tell them what to do. Rutledge looked up at the media booths, wishing for the same thing. But the view windows of the Broadcast Center were dark and partially shattered out. Furthermore, all of the stadium's display panels were dark, where moments before they had been flashing a plethora of team-spirit phrases, highlight videos, and advertisements. Clearly, the power was out completely.

He glanced at the dugouts. Most team members had vanished into interior corridors, but a few were either sticking it out where they were or venturing onto the field despite the trembling underfoot.

In addition to the players, many fans raced onto the field, perhaps to avoid falling objects or to find the quickest way out. They rushed past Rutledge in random directions with horror-stricken faces and cries of terror.

He stayed where he was for the moment, shaken and confused. He had come to the stadium to teach earthquake safety, but the quake had already come and gone. *What should people be doing now?* Was it better to leave, or had those who stayed in place made the right decision? The correct answer came in a flash when he recalled his own prepared remarks: *There may be a tsunami.* Given Lori's call of minutes before, he was instantly certain the quake had hit the Seattle Fault and consequently a tsunami was coming—probably within just a few minutes.

Suddenly he was in motion. Cupping his hands, he shouted at fans rushing past him. "People! You should stay in place! Don't run out! We're in a tsunami hazard zone. Stay here and move to higher locations!" He was reciting the speech he had planned to give, but no one was listening. Stepping to the highest point of the pitcher's mound, he raised both hands high and waved at people.

"Stop! Everyone!" he bellowed.

Still, no one paused or looked in his direction. He lowered his hands and stared at the pandemonium gathering strength. More and more people were fleeing. His situation struck him as almost comical—one panicky man shouting at a panicked crowd to stop panicking and listen to the voice of reason. But this was no comedy. And Rutledge felt a grim sense of responsibility.

Aron Carter stumbled to him over the still-moving playing field. "What do we do?" he shouted over the roar of thundering feet in the stands and shrieks of women and children.

"If I were you," Rutledge hollered back, "I'd get into the stands as high as I could go."

"What are *you* going to do?"

"I've gotta get to the broadcast booth. If they've got any power, these people need to be turned around. How do I get there quickest?"

"Come on!" Carter turned and motioned Rutledge to follow. "There's an opening through the foul-ball netting behind home plate. We can go up from there!"

As they raced toward the backstop, a new and terrifying

sight met their eyes. All along the left-field wall, mud gushed from under the stands like lava from a volcanic fissure. Thick and black—no doubt a liquified portion of the mudflat on which the stadium had been built—it spread across the playing field at an alarming rate. The third baseman and third-base coach were mired to their knees and struggling to avoid falling into what was essentially flowing quicksand. As the front raced toward them, Carter reached the place where the foul-ball netting could be parted and held it back to allow Rutledge through. Rutledge vaulted over the field bumper and went headlong into the stands. Carter quickly followed, but not before his feet were overrun by the surge. Making slurping noises as he pulled his legs free, Carter tumbled into the first-row aisle and got to his feet, coated to mid-calf with sulfurous, stinking muck. Rutledge watched in horrified fascination as the mudflow washed over home plate and then into the now-empty Mariners dugout, sweeping along dozens of hapless fans who had been knocked off their feet.

"This way!" Carter turned and ran along a corridor that led under the stands. Rutledge followed with the mudflow surging under the barrier and streaming close on his heels. Carter burst through a door labeled INTERVIEW ROOM and they entered a ground-level auditorium with massed camera gear and interview tables fronting a backdrop of Mariners' logos. They rushed down an aisle between rows of empty press chairs as mud gushed onto the podium, overturning the interview tables. Racing out a back door, they finally left the mudflow behind by running up a concrete ramp that led to the main concourse level. There, they encountered a chaotic mass of humanity rushing for the exits.

"No! People!" Rutledge began his entreaty again, but Carter seized him by an arm and dragged him to the nearest staircase. It was jammed with people rushing down to the streets—and whatever fate awaited them there. With some effort, the two found they could edge their way along one side by grabbing a handrail and pulling themselves upward one step at a time against the downward crush of fleeing, panicked humanity.

Within Devine's Emerald Tower, the floor and walls continued heaving—sideways, up, and down—as the force of the earthquake reverberated through the inadequately braced building. Still prostrate on the black tile floor, Eldon and Kelly Anton looked to each other desperately in the dim, dusty interior. A crack had opened across the entire width of the floor, separating them with a gap more than a foot wide. Eldon's side remained level, but the floor on Kelly's side buckled downward more with each reverberation.

Slowly, she began to slide toward the opening.

"H— Help!" She clutched at the smooth tiles while Eldon looked on, apoplectic with terror. She managed to scramble up the slope and catch hold of the jagged edge where the sagging part of the floor met a portion that had not buckled, being abutted to a wall. She managed to keep herself from sliding down the ever-increasing incline by clinging to a piece of iron rebar protruding from the edge of the flat floor above her. Another violent jolt caused the floor section she was on to drop and hang suspended vertically by the rebar she clutched and a dozen others. The broken floor section, and Kelly, swung suspended above a chasm that vanished into the dust-obscured depths. Many floors below, crumbling and smashing sounds could be heard.

Clinging to the rebar with both hands, she twisted until she could see Eldon. "You've got to"—she called to him breathlessly— "come over and pull me up!" She nodded her head toward a place where the rim of still-horizontal floor on her side joined the floor on his side via a ledge that ran along the wall's circumference. "Cross over that ledge!"

As the quake's energy passed and the most violent surges within the building subsided, Eldon rose to his feet, staring at her with eyes still wide with panic. "H— How am I supposed to do that?" He glanced where she indicated but stood frozen in place. "I can't cross that ledge."

"You've got to try. If you don't, *I'll* fall." Small tremors still rattling through the building were slowly undoing her grip on the rebar.

Eldon could see her fingers slipping. He glanced at the ledge again, and then at Kelly. "I can't!" he reiterated, shaking his head.

"Please!" she begged. Her voice became a childish, unhinged whine. "Ple-e-e-e-ease! Don't let me di-i-i-ie!"

Eldon took several steps toward the crossing point, but then he stopped. He faced her with outstretched palms. "What about me?" he demanded. "What if *I* fall?"

She stared him hard in the eyes. "Coward!" she raged, but the violence of her outburst made one hand slip off the rebar. Her voice choked off. Her face went ghostly white.

He approached the edge of the chasm carefully and glanced down. "I'm afraid your luck has run out," he said icily. "But *mine* hasn't."

"What?" she gasped. Terror and incredulity played over her face. Then rage returned. "Damn you, Eldon Devine!" she screeched. Then her grip failed, and she dropped into the dust cloud. "Damn you to he-e-e-e-ell!" Her curse ended in a heavy thud about four stories below. After that, the only sounds Devine heard were the grinding of concrete on steel inside the still-flexing building.

Chapter 13

Tim Carrington and Valerie Styles sat silently staring across the gap in the West Seattle Bridge. They had calmed enough to catch their breath but remained paralyzed by fear of falling if they made the wrong move. The Explorer hung in a precarious balance, teetering a little more with each jolt of the subsiding earthquake.

Suddenly, Valerie broke into tears. "I don't want to die!"

"I don't either!"

Moments before, their hopes had raised when they spotted a Coast Guard helicopter in the sky above them. The idea that it might somehow rescue them had faded when it swung away to the east and circled back toward downtown Seattle. Dust clouds and smoke emanating from a dozen tall buildings suggested the helicopter had greater problems to deal with than just one vehicle in jeopardy.

Although earth tremors shaking the bridge lessened with each passing second, the Explorer continued inching farther over the brink.

After a moment, Valerie wiped her eyes. She pointed ahead of them. "Maybe *he* can do something."

Across the gap, a man had gotten out of a station wagon that lay on its side not far from the point where the westbound lanes, like their eastbound counterparts, had crumbled into the river. Moving cautiously, he came to the edge of the gap and stared across at them. Perhaps he sensed that his hopes of survival where much greater than theirs. Perhaps he was considering ways to help them. A small dog stood beside him, glancing uncertainly from its master to the river below. The man took a cell phone from his pocket, touched some keys, and put it to his ear. After apparently getting no signal, he put the phone back in his pocket, put his hands out to his sides and gestured that he could be of no assistance.

Valerie fetched her phone from her purse and tried calling 9-1-1. The display read NO SERVICE.

"There's probably no reception for a hundred miles around here," Tim muttered.

On the south side of Alki Point, Ryan Hewitt and his daughters had just experienced something more horrific than a nightmare. Their tide-pool explorations had ended when the fault ruptured directly under their feet. Although they could not know it, no one was closer to the epicenter than they. The earth jarred upward in a stupendous surge that knocked them off their feet and flattened them onto the seaweed-covered rocks. For seconds that seemed like hours, one massive upward jolt followed another, each of which thrust the shoreline higher, and them with it.

In seconds, the entire beach had risen fifty feet skyward. Tide pools lost their charm and turned into frothing cyclones that splashed cold water on them as they floundered on slippery boulders. The girls' piping screams chilled Ryan to the bone, as did the spectacle around him. The waters of Puget Sound, which had lapped the shore placidly moments before, drained away from the uplifted land in foaming cascades. A huge volume of water that had risen with the seabed now poured back into the Sound, generating a huge wave in the process. Mercifully for the Hewitts, it moved offshore rather than on.

As the rumbling and vibrations subsided, Ryan struggled to his feet. Slipping on wet seaweed and uneven rocks, he gaped in confusion at the crazily up-tilted beachscape. Caylie was at his side, clinging to his waist and wailing. He picked her up, and she hugged his neck, shrilling, "Daddy! I'm so scared!"

Emily was on her feet too, though multiple small aftershocks in the still-rising land made it hard for her to keep upright. She bent to inspect a skinned kneecap. The sharp shells of barnacles had opened dozens of small bleeding slits.

"Are you all right, sweetie?" Ryan asked.

"I'll be okay," she replied bravely. "What happened?"

"Earthquake!" Caylie wailed, pressing her tear-wetted face

against Ryan's neck.

"Yeah, an earthquake." Glancing around, he could scarcely believe his eyes. The immensity of the earth movement was hard to conceive. Not only had the beach been uplifted, but the bulkhead above them and the houses across the street had risen fifty feet as well. An entire portion of West Seattle, as far as the eye could see, had been thrust skyward. Many of the beach-front houses were in various stages of collapse. Some had lost the glass of their picture windows. Others had caved in partially. Still others had crumpled completely.

Frightful as the shoreward view was, the scene offshore was more unsettling. Where gentle waves had lapped no more than ten feet from them, there was now a steep, seaweed-glazed slope that extended a hundred feet into Puget Sound. The previously calm waters churned on the back of the outbound tidal wave.

Other beachcombers staggered to their feet as the wave moved away southbound. But now Ryan saw a new and horrifying change. Nearest the shore, the outflow stopped. Almost imperceptibly, the water reversed direction and advanced onto the beach. Having rushed out too far, too fast, the waters stood below the general level of the Sound—and that imbalance was causing a rebound. The main wave might be moving away, but the hollow it left behind was being refilled massively.

"Come on, girls!" Ryan barked. "We've gotta get away from here!" He grabbed Emily's hand and clutched Caylie tightly, scrambling up the slippery slope toward the half-demolished ramp that led to the top of the bulkhead. Their car, parked on the roadway, appeared dishearteningly far above them. "Hurry!"

Eldon Devine peered down into the black, dusty void where Kelly Anton had disappeared moments before. Earthquake tremors were abating and the building at last was settling down. His heart pounded in his chest, but that too was subsiding. He took his cell phone out of a coat pocket, punched 9-1-1, and pressed it to his ear. A triple beep indicated a dropped connection.

"Come on!" he frowned at the NO SERVICE message. "Why don't you work when I need you?" He thrust the phone back in his pocket with a grunt of disgust. "Do you know the hit my pocketbook will take if I lose this place?" he blustered as if berating others who were not present. "Billions!" He glanced around in the dim light, searching for the land-line phone that normally sat on the front desk. Both the ruins of the desk and the phone had vanished into the hole.

"I'll contact the Governor, that's what I'll do. And I'll *demand* action from that dragon lady! I'll let her know, in no uncertain terms, Eldon Devine's tower is first in line for repairs! And if she can't make it happen, I'll call the President of the United States. Goddammit, I will!"

He choked on acrid concrete dust hanging thick in the air. And then an even more acrid smell drew Devine out of his obsession with money matters. "Smoke!"

He edged near the brink of the hole and leaned out far enough to get a good look down. Four stories below, orange flames flickered obscurely among the dust billows. "Oh my God! I could be burned alive!" His heart palpitating, he peered down at the hellish glow. "Kelly," he murmured, "you might be the lucky one after all."

Chapter 14

Moe and Zoey had watched from the elevated vantage point of their shop as the tidal wave moved northbound in the direction of Seattle proper. As it went, it swept along the side of the Admiral Heights bluff, crushing view homes and snatching fleeing cars off hillside roads like toys.

"Oh, man!" Moe groaned. "I'm thinking a lotta people are gonna get killed."

Zoey tore her eyes from the unfolding tragedy and glanced to the west. "Hey, look!" She elbowed Moe and pointed out over the drained beach. A new, lesser wave—although still huge—was coming ashore. Moving directly at them at right angles to the first wave, it was refilling the low-water area. They watched in mounting horror as it developed a curling crest about fifteen feet tall. "We gotta get outta this place!" she cried.

Moe stood impassively as the crest began to break with a thunderous roar. "No," he said in a strangely calm voice. "We don't need to get out."

"What?" Zoey gaped at him like he'd lost his mind.

"We need to go up, not out. We're on the flats of Alki Point, right?"

"Yeah? So?"

"So, it would take us forever to get to high ground."

"Oh. Yeah. You're right."

As if to emphasize the futility of flight, the wave swept across the tide flats and consumed the sandy part of the beach in seconds, enveloping terrified beachgoers who had only just gotten back on their feet. It overwhelmed the sidewalk and Alki Avenue, gathering up parked cars like chips of wood, and then surged straight at the line of businesses on the landward side of the street. It mowed down pedestrians who had fled from buildings, and then slammed into the buildings with crushing force.

Zoey screamed and Moe cried out "Ya-a-a-a-aah!" as their own building shuddered with the impact of the wave, which surged in and through the first floor and raced past on either side. Shattering and crashing sounds beneath their feet made clear that the Thai Mi Down Restaurant below them was being annihilated along with its staff and clientele.

"What do we do now?" Zoey cried.

Moe stood dumbstruck as the flood rumbled under and around them, making horrific sucking, splashing, roaring sounds as it inundated the neighborhood. He and Zoey watched breathlessly as the surging brown water carried driftwood logs, street trees, cars, and people swimming feebly in its overwhelming clutches. Flimsy buildings splintered and were carried off as flotsam. But the old, solid, reinforced two-story building that housed Blazes Emporium had withstood the torrent—so far.

"Water's still rising," Moe observed. "We'd better get to the roof if we can." He led the way through a bead-curtained door at the back of the shop to the stock room where dozens of shelves of marijuana boxes had spilled their plastic-bagged green contents on the floor. Scarcely noticing, he opened the rear door marked EMERGENCY EXIT and they were surprised to see daylight in what had been an enclosed staircase. Sections of the outer brick wall had peeled away, and sunlight streamed around the retrofitted steel cross-beams. The steel-reinforced concrete stairs had also survived, though they were strewn with fallen bricks.

Moe began to carefully ascend the unstable rubble. "Come on, babe. We've gotta get up there somehow. I think the water is still rising."

"It sure is." Zoey pointed through one of the new holes in the wall. Water encircling the building had nearly reached the second level where they stood. She called behind her, "Here, Rexy!" The little mutt came from the shop, making low moans and reluctantly following as they clambered up the brick rubble. When Moe reached the top of the steps, he shouldered a jammed wooden door open and pushed it out against resisting debris. "Thank God! The roof's still okay!"

Zoey and Rex followed him onto the flat, tarred surface and gazed at the neighborhood in dull astonishment. Less substantial buildings were folding one by one, their wreckage rafting away on the overwhelming current. The water level had risen until Blazes Emporium must surely be awash.

"How—how high will the water get?" Zoey asked.

"I don't know, babe."

The *maître d'* of the Space Needle Restaurant, a portly balding gentleman, circulated among tables, overturned or otherwise, with an announcement. "People! The elevators are out, but the stairway is right through there." He gestured with the flat of a hand to an exit door. "You can walk down. It's a long way—over a thousand stairs—but you'll do fine if you keep calm."

Carrie hurried to the man. "My fiancé is hurt! And he's trapped!"

The man followed to where Earl half-sat, half-laid with his right leg pinned to the floor by the air conditioning unit. The huge, box-shaped machine, four feet on a side, had crushed his calf just below the knee, and he was bleeding badly. The man put his hands on the unit and shoved with all his might, but it didn't budge.

"I tried that," DeWayne Pettijohn explained as he came from the kitchen with a first-aid kit. He knelt and got out a tourniquet, which he wrapped around Earl's thigh and twisted to apply pressure to the femoral artery. "I was a combat medic in Iraq," he told Carrie as he cinched the tourniquet tight and stanched the blood flow. "There!" He sat back on his haunches. "That's better."

"At least the spurting stopped," Carrie turned a little green at the sight of blood pooled on the carpet under Earl's leg.

Matt and Grace arrived while DeWayne worked. Matt knelt to inspect Earl while Carrie and Grace shared a tearful hug. Grace stared at Earl's face, wearing a haunted look as if fearing a replay of the Kathmandu scene.

"C'mon," Matt said. "Let's see if we can get this thing off of him."

Acting together, the four put their combined force into trying to move the unit off Earl's leg, but the effort was wasted. The unit weighed half a ton at least.

"Has anyone called 9-1-1?" Grace asked.

"I tried," DeWayne replied. "Cell phones aren't working. Land lines either."

"Then somebody's got to go for help. But where to?"

Waitress Monica Morales overheard the question and came to them. "There's a fire station down there." She pointed through a shattered window at the neighborhood below. "See? It's on Fourth Avenue and Wall. Maybe they can send someone to help you. It looks like their building isn't too messed up."

"You're right!" Matt agreed. "I'll go there!"

"I'm coming with you!" Grace followed him as he hurried toward the exit.

"Tell them to bring blood plasma," Earl called after them. "I feel a little faint."

"Will do!" Matt called over his shoulder as he hurried out the exit with Grace. "Keep chill, dude!"

When they had gone, Carrie sat down on the carpet beside Earl and took his hand. The Space Needle was still swinging back and forth, more gently now as the energy imparted by the quake dissipated. "Please, God, let them find help quick," she prayed.

DeWayne patted her shoulder. "Don't worry. I saw worse cases than this in Iraq, and they pulled through."

Earl said, "Mind if I worry just a little bit?"

"You're entitled," DeWayne said. "I just wish we could get this thing off you. I'll go look for something we can pry it up with."

"Good idea," said Earl.

The *maître d'* had cleared the rest of the people from the restaurant. Now he stood at the exit. "Come on folks," he called to the group. "Those who can leave, should go."

"Nah!" DeWayne shot back. "I'm staying with this guy."

"Me too," said Monica Morales.

"Okay," the man said. "But this place might not be safe. It's your call. Good luck to you all!" He turned and went down the stairs.

Kyle Stevens and Lori McMillan had bolted from the seismology lab when the quake hit, but the building withstood the shaking well. After waiting several minutes under swaying campus trees, they cautiously re-entered the dark ground-floor corridors, using a cell-phone light to make their way back to the lab. They knew a trove of information awaited them if and when the power came back on.

Some of the lab's tables and desks were overturned and some of the electronic equipment lay smashed on the floor, but most of the hardware was in place and intact. "I wish we could see the screens," Lori said, eyeing the bank of dark seismograph monitors. A moment later, her wish came true. Overhead lights came on with a buzz and the monitors flickered with restored electricity.

"Snap!" Kyle exclaimed. "That's gotta be the campus auxiliary power." All around them, display screens flickered to life. Printers and other electronics whirred and beeped through re-boot routines. Several of the seismograph-monitoring screens lay shattered on the floor, but most were still in place and reviving themselves automatically. And miraculously—or more likely by preplanning—the seismographic traces started appearing on them at once.

"Check this!" Lori indicated one. "The first station to register a jolt was in West Seattle. God! That's a huge spike! What magnitude do you think it is?"

Kyle frowned at scribbles sweeping from the top to the bottom of the screen. "It's, like, completely off-scale! I can't imagine the magnitude."

"Whatever it was, it was hella big!"

"I've seen seven-point-one, but that spike looks bigger. Insanely bigger!"

"The destruction must be epic," Lori wheezed. "People are going to die—"

"People have already died," Kyle corrected. "And the dying

may not be over."

"How do you figure? The spikes are a lot smaller now."

"I'm thinking, tsunami."

"Tsunami!"

"Could be major," Kyle said. "Especially if the bottom of the Sound shifted in a big way."

Lori's eyes widened at the thought. "Are we safe here?"

"I think so."

"But you're not sure?"

"Pretty sure. I've been researching some of the biggest tsunamis ever recorded, and—" He thought a moment. "You know, they can be pretty awesome."

"Kyle, you're scaring me. How awesome is awesome?"

"The earthquake that hit Valdez, Alaska in 1965 was bad-ass. It caused a tsunami that was forty feet tall on some of the islands in Prince William Sound."

"But we're like, a lot higher than that, right? We're pretty far uphill from any water."

"The Montlake Ship Canal, you mean. Yeah, it's downhill quite a bit from here. And it's above the Chittenden Locks, which are like, a good fifteen feet above high tide. So, yeah. I guess a forty-foot wave probably wouldn't get us here."

"Probably?"

"Well… You've gotta add the run-up factor."

"Run-up factor?"

"You know, like when a wave washes ashore on a beach. It spills on the sand and then it runs uphill before it turns and goes back out again. So, a tsunami doesn't just go as high as its original height. It goes a lot higher."

"You're definitely freaking me out. How high?"

"The forty-foot wave at Valdez knocked down a forest on a mountainside. It got up to one hundred seventy feet high in one place."

"Oh my God. We're not *that high* above the Sound!"

"No. We're not. And we gotta consider what happened at Lituya Bay in the '58 Alaska quake. That wave had a run-up of almost two thousand feet."

"Oh my God! Let's get out of here!"

"Nah."

"What?"

He shrugged. "We don't know for sure if there *is* a tsunami. Maybe there's nothing happening in Puget Sound at all."

She set a toppled chair upright and sat down on it as if her knees were about to buckle. "Can't we tell from any of these instruments?"

He picked up another chair, sat on it backwards, and rested his arms on top of its back. "Not these instruments. We might be able to get some information on the internet, but I doubt it's working right now."

"So, what are we supposed to do?"

Kyle shrugged. "Keep chill. And listen for a roar. If it comes, we'll book it up the staircase across the hall. Get above it."

"Gotcha." Lori took heart. "I guess I'd rather be in a solid building than out running around on campus."

"Totally."

As Ann Butterfield raced the wave up Bonair Drive, she repeatedly glanced in her rearview mirror, watching the wall of muddy water hurtle toward her. As it came, it smashed houses and apartment buildings lining Bonair in a thunderous symphony of splintering wood, shattering window glass, and faint human cries that were quickly drowned out. She watched cars in line behind her disappear one by one.

"It's gaining on us!" Leon moaned, unable to turn his eyes away.

"I know!" She watched death draw near with one eye on the mirror, one eye on the road ahead, and her foot jamming the accelerator. Her hands trembled on the wheel from an overdose of adrenaline. The wave diminished somewhat as it came uphill, and she hoped it would lose its momentum. But when it consumed the jeep immediately behind them and splattered against the Blazer's rear hatch, Ann let out a scream of pure terror. An instant later, the water swept up the Blazer with an impact like a bomb detonation, snapping Ann's and Leon's heads back and pushing the car forward faster than it had been going. Ann screamed again as they crunched into the sports car ahead of them and were forced up and over it, crushing the small vehicle and its driver. Then frothing dark water enveloped them on all sides. Immersed in nearly total darkness, they were buffeted fiercely and soaked in chilly spray gushing in through the door seams. The glass beside Ann's head cracked from water pressure, but it held.

"The car's filling up!" Leon cried.

"I know!" Pressurized jets of water sprayed across Ann's face and shoulders, chilling her and deepening her terror.

Then, miraculously, the water cleared from the windshield. The car was afloat, buoyed by air in the passenger compartment. Tossed by the chaotic waters, the Blazer whirled like a mad carnival ride. At first, it stayed upright with only its floor awash, but as the compartment filled, the SUV tilted alarmingly to the right.

"We're tipping over!" Leon shouted. Then they hit a massive object and their forward motion stopped with a grinding crunch. The brown deluge surged around and over them for what seemed an eternity. When the water at last drained away from the windshield, it was clear what had stopped them.

"A tree!" Ann could scarcely believe her eyes. "A huge tree!" Surrounding them were five massive, two-foot thick trunks of a bowl-shaped bigleaf maple, holding the Blazer like a gigantic catcher's mitt. Leafy branches overhead shuddered with the force of the water still flowing past, but the old maple withstood the tsunami's pull.

Ann realized she was tugging the wheel this way and that, trying to steer. The car, of course, wasn't responding. Its wheels were not in contact with anything solid and its engine had long since been killed. She let go of the wheel and sat back, taking deep breaths to regain some composure. The wave began to subside, having crested more than a hundred feet up the bluff. As it drained away, it carried a hellish mix of building wreckage, snapped-off trees, tangled telephone lines, and other detritus all but impossible to define.

"I think we made it," she sighed.

"Just barely," said Leon. "Nice driving."

"Even if I did drive us up a tree." She giggled, burning off nervous energy. Leon joined in, and they guffawed heartily, compelled by adrenaline and the preposterous situation they found themselves in.

While the main tsunami swept a path of destruction along the bluff north of Alki, the lesser surge south of the point did not act like a wave as much as like a tide rising impossibly fast. As Ryan Hewitt and his girls ran up the ramp, the waters moved like a living thing, mounting the beach in crawling, snake-like surges that quickly reached the base of the ramp. Climbing behind the sprinting family, the flood came on without a roar, but with an evil mix of gurgling, sucking, and sloshing sounds as unnerving as the full thunder of a breaking wave would have been. When the Hewitts reached the top of the ramp, they rushed to the station wagon without an instant to spare as the surge spilled over the top of the bulkhead and raced after them.

"Get us out of here, Daddy!" Caylie wailed, buckling herself into the passenger seat beside Ryan as he started the engine. He put the car in gear but paused with his foot on the brake.

"Go, Daddy!" Emily cried from the back seat. "What are you waiting for?"

Ahead of him, Ryan saw that the quake had split the pavement of Beach Drive wide open. In places, the concrete was jiggered up at odd angles or crisscrossed with cracks wide enough to swallow a tire.

"Daddy!" Emily urged again from the back seat. "Get going!"

Ryan let off the brake and moved forward, feather-footing the gas pedal. He swerved one way and then the other, moving past deep cracks in the pavement. He gained confidence and accelerated, mindful of the water not far behind. As he skirted a gap between two concrete slabs, the right-front tire dropped into it and the car smashed onto its undercarriage and scraped to a halt.

Both girls screamed.

"Sorry, girls," Ryan muttered. He put the shifter in reverse and gunned the engine. The rear tires screeched and threw out blue smoke, but the front wheels didn't budge. When the water reached the rear tires, they ceased screeching and spun freely, lubricated by muck. Ryan let off the accelerator and glanced desperately in all directions. Across the street the ground was higher, but the row of houses there looked threatening. In various stages of collapse, they were still shedding boards and sharp widow glass from their upper stories.

The girls squealed and screamed until Ryan silenced them. "Calm down, girls! I can't hear myself think!"

They obeyed. Caylie pressed her face against his arm to shut out the sight of the rising water. In the rearview mirror, he saw Emily looking at him with fear-widened, tear-streaked eyes. Meanwhile, the flood had washed completely over the street, surrounding the car in moving currents of murky, seaweed-laden water.

"What do we do now, Daddy?" Emily cried.

Ryan was at a loss. The water around them was already a foot deep with no sign of cresting.

Inside his tower, Eldon Devine stood near the brink of the hole that had consumed Kelly Anton. Shaken, he babbled to himself. "Maintain, Eldon. Don't lose control." The floor under him shuddered, clarifying that he by no means controlled the situation. Though the rumbling below abated as the earthquake rolled on, the thundering sounds above him seemed to be increasing.

A green EXIT sign glowed over a door across the gap. Its emergency battery made it a beacon in the otherwise dim and dusty room. "Gotta get over there," he mumbled. "But how?" The chasm in front of him was far too wide to jump. He glanced at the ledge Kelly had begged him to cross. Seeing it led to the exit and salvation, he went over and cautiously edged onto it.

Hugging the wall and glancing over his shoulder into the pitch-black hole, he said, "Sorry, Kelly. I wouldn't cross it for you, but I'll cross it for me."

PART THREE: FLOODS

Chapter 15

The canoers had stopped in the middle of Elliott Bay, watching in mute horror as the city shook and crumbled. Now, Kenny Helm called out, "People! Remember the legend of A'yahos! A wave will come!"

Ginny and Arnie Musselshell faced backwards in their honorific seats in the bow of the *Tatoosh.* Suddenly Ginny cried, "There it is!" Pullers in the *Tatoosh* and the other canoes turned to look where she pointed. A huge swell rounding the north end of West Seattle made people cry out in terror. It was bearing down on them with incredible speed. Kenny Helm glanced at it for only a moment, then addressed his paddlers. "Pull hard left! Turn to face it!"

The pullers splashed their paddles in a panicky, uncoordinated way that got them nowhere fast. Driven by necessity, Kenny calmed himself and called out his paddling chantey loud and clear. Johnny Steele and the other pullers responded with an answering chorus and settled into a disciplined stroke. In response, the *Tatoosh* swung to starboard just as swiftly as the big boat could move. Following their example, other canoe teams brought their craft around as well.

Dismayingly, as the wave neared, it rose to a crest in the shallower waters of Elliott Bay, reaching a height of fifty feet or more. The flotilla rode up its ascending face with stomach-churning swiftness. Then, one by one, the canoes launched into the air off the crest and plummeted over the far side. Choruses of screams went up as crews felt themselves dropping weightlessly until their wooden hulls splashed down. Still, none of the seaworthy vessels foundered.

The waters rose swiftly around Ryan Hewitt's station wagon. The engine compartment, tilted lower than the rest of the vehicle, flooded quickly and the engine killed. Ryan took his hand off the now-useless shifter.

Both girls screamed as water welled onto the floor of the car. Within seconds, it was filling Ryan's shoes and chilling his feet. It dawned on him that the weight of water rising around the car could press the doors shut and trap them inside. He grabbed the latch and tried to force his door open, but the flood was halfway up the sides of the station wagon. The door wouldn't budge. He glanced at the girls, who knelt on their seats to keep their feet out of the water. Both were trembling in terror and looking to him with desperate appeal in their eyes.

He got the idea to open a window and scramble to the top of the car, but the electric window button was shorted out. By now all traces of the beach, the bulkhead, and the road had vanished underwater. The station wagon was an island in a rising sea, with water gushing in through every seam.

Yet matters got worse. The flood developed a longshore current paralleling the beach. When the car's buoyancy freed the front wheels from the crack, the station wagon began moving with the flow, rocking crazily as it went. Both girls screamed shrilly. Ryan added his own outcry as a thought struck him: *If we get swept off the bulkhead and sink, we'll all drown!*

Moe, Zoey, and Rex stood on the flat roof, staring at the surge flowing on all sides of their building. It had risen to second-story level with terrifying swiftness. The building shuddered under them but showed no sign—as yet—of collapsing.

"I think the water might have peaked," Moe said.

"No, it hasn't!" Zoey stared, transfix with fear, at a second wall of water coming from the south and overriding the first. It appeared to be a reflection of the first wave, rebounding off the new hill that had risen along Alki Point. When this crosscutting surge reached the building, it submerged the last portion of the second floor and overtopped the low parapet that rimmed the asphalt roof. Only the topmost portion of the wave reached the roof, but it formed a two-foot wall of water rushing at them like a beach breaker.

"Over here!" Moe ran to an air-conditioner cabinet in the

center of the roof, about five feet on a side and three feet tall. They grabbed its door handles and other fixtures to steady themselves just as the wave roared into them. Rex leapt up and Zoey caught him, one-armed, and held him to her. Bracing themselves, they withstood the first sweep of the water, which inundated the entire roof and poured off the far side. For a moment they resisted the swirling, sucking drag but then Zoey lost her one-handed grip and splashed down. Moe caught an arm and held her against the flow one-handedly. Then, as quickly as it came, the water receded from thigh-deep to ankle-deep.

As the last of it drained from the roof, Zoey got to her feet. *"I lost Rex!"* she shouted. "I couldn't hold him! Where is he?"

"There!" Moe pointed off the downstream side of the building.

Rex was a hundred feet away, caught in the receding but still-furious current. His little feet dog-paddled frantically, but he was losing headway.

"Re-e-e-ex!" Zoey wailed as he was swept around the corner of a damaged building and disappeared. "Re-e-e-ex!" She turned and buried her face against Moe's soggy chest. He wrapped his arms around her and held her as she wept.

Aboard the fireboat *Leschi*, all was controlled chaos. The team had been preoccupied with the procedures and details of holding station and running four simultaneous jets from the ship's monitor spouts. Their attention had been fixed on the canoes and other shipping, and no one had noticed the quake hitting Seattle astern of them.

Now that situation had changed dramatically. The first inkling had been a rush of communications over the 800-megahertz police and fire radio system. In rapid succession, unidentified voices called, "Got a bad situation here!" "Emergency!" and "Earthquake!"

The three crewmen in the wheelhouse had turned to look back at the stricken cityscape of Seattle, at a loss for words until Chip Sandoval spun them around again with a cry. "What the hell is that?"

Off their port bows, less than a quarter mile away, the canoes were launching off a great ridge of water that was now bearing down on the *Leschi* as well.

"Tidal wave!" Rick Lester exclaimed. "A huge one!"

Captain Klimchak snapped out of a momentary state of shock—and came out shouting orders. "Kill the guns, Rick! All of them!" The arcs of water from the monitor spouts dwindled one by one. "Chip! Come about and face that wave squarely."

"I'm on it!"

"Ahead slow."

"Ahead slow."

"Steer straight into it!"

"Steering straight!"

"Everyone brace for impact!"

The canoes had vanished over the top of the wave—their status unknown. Just as Chip got the *Leschi's* bow squared with the tsunami, she was swept up by the wave's towering front. Plowing in deeply, her hull sprayed out great walls of white water on either side. An instant later, she was lifted entirely into the air off the wave's crest. There was a moment of gut-churning weightlessness as the *Leschi* fell through space, and then her hull crashed down on the back of the wave. All three men were thrown down heavily.

Walls of white water shot out around the *Leschi*, drenching her windows and sweeping her decks. A few breathless moments went by in which each man struggled back to his station and frantically checked equipment to see if the boat was intact or mortally wounded and sinking.

Rick spoke first. "Where's Rita?"

His question sent a fresh jolt of fear through the others. They glanced at one another with horror written on their faces.

"Last time I saw her," Chip began, "she was—"

"On deck!" Klimchak concluded.

They surveyed the boat out each window but the *Leschi's* decks, still shedding sea water, were barren of anything—or anyone.

As the crew of the *Leschi* rode out their ordeal, Dolphin 224 hovered overhead.

"Man!" Ramon Valenzuela cried as the fireboat splashed down beyond the wave. "What a ride!"

"Look there!" Jason Chow hollered, pointing to the north of them.

The Elliott Bay Marina had been overwhelmed. Hundreds of yachts and sailboats were jumbled against the base of Magnolia Bluff, riding a high surge of water in various states of capsizing, foundering, or shattering into splinters. The great mass of masts, keels, bows, sterns, and detritus were driven a hundred feet up the face of the bluff. There, the surge divided, and a portion of the wreckage flowed inland to the northeast of Smith Cove. An equally huge mass moved northwest, flowing over and past West Point. This surge reinforced the northbound wave as it overtook the departing cruise ship *Alaskan Queen*. Catching her at the stern, it propelled her like a colossal surfboard riding an equally colossal wave. The tsunami then left the liner behind, but not before her crazily tipping hull sloshed water out of upper-deck swimming pools and cast dozens of people from promenades into the Sound on either side.

"Woah!" Valenzuela exclaimed as the ship settled. "They were lucky to survive that—most of 'em anyway."

Meanwhile, the water in Smith Cove reversed direction, carrying its load of wreckage back into Elliott Bay in a rebounding wave almost as huge as the original tsunami.

Chapter 16

The water had roared around Ann Butterfield's SUV for what seemed an eternity but in reality, had been mere seconds. Speechless and trembling, she and Leon had watched the waters subside as the tsunami rolled on to the north. As the hillside resurfaced, it became clear there were no cars left on Bonair Drive. Those following them had been washed away. Those ahead had escaped around a bend where the road reached the top of Admiral Heights.

The hillside itself was entirely changed. Houses and apartment buildings below their level had been crushed and carried away. What had once been roofs, dining rooms, and bedrooms had become a logjam of plywood, two-by-fours, and wreckage floating offshore. Other logs in that jam were the remains of trees torn from the greenbelt along Bonair Drive. The huge tree in which the Blazer had come to rest was one of very few that were stout enough to resist being ripped away to join the flotilla of trees now bobbing on the Sound.

Ann and Leon were left in an odd condition: they sat in water up to their chests inside the car while outside, the water was entirely gone.

"This is preposterous." Ann finally found her voice. "Not only are we literally up a tree, but we're sitting in a bucket of water!"

"C-Cold w-water," Leon stammered as his ability to speak came back.

"What are we supposed to do?"

Leon reached underwater and felt for his door latch. When he found it, he said, "This!" He gave a solid tug and the door flew open. Water around him drained so quickly that it nearly swept him out with it. He reached out and grabbed one side of the steering wheel and held on while a waterfall poured onto soggy blackberry brambles ten feet below.

Once the water was gone, he looked down with dismay. "We *really are* up a tree, aren't we?"

"How will we get down?" Ann asked.

Leon shrugged. "Parachute?"

"Do you think we can shinny down one of these trunks?"

"You, maybe. Not me." Leon patted his stout belly. He looked apprehensively down from his open door. "I'd hate to fall that far. Any other ideas?"

"Ah!" Ann said. "I've got jumper cables in a compartment under the back floor." She turned and glanced back, where the boxes containing the chief's bones had somehow weathered the catastrophe with no more than a soaking. "All we've got to do is get those cables out and tie one to the other to make a rope long enough to get us near the ground."

"Sounds like a good plan." Leon reached back and tugged at one of the boxes. "If we can get to them."

Ann gazed again at the chaos offshore. The wave had disappeared to the north but had overwhelmed the full length of the bluff. The wreckage of houses and condominiums that had lined the landward side of Alki Avenue, and much of the greenbelt forest behind those buildings, now comprised a miles-long log-and-debris jam. Massive roots and branches jutted up among shattered roofs and twisted timbers. Here and there, survivors wallowed in the churning waters or clung desperately to flotsam.

She turned away and shut her eyes. "It's too horrible to watch."

"Come on," Leon said. "Help me shuffle the chief around and dig those cables out."

The water had risen both inside and outside as Ryan Hewitt's car floated on the longshore current. The girls had crouched on their seats to avoid the water, but Ryan had stuck it out behind the wheel. As the water had risen to his waist, he had kept a grim watch out the front windshield while the car was dragged for half a block or more. Then, as the tidal surge began to recede, things went from bad to worse. The car was dragged onto the submerged sidewalk by the tug of outgoing water, drawn toward deeper waters beyond the bulkhead—fatally deep, Ryan was sure.

Their only hope of salvation was a pedestrian handrail of steel pipe that paralleled the sidewalk. The station wagon plowed into it sideways and scraped along it, and it seemed the sturdy rail couldn't resist the power of the outflowing water. Everyone reflexively held their breaths as the car teetered sideways against the railing while the outgoing water rushed around its front and rear ends. Somehow, the railing held them back from certain death.

The torrent ebbed quickly, and the station wagon toppled back and settled onto all four wheels, two on the sidewalk and two on the street.

Ryan glanced around, searching for any new threat and scarcely daring to hope that the flood had truly left them unharmed. Soon he realized it was true. "The water's gone down!"

"It has, Dad!" Emily cried. "The water has totally gone down!"

Caylie was still incapable of speech. Trembling with cold and fear, she clutched his arm and kept her tear-soaked face buried against his shoulder.

"It's okay, honey." He petted the back of her soggy head. "The water really has gone down!"

She turned slightly and peeked with one eye, still keeping a solid grip on his arm.

Aron Carter and Professor Rutledge had almost reached the level of the announcer booth. But as they hurried up staircase after staircase, the crowd moving down swelled with more and more people rushing for the exits. Progress up the stairs was all but impossible. Trying to push their way up one side, they could only manage a step or two before having to yield to the momentum of the crowd coming down. At each pause, Rutledge cupped his hands and shouted. "No, people! You don't leave the stadium after an earthquake. That's what I was going to tell you!

A tidal wave may be coming!"

Those nearest him paused, looking all the more confused and frightened. But people above continued pressing down, and they were forced to move on. The whole process of people stopping and then going again only made the congestion worse for Carter and Rutledge.

Eventually Carter, who had taken the lead, turned to Rutledge. "Maybe we should just give up!"

"No! They've got to be told not to leave."

"How you gonna tell them? Go up there and shout? The power is out."

"I don't know. Maybe I will shout. But we can't just let everybody run out. A wave really might be coming."

"All right!" Carter turned and bulled his way into the crowd with renewed vigor and Rutledge followed.

As they went, the scoreboard lights flickered on and then went off again.

"Someone is trying to get the power on," Rutledge called to Carter. "I wanna be in that booth when they get it."

"Stand aside, folks!" Carter bellowed at the mob above him. "Out of the way!"

A tall, muscular man in a Mariners fan jersey refused to make way and instead gave Carter a heavy shove. Undaunted by the man's much greater size, Carter grabbed him by the shirt and bulldogged him down on the steps. Leaving the man flat on his face, Carter was up in an instant and charging up the staircase again.

"Come on!" he called to Rutledge. Behind them the tall man got to his feet, cursing, but rejoined the throng moving down to the exits.

When the earth tremors subsided in Fire Station Number 2 at Fourth Avenue and Wall Street, dust that had fallen from the ceiling billowed out the open bay door in front of Engine Number 9. More than dust had come down from the ceiling. Ventilation ducts, wiring, and light fixtures were strewn across the floor and over the tops of the fire engine and a smaller aid car also housed in Station 2.

A fireman was down, too, clobbered by some of the fallen sheet metal. Two of his comrades were tending his wounds, which were minor: a badly scraped shoulder with a purple bruise forming on it.

Battalion Chief Bob Jensen stood near the team and their patient on the still-vibrating concrete floor of the engine bay, surveying the condition of the station house with his colleague, Fire Sergeant Gary Dawkins. Both men's faces were grim.

"So, the day has come," Jensen said.

"Yeah. The day has come," Dawkins agreed. "It looks worse than what we were trained for."

"Could have been a lot worse than this. I thought the building was about to come down around our ears."

Three men approached from the crew facility wearing full fire-response gear. With a gesture, Jensen directed them toward the fire engine. "Let's get her cleared off and on the street ASAP!"

All three men responded, "Yes sir!" and went to start pulling segments of fallen duct work and wiring off the big rig.

"We've got one hell of a lot of work ahead of us," Dawkins said.

"Yes, we do. How are things in the EMC?" Jensen pointed through a doorway that led into the Emergency Management Center, a quake-hardened facility within the station that was intended to control and coordinate multiple fire and police stations in an emergency like this.

"The auxiliary power generator is damaged."

"Oh, boy."

"But the guys are working on it. They think they can get it going pretty quickly."

"I hope so." Jensen leaned near the injured fireman and his helpers. "You'd better get a compressive wrap on that. It looks like it might have a hematoma developing. But wrap it so the arm stays functional. I'm gonna need every hand I can get."

As the men went to work with gauze wrap and Ace bandages from an EMT kit, he turned back to Dawkins. "We've got one bay door open and one closed, and no power. See if you can scare up a couple of men to manually crank that other door up. We might be able to get the aid car on the street before the engine, depending on how much crap fell on it from the ceiling."

As Dawkins hurried toward the crew facility, Jensen glanced out the open bay door at rows of apartment buildings in the area. Some had lost parts of their façades. Some showed signs of internal collapse—sagging roofs, off-kilter shifts of whole buildings—but none were on fire. That didn't mean no one inside them needed emergency assistance. Only time would tell about that. More ominously, wisps of black smoke were drifting into the neighborhood from somewhere nearby.

Jensen was wearing a standard black light-duty fire service uniform. He went for the crew facility to put on heavy-turnout gear. As he walked, he tried to mentally prepare himself for the succession of horrors the day would surely bring.

Aboard the *Leschi* the initial chaos had settled somewhat after the wave passed. But all was not normal. The 800-megahertz channel in the walkie-talkie units attached to each man's shoulder had at first swelled with dozens of voices reporting or calling for assistance. But then the sheer volume of communications had sent the 800-megahertz system into buzzing waves of static. Klimchak had called into his own unit, frantically begging Rita to respond, but malevolent crackling noises had been the only reply.

As the *Leschi* rocked side to side in heavy seas Klimchak stood in shock, trying to imagine what to do next. Could he justify ordering a search for his missing crew member? Or should he go in search of many others who might be in desperate need? His mind blanked briefly. He closed his eyes and shook his head slowly. Then he heard the cabin door behind him open. Turning, he saw—

"Rita!"

She was soaked from head to foot and trembling from cold. He opened his arms and she rushed to hug him.

"I went overboard," she sobbed as he wrapped her in his

arms. "But I grabbed a cable and held on for dear life! I had a hell of a time climbing back onboard."

They hugged each other tighter, both weeping with relief.

Chapter 17

The canoers had survived their encounter with the tsunami with no losses and few effects beyond frazzled nerves and the need to empty substantial amounts of water from their craft—with perhaps a little pee mixed in. They accomplished this quickly with ornately carved traditional wooden bailing scoops. The wave was far beyond them, having rounded the north end of West Seattle while reflecting off Magnolia Bluff, the net effect of which had been a hard turn southeast into Elliott Bay.

Although the main body of the wave was past, the canoe flotilla was by no means at rest. The surface of the Sound heaved chaotically. Mighty peaks of water rose and fell all around them. The canoes were lifted high and then dropped low in gut-churning plummets that felt like a mad roller-coaster ride. And each time they rose high, the occupants could see huge reflected waves crisscrossing Elliott Bay from shore to shore, intersecting with each other and rising doubly-tall one moment and dropping precipitously the next. The Sound's surface had become a maze of crisscrossing waves that traveled nowhere but surged up and down repeatedly. It was no place for anyone prone to seasickness—or anyone even slightly fainthearted.

"I hope this is as rough as it gets," Kenny Helm called from the stern of the *Tatoosh*. "I've never seen water like this before."

"What do we do?" Arnie Musselshell called from the bow.

"Ride it out. Pullers, keep your paddles ready. We're not out of this yet."

The tidal wave had traveled nearly a mile southeast since passing under the canoes and the *Leschi*. Becoming a long semicircular arc as it swept past Seattle, it crisscrossed its own reflections, gaining strength here and dissipating force there. It raked the waterfront, tearing at piers and buildings along its path. But it did so unevenly, sparing one pier while destroying the next.

Choppy and chaotic on a titanic scale, it rolled on toward the stadiums and the ferry *Issaquah.* As it neared the south end of Elliott Bay, the narrowing waterway constricted it and forced its face higher.

David and Zack McGee were on the deck of the *Issaquah* near the passenger gate at the front of the upper level. From their high vantage point, they had watched the earthquake shake the city's foundations. The ferry had slowed as if the captain were unsure whether to approach the terminal or not. Now Zack bumped David's arm and gestured astern. "That looks totally badass." The wave was less than a quarter mile away and bearing down on them swiftly.

"It does look badass," Dave agreed.

"Let's go inside, Dad."

David thought a moment, while the wave rose so tall he had to tilt his head back to watch it. "No way I'm going inside. If we capsize, all I know is I don't want to be trapped in there. I'll take my chances out here."

"Okay. But what are we supposed to do?"

"You just stick close to me and do what I do."

"What's that?"

"I'm making this up as I go." He moved to the steel handrail and grabbed it tightly. Zack did the same. "Get ready to hold on for dear life."

The wave drew the dark green water into a wall so steep that when it hit the ferry's open stern, the upper half of the wave didn't break so much as part from the lower portion cleanly and rush onto the car deck intact. At the same time, the lower portion lifted the boat's stern and accelerated her.

Dave and Zack were buffeted but had braced themselves well at the side railing. They heard a thunderous roar on the car deck as the wave smashed into dozens of parked vehicles. Seconds later, a frothing mass of white water burst out the front of the car deck, carrying cars and trucks like child's toys. David and Zack gaped from above as the surge swept everything and everyone off the bow of the ferry. The formerly smooth water ahead became a roiling mass of foam, wreckage, and luckless people—some of whom struggled among the sinking vehicles, while others floated limp. The *Issaquah* was out of her captain's control. Caught in the tsunami's grip, she surfed toward Colman Dock, thumping and rumbling over jettisoned cars and trucks and racing forward with terrifying speed.

David hollered, "Brace yourself again!" as the ferry slip loomed—a threatening mass of metal towers, black composite-rubber bumpers and raised steel draw-spans, backed by an immovable-looking terminal building.

The *Issaquah's* spade-shaped prow cut into the dock, crumpling impact bumpers, shattering concrete pilings, and twisting steel girders. Dave and Zack lost their grips and were tossed onto the deck. Shouting, they tumbled forward over each other and came to a stop pressed against the front handrail's screened understructure. Meanwhile, the terminal's superior mass absorbed the impact and held firm.

Battered but otherwise unharmed, the two stared as the wave surged through and around the *Issaquah,* inundating the terminal's vehicle waiting area. Scores of cars and trucks were swept into its flow amid hellish noises—shattering glass, crunching metal, and a few faint screams. The *Issaquah* wallowed against the pier while the wave went on to flood the lowest areas of the city with an awful slurry of muddy water, smashed vehicles, and human bodies.

Matt and Grace had hurried down the Z-stacked staircases that descended from the restaurant to the base of the Space Needle. They had moved far faster than everyone else by dint of their youth, agility, and the urgency of their mission. As they pursued their zigzag descent, the open-air staircases afforded views in all directions whether they wanted to see what was there or not.

They witnessed a city that had undergone a horrific transformation. Most buildings still stood but lacked the majority of their windows. Some towers billowed smoke from fires unseen inside them. In Elliott Bay, the tidal wave was rending Seattle's waterfront with furious surges of brown frothing water. For all the visible chaos, however, the scene was eerily quiet. There were a few distant rumbles, but no fire engines wailing, no police car sirens blaring. It was as if the city were too much in shock to react to what had happened.

On one staircase about one hundred feet above ground level, Grace caught Matt's arm and stopped him. "Oh my God!" she shrieked. "Look at that!"

One of the tallest buildings in the downtown cluster, a green-hued tower, had been belching black smoke as they descended. That smoke had billowed among other skyscrapers and curled around the Smith Tower, whose smaller white-stone pinnacle had somehow withstood the quake in good condition. But it wasn't the smoke or the Smith Tower that caught Grace's attention. Atop the unfinished green monolith an orange construction crane, bent by the quake and tilted far to one side, tore loose of its underpinnings. It plunged earthward, dragging a portion of the top story with it. Other pieces of the top floor dislodged in succession and followed the crane down, silently, it seemed, as distance delayed the sound. Then came the muffled thunder of the crane's impact, followed by the rumble of multiple falling pieces echoing among the still-standing towers of the city.

"Let's get moving again." Matt turned to start down.

Grace still hesitated. "What is that?" She gestured at Elliott Bay, where peaks and valleys of waves surged chaotically, in places overwhelming waterfront buildings. "That's only a few blocks away. Will we be safe on the ground?"

"I don't know, but Earl's in a bad way. We've gotta keep moving."

"Okay, although I have my doubts about getting near that waterfront."

Once they'd caught their breath, they descended the last few flights at a run. Hurrying out the emergency exit gate, they jogged south across a broad lawn. Around them everywhere were shards of glass from the restaurant—and the crumpled bodies of unfortunate people who had joined that glass in plummeting five hundred and twenty feet to the ground.

Chapter 18

Councilwoman Mariah Rey had been at her massive oak desk at City Hall when the quake struck. Thrown from her high-backed chair, she had scrambled into the knee-space under the desk and remained there through the most violent shaking. She had stayed put as shock followed shock, huddled with her head between her knees and her arms around her legs, wailing like a baby.

Outside her office windows, glass cascades had roared down unseen but heard in terrifying detail. She had stayed frozen in place for minutes after relative calm had returned, then had peeked out over her desk. A pall of dust had settled on the desk and overturned furniture. Picture frames were cocked at odd angles. A vase of flowers lay shattered on the floor. Outside, the pavement was strewn with piles of window glass from tall buildings. A haze of dust made it hard to see across the street. Mariah's own tall windows had remained intact except one with a diagonal crack running from upper right to lower left.

For a brief moment, Mariah felt a sense of relief and joy at having survived. Feeling weak in the knees, she moved back into her chair. She took some deep breaths and released them slowly to calm herself. But her complacency was short-lived. Right before her eyes, something stupendous crashed down onto the street outside. It was a huge I-beam, thirty feet long and two feet thick, weighing many tons.

Mariah screamed as a second beam joined the first, falling from great height and impacting with thunderous *Clang!* that shook the floor beneath her feet. Stunned, she gasped, "The tower is coming down!"

More beams followed the first two and their clangor built to a deafening roar. Mariah shrieked and shrieked again, certain the tumult would crush City Hall and her office along with it. Through the thunderous rumble of falling beams, a still louder noise made itself known—a repetitive *boom! Boom! BOOM!* from high above, made it clear the entire monolith was collapsing.

"Oh God!" Mariah prayed. "Please help me!" She stayed at her desk, clasping her face in her hands and letting tears flow. *What was the point of ducking under the desk?* She was certain the disintegrating skyscraper would crush her whether she hid or not.

Moving with infinite caution, Eldon Devine sidestepped to the middle of the ledge. As he moved, he listened with growing concern as the rumbling overhead increased to a roar punctuated by louder sounds with an ominous rhythm. *Boom! Boom! BOOM!* The sounds repeated until it dawned on Devine what he was hearing.

"The building is pancaking!"

A chill ran through him. He remembered inspector Federly warning how one floor would drop onto another and then both would drop onto the next until the building compressed like a stack of pancakes. He could almost count the succession of floors thundering down. But he was in no mood to do so. "Eighty-one stories," he groaned. "All coming down on my head!"

Scrambled thoughts crisscrossed his mind as the thunder of falling floors became deafening. Vibrations shook the wall he was pressed against, loosening his tenuous grip. A particularly violent shudder pushed him away completely. He toppled backwards and hurtled head over heels into the depths—his shrieks lost in the crescendo of thundering debris.

His end came in blackness, impacted from below and above by masses of steel, concrete, and stone. The tower's continued collapse was unaffected by the pulverized bits of flesh that had been Eldon Devine and Kelly Anton. They were merely incorporated into the rubble.

Aboard Dolphin 224 hovering five hundred feet above the waterfront, Jane Hewitt and her crew were so absorbed by second-to-second events that they scarcely had time to think. One calamity after another riveted their attention. They had watched, open-mouthed, as the Emerald Tower collapsed into its own excavation, leaving nothing above ground but a pall of dust and a column of smoke from a fire burning in the rubble. They were spellbound by the seiche on Elliott Bay, where intersecting reflected waves still resonated from shore to shore. Some near-shore peaks crashed onto waterfront buildings while lower spots in the wave pattern left other structures almost unaffected.

"Dios mio!" Valenzuela exclaimed. "Check that crazy mess on the waterfront!"

Suddenly, Jane Hewitt cried out in a high-pitched, panicky shriek, *"Oh, my God! Oh, my God! Oh, my God!"*

"What's wrong?" Valenzuela reflexively scanned for trouble on the gauges in front of him.

"My family is at *Alki Beach!"* Hewitt spun Dolphin 224 away from the city and steered onto a straight vector for West Seattle at top speed.

"Aren't they safe in Port Angeles, like our families?" Valenzuela asked. "Sixty air miles away?"

"Not my family! They came here to watch the fly-over. But they were supposed to go to the beach first. *Oh, my God! Oh, my God! Oh, my God!"*

She held Dolphin 224 on a beeline for West Seattle, her trembling hand forcing the thrust lever as far forward as it would go. If she could have coaxed another ounce of power from the whining turbine, she would have done so.

By the time Aron Carter and Ron Rutledge reached the announcer facility, the emergency power was on. It surged and flickered but would do what was needed if it only stayed on for a minute or two. Rutledge rushed to the broadcast sound stage, where the hosts and crew stood looking shell-shocked and uncertain what to do. Meanwhile, out the shattered windows and across the playing field, an inane graphic was showing on the scoreboard screen. A TV camera, abandoned by its technician, had swung to point at a ceiling with several missing tiles and dangling wires.

Rutledge rushed onto the set, filled with a purpose these

people had not yet found. "Come on, folks," he snapped at the crew, several of whom still wore headphones. "Get a camera on me and give me some sound."

Brett Stertzel and a network sports announcer stood near a pair of overturned newscaster chairs on a low dais, looking dazed and confused. "You, I don't need!" Rutledge growled, pushing Stertzel and the network man hard and propelling them off the stage. He and Carter set the chairs upright and Rutledge sat down in one, motioning Carter into the other. A crewman handed them headphones and they put them on. Another swung the up-tilted camera around and focused it. On the screen across the stadium and in several TV monitors around the broadcast facility, Rutledge suddenly saw his own gaunt face staring back at him.

Everything was in readiness—*but what was he supposed to say?*

The set director had appeared out of nowhere. "Tight shot please!"

Rutledge glanced out the shattered window of the broadcast booth and saw his face grow to eighty feet tall on the screen as the cameraman zoomed in.

"A-a-a-a-nd sound!" the director called.

"Hello?" Rutledge spoke into his headset mic as he turned to face the camera. *"HELLO,"* his amplified voice reverberated from dozens of giant speakers around the field.

"You're live," the director affirmed. "Go ahead."

Rutledge stared at the camera lens and, for just a moment, was speechless. He shook his head to clear his thoughts. "People," he began, his voice reverberating powerfully. "People, please be calm. Please don't leave the stadium. Please move from wherever you are to a higher level if you can. I repeat, you will be safest if you move to a higher level. Do not go down."

The director cupped his hands and hissed a prompt. "Why?"

"Oh. Yes. Because there may be a tsunami." The words slipped out with such ease that Rutledge was surprised how understated they sounded. "There is a real danger," he stated more firmly, "that a tidal wave could follow an earthquake of this size. If you go out, you may be in danger. So, I repeat. Stay inside the stadium. And move to a higher level if you can."

In the few minutes it had taken Rutledge and Carter to reach the booth and get Rutledge's plea delivered, a large portion of the crowd had moved down and jammed the exits. The playing field was covered in a foot-deep layer of muck as if the mudflat on which the stadium had been built was trying to re-establish itself. Fans and players who had endured the mud volcano now slogged through the sticky glop, still going in different directions with no coherent plan to their actions.

"Please, people!" Rutledge admonished. "This is what I was going to tell you later. The whole SoDo District is a tsunami hazard zone. If there is any tidal wave at all, it will flood the streets and parking lots around the stadium. Those are not safe places to be. Please return to your seats. And if people can hear me outside, please come back inside quickly. You will be much safer."

Rutledge's words echoed in the streets outside T-Mobile Park. There, in a crush of people leaving the stadium, were Craig Palmer and his boys. Having extricated themselves from under the placard, they had just exited the Home Plate Gate.

The fleeing crowd, thousands strong, heard Rutledge's message but had varying reactions to it. For some, it only goaded them to run faster. For others, it was compelling logic. These people turned and began making their way back against the flow of those still bent on leaving. Craig drew the boys aside in a clear space where the tangle of fleeing and returning fans parted around the bronze statue of Ken Griffey Junior, poised as if his bat had just knocked a ball out of the park.

"Wait a minute, boys. Let's catch our breath." What he really wanted was time to think.

"I don't need to catch my breath!" Liam wailed. "I wanna get outta here!"

"It's not that simple."

"I don't care!" Liam began to cry. "I wanna go!"

"Dad!" Willy interrupted.

"Just a minute, Willy. I'm talking to Liam."

"But Dad!"

"All right Willy! What is it?"

"That!" Willy pointed north up First Avenue, at an almost incomprehensible sight. A wall of brownish-black water had come into view from a side street. Three or four feet tall, the mass of moving water swept up everything it encountered including parked cars, trash cans, landscape trees—and dozens of luckless fans who had run in that direction after leaving the stadium.

Craig grabbed each boy by a wrist. "We're going back inside." As he hurried them toward the entrance through a milling crowd, with Liam trying to pull away, he was glad the announcer's words had made him pause long enough to avert tragedy. At least, he *hoped* it had been averted.

Inside the announcer booth, Ronald Rutledge was gratified to see many people moving back into the seating areas. Some walked. Some ran, pushing past others, reversing their direction but maintaining their panic.

"And now," the director prompted, "what are they supposed to do?"

"And now," Rutledge replied into the microphone, and then he paused. He said, off-mike, "I guess we wait."

"Wait for what?"

"I'm not sure. I guess we wait until we're sure there's no tsunami."

"Will there be one?"

As if in answer, a fresh chorus of screams went up from the crowd. A surge of muddy water gushed through the bull pens on the ground level at the north side of the field. It spilled onto the already muddied turf and quickly swelled to a three-foot flood that knocked down the people crossing the playing area and carried them along. In seconds, the field was inundated by swirling, debris-laden brown water in which fans struggled to rise but were dragged under by chaotic currents. The water level rose to four feet and a giant vortex began rotating over what had been the baseball diamond. In the stands, terrified people fell over each other in efforts to get to higher locations.

Kyle Stevens and Lori McMillan were in the lab watching seismographs register a succession of small aftershocks. Fear that a tidal wave might reach them had faded with passage of time. They ported data to a computer capable of computing the quake's epicenter and depth with high precision, but found it added little to the conclusion they had already drawn from the seismo feeds. The event had happened in West Seattle and under the adjacent Sound. Its depth was indistinguishable from the surface.

While they were looking over the computer-generated data, Kyle cocked his head and frowned at one seismometer display.

"What?" Lori turned to follow his gaze. On that screen, a new scribble had appeared. "Another aftershock?"

"Yep. And a huge one!"

Chapter 19

When the aftershock struck, Tim Carrington and Valerie Styles were still trapped in the Explorer, teetering half on and half off the broken edge of the bridge. They had gingerly crawled into the back of the car and Tim had opened the hatch door. They were discussing how to get out without tipping the car's delicate balance when the aftershock's rumble ended the discussion.

"Jump!" he shouted. "Now!"

Valerie scrambled out the hatch while Tim held the door open. As she tumbled to the pavement, he was already in motion—but too late. He clambered out the hatch opening, but the loss of Valerie's weight unbalanced the car and it nosedived into the void. Tim got a foot on the back bumper and leapt with every ounce of his strength. He hovered momentarily in mid-air as the car dropped away from him—*but had he given himself enough momentum to reach the roadway?* He landed against the broken concrete edge with a thud that knocked the wind from him, but by desperately grabbing at jagged stone and bent rebar, he managed to hang on. His feet dangled in thin air as the Explorer cartwheeled into the river a hundred feet below and threw out a huge splash.

Valerie crawled toward him as if wanting to help, but help wasn't needed. Propelled by adrenaline, Tim pulled himself onto the road surface and flattened himself on the shaking concrete. Valerie threw her arms around him, and they peered down at the swirling eddy where the Explorer had disappeared beneath the surface.

"My God!" Tim wheezed, having trouble regaining his breath. "I almost went down there!"

"It still could happen," Valerie said edgily. "What's happening to Harbor Island?"

Across the Duwamish River channel, the columnar uprights of the far side of the West Seattle Bridge had their foundations set on Harbor Island. The island was an artificial construct of flat, mostly paved land, roughly rectangular in shape. More than a mile north-south and nearly a mile east-west, it was the product of a massive dredge-and-fill operation that had reshaped the Duwamish River in the early 1900s. Built on top of a mudflat at the river's mouth, it lay on waterlogged, unsolidified ground.

Now its muddy substrate, liquefied by earth tremors, had begun to slide into Elliott Bay, carrying the entire northern two-thirds of the island with it. The formerly solid surfaces of container terminals split into segments rafting on the mud as it flowed north. The terminals' immense cranes were undermined and crashed into heaps moving along with the flow. Stacks of red, yellow, and blue train-car-sized cargo containers were scattered like children's blocks and carried along on the liquefying land. Tim and Valerie watched in horrified fascination as the entire north end of the island began to slip beneath the waters of Elliott Bay.

"Things just keep getting worse!" Valerie murmured.

"I've seen enough," Tim said. "Let's get away from this edge."

In the seismology lab, huge new surges were registering on each of two West Seattle seismometer traces. The feeds from HART HNZ UW on Harbor Island and QDHS HNZ UW at Duwamish Head seemed to have gone crazy.

"Look at that!" Lori cried. "It's another huge event!"

"But it's a weird one," Kyle said. "It's lasting insanely long."

The signal from HART HNZ UW on Harbor Island grew in magnitude rather than tapering off. Then the screen abruptly went blank.

"Whoa!" Lori blinked in amazement. "What just happened?"

"I hate to think." Kyle stared, half-mesmerized, at the continuing Duwamish Head feed. "There's been, like, dozens of shocks already. And they're still going on. This has to be something else besides an earthquake."

"What else could it be?"

"I'm thinking it's like what happened at Valdez in '64. The whole waterfront collapsed after the quake."

"What are you saying?"

"Valdez Harbor was built on mudflats, just like the Port of Seattle. The quake turned the mud to liquid and the land sank into the harbor."

"You're saying that could happen here?"

"I'm not saying it could. *I'm saying it is!* Why else would the Harbor Island seismo feed stop? It sank!"

The *Issaquah* wallowed in rough seas south of Colman Dock. Without power to her propellers, the ferry drifted on a southbound current left by the first wave. Black smoke belched from her stacks as the crew tried desperately to restart her drowned engines and regain some maneuverability.

David and Zack McGee leaned against the foredeck railing, braced against the violent pitching of the ship. They gawked at a cityscape of windowless skyscrapers, swirling dust, and billows of black smoke. The current drew the *Issaquah* to the southeastern corner of Elliott Bay, where Coast Guard Station buildings and ships loomed just east of her. A huge red-hulled icebreaker bobbed violently at its moorings as the *Issaquah* drifted dangerously near.

"I've got a bad feeling about this," David muttered.

"Well, your gonna feel worse! Check that!" Zack pointed astern, where the entire surface of Harbor Island was in motion and sliding into Elliott Bay.

"Oh my God!" David cried. "Am I seeing this right?"

The huge volume of earth sliding into the Sound pushed up a mountainous wall of water spanning the entire south shore of Elliott Bay.

"Another tidal wave!" Zack cried. "As if one wasn't enough! And it's bigger than the last one!"

"I still don't want to get trapped inside!" David shouted above the thunder of the crumbling island. He held firm to his place at the rail, and so did Zack.

Most of the new wave moved north toward the already

ravaged shoreline of Seattle, but its eastern end curved and came at the *Issaquah's* stern. When it hit, it made the ship shudder. White spray jetted higher than the upper decks. Frothing water crushed the rear windows of the passenger level and burst into the seating area, enveloping screaming victims where they sat. The only exceptions were David and Zack, who were farthest from the wave's impact. Sheltered from all but a drenching spray, they braced themselves at the railing with all their might.

When the pelting rain of salt water subsided, they found themselves perfectly positioned to witness a series of incomprehensible events. The *Issaquah* rode the stupendous surge of water, careening dizzily toward shore. Dead ahead, the violently rocking icebreaker snapped its mooring ropes.

"Tell me this isn't happening," Zack cried.

Chapter 20

David and Zack watched open-mouthed as white water surged over, around, and through the Coast Guard station. The *Issaquah* came abreast of the icebreaker, whose side placard they could easily read: POLAR STAR. The ultra-seaworthy and self-righting icebreaker rode the wave without capsizing, but the gap between the two ships closed to a few feet and then a matter of inches. David and Zack shouted in terror as the *Issaquah* struck the *Polar Star* a powerful glancing blow. Accompanied by thunderous metal-on-metal scraping along the length of both vessels, the sideswipe had dramatic effects. The *Issaquah* was deflected onto a northward course paralleling the shore, while the *Polar Star* was forced up and onto the pier to which she had been moored. David and Zack were pitched forward and back and side-to-side as the torrent surged under and around the *Issaquah* and then rolled inland.

"That was close!" David nervously eyed how the ferry skirted the sunken shoreline.

"It could be worse," Zack gestured to the east. "How'd you like to be over there?" Ashore, roiling debris-laden water had inundated Alaskan Way, the waterfront boulevard. Just inland of that, the elevated roadway of Highway 99 dropped to street level after passing the Coast Guard station and then descended into a northbound tunnel under downtown Seattle. The portal had been inundated by the first wave and was now a colossal whirlpool whose swirling maw had accumulated a chaotic mix of cars, debris, and struggling people. All of these were being sucked under as the tunnel filled.

"The poor people!" David cried as the new, bigger wave washed over the previous maelstrom and annihilated any trace the wreckage and people that had been there moments before.

"Look over there!" Zack pointed south toward a container terminal on what had been the east bank of the Duwamish channel. There, the wave that had just struck the ferry was impacting a large freighter at its moorings. Stacked high with cargo containers and not nearly as seaworthy as the *Issaquah* or the *Polar Star,* the ship listed heavily and spilled its containers at the foot of a giant crane. With its legs cut out from under it, the crane toppled onto the freighter, crushing a huge hole amidships. As the stricken vessel took on water and settled on its side, other cargo ships farther south seemed doomed to a similar fate as the wave rolled on.

"Can you believe this?" Zack cried.

"No, I can't," David responded.

Meanwhile, the aftershock that caused havoc at Harbor Island had propagated under downtown Seattle without causing much additional damage. The land had rippled again like writhing A'yahos, but the effect on the skyscrapers was only to stir more dust into the air and dislodge the few shards of glass that were still in place. When the impulse reached the Space Needle, the building shuddered and began a second metronomic swing.

DeWayne Pettijohn had come from a back room moments before, carrying a wooden-handled mop. He had worked it under the air conditioner and pried upward with all his might but had been unable to budge the heavy machine. Now, as the aftershock's force rocked the floor, he tried again.

Earl let out an agonized cry as DeWayne's effort, coupled with the quake's impulse, rocked the unit away, only to let it fall back onto his leg again. DeWayne forced the mop handle farther under and pried up hard, shouting to the others, "Come on! This is our chance to get it off him!" Carrie and Monica put their shoulders into the unit and all three groaned with the most extreme exertion they could muster—and the air conditioner tipped away.

"Now, Earl!" DeWayne shouted. "Pull yourself out!"

Though feeble from loss of blood, Earl rolled over and dragged his leg out from under the unit. An instant later, it crashed back down. DeWayne cast the mop aside, grabbed Earl by the shoulders, and swiftly tugged him a safe distance from the machine. The wounded leg left a streak of blood across the carpet. Blood gushed from the lacerated calf muscle, but it slackened when DeWayne twisted the tourniquet and stanched the flow. Carrie and Monica crawled from the air unit to Earl's side.

"Am I gonna die?" Earl mumbled groggily, his eyes dulled by pain and shock.

"Die?" Carrie was horrified. "No, you won't!"

"That's *not* gonna happen," DeWayne snapped.

"I hope you guys know what you're talking about," Earl murmured.

"I've done this under enemy fire," DeWayne shot back. "I'm *sure* I know what I'm talking about."

Inside the press box at T-Mobile Park, Professor Rutledge continued addressing the crowd. "I am serious, folks. Please remain seated or return to your seats if you have moved toward the exits." However, the crowd had grown more restless with passage of time. Once again, people were moving toward the exits, amid scattered choruses of boos.

"Tidal waves can come in a series," he cautioned. "This might not be over—" His voice trailed off as a new surge of dark water burst onto the field from multiple directions, and with much greater force than before. The original flood had been draining away and a few brave—or foolhardy—souls had ventured onto the field. Perhaps they were searching for lost loved ones among the bodies scattered on the muddy grass or tangled in wreckage. But now those who had gone down confronted an even larger flood than before. The fresh surges quickly rose to ten feet high and, though many turned and rushed for the stands, they were swept under in seconds.

"Oh, my God," Rutledge gasped into the mike. "That's exactly what I was talking about."

By the time he got those few words out, all who had been on the field were consumed by converging walls of brown water. Much more massive than the flood before it, this new wave quickly overtopped the playing-field barriers and surged into the lower sections of the stands. Fans there were overwhelmed or—if they reacted quickly enough—managed to scramble to safety above. Another churning whirlpool formed on the field, in which a few desperate souls swam or clung to debris.

Two exceptions among the bystanders were Willy Palmer and Liam Beasley, who stood on the concourse level where they had escaped the first wave. Craig Palmer held them close and pressed their faces to his sides to shut out the horrors on the field below. For good measure, he covered their eyes with his fingers to shield them from sights he knew would live in his own memory for a lifetime.

As the rocking of the Space Needle subsided, DeWayne and Carrie made Earl as comfortable as possible. Keeping him flat on his back to avoid passing out from shock, DeWayne and Carrie arranged some folded cloth napkins under his head as a cushion.

Suddenly Monica cried out, "Look at that!" She stared out a shattered window at an awe-inspiring new sight on Elliott Bay.

"It's another tidal wave!" Carrie said. "A bigger one!"

The tsunami from Harbor Island was spreading northward in a semicircular arc across the already-chaotic bay. At its west end it washed the shore of West Seattle with a wall of water nearly a hundred feet high. At its east end, it raked the city shore, flooding into and around tall buildings near the waterfront. Although the hill on which Seattle stood limited the inundation, one strong surge penetrated the downtown business district and washed over the brink of the giant hole that had been Devine's Emerald Tower. Swamping the wreckage and extinguishing fires raging there, it transformed the black smoke columns into billows of white steam.

As the main body of the tsunami came north, it overran the peaks and valleys of the seiche, adding its bulk to those already towering surges of water. This crazy mélange of rippling wave-forms inundated parts of the waterfront unevenly. In some places, fifty-foot floods overwhelmed entire buildings, while other areas were bypassed completely. Streets running uphill from the waterfront received similarly uneven flooding. Some surge fronts traveled many blocks, while others scarcely moved inland at all. As the tsunami neared the north end of the waterfront, it combined with one of the largest seiche peaks and the resultant mass of water rushed ashore at the foot of Denny Way. It overwhelmed two five-story buildings, crushing one and surging around and over the other. Then it rolled uphill like a fast-moving tide, heading toward the Seattle Center and Space Needle.

"Oh, no! Oh, no! Oh, no!" Carrie cried as the muddy water surged nearer.

"No worries," DeWayne responded. "It can't get us up here. And it won't knock this place down either. The foundations are way too deep."

"It's not *us* I'm worried about," Carrie wailed. "Matt and Grace are down there!"

Matt and Grace had left the Seattle Center campus and were moving along city streets toward the fire station. The neighborhood of five-to-ten-story buildings had been damaged but not destroyed entirely. Some buildings had partially collapsed. Others were almost intact but had shed glass and debris onto the sidewalks. This made the going difficult for Matt, Grace, and the dazed people who were wandering the area or tending to the inured.

After they had gone a few blocks, Grace paused. "Are you sure you know where you're going?"

"Here's a street sign," Matt said. "Fourth Avenue and Denny Way. I think that's where we want to be..." His voice trailed off as something caught his eye. Grace followed his gaze down the slope of Denny Way—and caught her breath.

A few blocks from them, buildings along the shore of Elliott Bay were disappearing beneath a chaotic wall of brown water, which had begun to surge up Denny Way. The persistent roar of the seiche was drowned out by a tenfold louder roar as the tidal wave rolled inland, sweeping up cars and people in its path.

Grace was paralyzed, but Matt broke the spell by grabbing her wrist and tugging her into motion.

"Where are we going?" she cried.

"Uphill!" he shouted over the growing roar.

PART FOUR: SEATTLE TSUNAMI!

Chapter 21

As Matt and Grace fled uphill on Denny Way with the tsunami steadily gaining on them, Matt made a snap judgment: buildings along the way might represent death traps rather than salvation. So they ran on at top speed, hoping to gain enough elevation that the flood would ebb before reaching them. As they neared Fifth Avenue, Matt glanced back and realized such hopes were in vain. The churning waters were almost upon them. In seconds, they would be swept into a maelstrom carrying splintered wood, half-buoyant cars, and a few people desperately struggling to stay afloat.

"This way!" On an impulse, he pulled Grace into Tilikum Place Park—a small, tree-lined, triangular open space just off Denny Way.

"What now?"

"We go up!" He glanced around at the trees—sycamores with widespread branches tall enough to remain above the flood. But every trunk was unbranched up to the fifteen-foot level.

"The wave will turn the corner too," she reminded him as he stared at the un-scalable trunks. "What have you got in mind?"

"This!" He pulled her toward a fountain where a statue of Chief Seattle stood. The life-size bronze of the old chief with a hand raised in greeting was mounted on a seven-foot-tall white marble pedestal, surrounded by a foot-deep pool. Matt splashed in and started circling the wide pedestal, looking for a way up.

"You want to climb up *there?"*

"It's taller than that!" He pointed at the wall of water, which was just spreading into the park from Denny Way. It had thinned, coming uphill, but was still a six-foot wall of muddy, frothing death bearing down on them.

She stood with jaw agape, staring at annihilation approaching.

"Here!" he shouted. "Put your foot on this." He indicated a bronze fountain in the shape of a bear's head on the side of the pedestal. Grace stepped up on it but could find no handhold on the pedestal's smooth vertical face. She flattened her hands on the un-scalable marble.

"I can't—" she began, but he put both hands on her rump and boosted her up with all his might. She got her hands and elbows on top of the pedestal and then Matt gripped one of her dangling feet and pushed her higher. With that, she scrambled up beside the statue, safe for the moment.

Matt stepped on the bear's head, reached up, and grasped the rim of the pedestal. He kicked a leg out, trying to hook a heel on the top of the pedestal, but could get no purchase on the smooth marble. By now, the flood was surging around the trunks of the sycamores. When it impacted the far end of the pedestal it made a colossal roar and sent spray twenty feet in the air. A thick rain of dirty water showered down on Grace's shoulders and almost swept her over the edge to join Matt.

Matt had wisely chosen the end of the ten-foot-long pedestal farthest from Denny Way for their ascent. Now he pressed himself flat against the marble as the main surge swept past on both sides. Eddying water closed on him, nonetheless.

"Here!" Grace knelt and reached for him. "Take my hands!"

"I can't let go!" His body was afloat in the swirling water. After a moment, his hands slipped off the pedestal, but Grace grabbed his wrists in that instant and held them tightly.

"Don't let me drown!" he begged.

"I won't!"

Matt's position on the far side of the pedestal from the main flow provided an unexpected benefit. Not only did he avoid being swept away, but he was also buoyed up by the back eddy as it rose around him. Grace maintained her grip on his wrists and got some leverage by wrapping one leg around the base of the statue to keep from being pulled in with Matt. As the water rose to the rim of the pedestal, Matt kicked his feet and, with Grace's help, drove himself onto the top. He got to his knees and they embraced. "Oh my God!" she cried as the water roared around them. "You're safe! I can hardly believe—"

"Come on." He gently unwrapped her arms. "We're not safe yet. The water's still rising."

She glanced around and saw that he was right. Although the front wall of water was past, the body of the surge was still deepening. Several of the sycamores snapped off, riding with the flow. Muddy ripples sloshed across the top of the pedestal as they got to their feet.

"We've got to go up some more!" Matt turned to Chief Seattle's statue, now the only part of the monument still above water. He helped Grace scramble up and onto the chief's shoulders and then shinnied up after her. Around them in the surge, more uprooted trees rafted away, issuing loud cracking, splintering, and sloshing sounds.

And still the water rose.

In Fire Station Number 2, Bob Jensen, now in his fire-response gear, watched two men carry a large, dented sheet-metal duct out the bay door of Engine Number 9. He nodded in satisfaction. That was the last piece of fallen ceiling hardware. Soon E9 would be revved up and ready to go looking for trouble, which wouldn't be hard to find.

Suddenly, the two men dropped the duct squarely in front of the door and retreated inside the facility.

"Don't leave it there!" Jensen called, thinking they had temporarily lost their minds. But as they sprinted past him without a word, he saw a reason a man might lose his mind. A two-foot-deep rush of muddy water was flowing south on Fourth Avenue, coming from the direction of Denny Way.

As the two men raced up a staircase, one called back, "Get to higher ground, Chief!"

Caught with less warning than his men, Jensen backpedaled as the water rushed into the station. He jumped onto a running board of E9 as the flood churned under it, and then climbed into the driver's seat as the truck was surrounded. Trapped, he could do nothing but watch the frothing brown water rise.

At Tilikum Place, the waters rose until Chief Seattle's statue was submerged to the chest. Matt and Grace perched on his shoulders, their feet dangling in the deadly swift current.

"Look there!" Grace pointed between two nearby buildings. An entirely new wall of water was rushing at them. Three feet taller than the original surge, it had been channeled up an alley and entered the park from a different angle.

"We can still go up," Matt said resolutely. Half-standing, he perched on Seattle's shoulder and clasped the statue's right arm, which was upraised in the greeting the old chief once gave pioneers. Reaching out his free hand, Matt beckoned Grace to him as the wave bore down on them. She clambered over the chief's head and leapt into Matt's one-armed embrace just as the wave crashed onto her back. He caught her and held her tightly, keeping his other arm firmly entwined around the chief's arm. The wave washed entirely over them. Assailed by an all-but-overwhelming force, they were submerged for many seconds, holding their breaths against choking water. Above them, nothing but Chief Seattle's hand remained above the surface.

Then the wave crested. The water level fell. They clung to each other with their intertwined arms and legs awash in the still-powerful current, gasping for breath. Matt kept one arm locked around the chief's arm and one arm wrapped around Grace, as the abating but still dangerous torrent swept around them.

Chapter 22

At T-Mobile Park, the chaos and catastrophe appeared to have ebbed as well. The brown waters that had risen into the lower stands began to fall.

Ronald Rutledge sat on the sound stage, the giant video image of his face with headphones and mouthpiece still filling the centerfield screen. Around him, the set director and staff were offering each other expressions of relief and congratulations, both for having survived, and for having saved the crowd from a greater disaster. A man in a bright yellow T-shirt marked SECURITY approached Rutledge.

"We've had a quick look around. As far as we can tell, the building didn't take any major damage. You can let people know they're safe where they are."

He did so.

The security man asked, "Do you think there'll be another tidal wave?"

"I'm not sure." Rutledge's voice inadvertently came across the stadium speakers.

"Can you give me an educated guess?"

Rutledge covered his mic with a hand. "No education prepares you for this. But basically, I don't expect another tsunami, unless there's another big aftershock."

"Will there be another big aftershock?"

"I can't say. I wish I could see my seismographs."

Only now did it dawn on Rutledge that he had been trembling with emotion the entire time he was on the sound stage. Suddenly, he felt exhausted.

The waters receded from Tilikum Place almost as quickly as they had come, draining from the high ground at Fifth Avenue both east and west, forward into Lake Union and back into Elliott Bay. Tilikum Place was soaked with grimy water, strewn with wreckage, and tangled with the branches of several downed sycamores. Matt scrambled down from the statue pedestal and then assisted Grace with her hands on his shoulders and his hands gripping her waist.

"Which way?" She was disoriented by masses of criss-crossed sycamore branches around them.

"I'm not sure," Matt said. "I'm all turned around, too. This way, I think."

They pushed through the branches and moved out of the park past soggy storefronts and buildings with windows shattered out. Turning a corner, they followed an avenue made tortuous by what had been parked cars, now scattered across sidewalks or pushed into clusters of crumpled, overturned, and mud-soaked wreckage. Here and there, dazed people moved randomly through a maze of building debris, mangled storefront frames, soggy furniture, and tangles of splintered street trees.

"Are you sure this is the right direction, Matt?"

He paused. "I think we're heading south or southeast, judging by the sun. Let's find an intersection sign just to be sure—if there are any still standing."

Bob Jensen sat in Engine Number 9 until the last of the water drained out of the station, leaving behind wet, grimy, litter-strewn floors. The surge of brown muck had risen until it half-covered the engine's tires, but it hadn't gone higher.

As he stepped down, a man appeared at the base of the stairs where the others had disappeared minutes before. It was Torrey Vega, E9's assigned driver. Jensen asked him, "Do you think this rig will start, after taking all that water?"

Vega shrugged. "Let's give her a try."

Ryan Hewitt sat behind the wheel of his car for a long time with his door open, letting water drain onto the seaweed-strewn pavement. Beach Drive, which had been submerged three or four feet deep at the height of the wave, had re-emerged as the tidal surge subsided down the bulkhead.

The station wagon was tipped at an angle, half on and half

off the sidewalk. Ryan and his girls were too numbed by terror and too chilled by cold water to do much more than sit and tremble as the receding flood cascaded down the rocks of the uplifted beach. He stared at the metal sidewalk railing that had kept the car from being swept over the brink of the bulkhead. It was bent but unbroken, pressing against the passenger side of the car—or rather, the car was pressing against it. The humble railing had been the arbiter of life and death. If the car had gone off the bulkhead when the beach below was awash in twenty feet of water, they surely would have drowned.

Caylie had crawled into the space between him and the steering wheel, put her arms around him, and collapsed in exhaustion. Her only movements now were little sobbing breaths and an occasional shudder. Emily sat in the back seat, crying quietly. He reached back and patted her shoulder.

He watched as an immense new swell came ashore. It rose halfway up the seawall, then subsided. "Come on, girls. I think we'd better get away from here." He scooped Caylie up in his arms and stepped out onto the cracked pavement. Emily got out the back door and joined him. They looked in disbelief at the changes the earthquake had wrought on the street. Rectangular sections of pavement had been shuffled like Scrabble tiles. Some had tilted up. Some had dropped down. Uneven gaps between the sections made it clear no car would get through anytime soon. The row of houses across the street had suffered a wide range of damage, from almost none to complete leveling. Here and there, dazed residents wandered in confusion or conversed with neighbors in varying degrees of urgency or hysteria.

"What are we going to do now, Daddy?" Caylie murmured.

"Let's get up a little higher." Ryan nervously eyed yet another surge on the Sound. This third wave was smaller than its predecessor, but he wasn't about to take chances.

"Where?" Emily asked.

"There." Ryan nodded at a house directly across the street. A small, sky-blue, one-story cottage built in earlier and simpler times, it had withstood the quake much better than several multi-story modern monstrosities on either side of it.

They crossed the street and climbed concrete steps that went up about six feet to a flat yard fronted by a basalt rockery dotted with flowering shrubs. The yard had stayed just above the flood level. Its green lawn, cherry tree with a hammock hung from it, picnic table, and gas barbecue grill had somehow retained their pleasant suburban appeal through the catastrophe.

They paused on the house's front walk to gaze at profound changes the quake had worked on the south shore of Alki Point. With the surface of Puget Sound settled to its normal sea-level position, it was clear the shore stood fifty feet higher than when they arrived a seeming-eternity ago. The shoreline had been thrust upward by stupendous forces within the earth and the entire neighborhood had gone up with it. The seawall was now far from the water's edge, as was Beach Drive on top of it, as well as the yard where the Hewitts stood.

An entire new hill had risen in seconds, starting somewhere in the middle of West Seattle and running west through Alki Point, then sinking beneath Puget Sound. The Alki Lighthouse, though cracked and damaged, still stood on what had formerly been the farthest point of land. Now it occupied a location midway along the new ridge.

"I see somebody got wet!" a friendly voice called from behind them.

They turned to see a small, wiry old man standing on the front porch above them, an additional four feet higher than where they stood. Dressed in shorts, sandals, and a plaid short-sleeved shirt, he rested his elbows on the porch rail and smiled down at them.

In response to his remark, the Hewitts looked themselves over. Although they were mostly dry on top, their clothes were soaked below the waist.

"Come! Come!" the old man encouraged them in a voice inflected with an Eastern European accent. "I have some dry towels inside." He gestured at a set of wooden steps and motioned for them to come up.

Emily looked to her father for reassurance.

"Sure," Ryan ushered Emily toward the steps and carried Caylie, who still clung to him. "We won't be able to get out of this neighborhood anytime soon."

"I'm Joe," the old fellow said. Sparkly-eyed and spry for a man of eighty years or so, he went inside as they came up the steps and returned with three large beach towels, which they took gladly. This especially pleased Caylie, who had begun to shiver from the wet chill on her legs when Ryan set her down.

"Would you like hot chocolate?" Joe asked while they blotted water off their legs and wrapped themselves. "The power is out to my stove, but I could heat up some milk on the barbecue grill. The milk in the fridge will go bad anyway, so we might as well use it up!"

Lulled by his calm and smiling demeanor, they accepted his offer gratefully. As they did so, a distant sound grew louder until it resolved into something quite familiar to the Hewitts—the powerful thumping of helicopter rotors.

Chapter 23

Jane Hewitt was still trembling with panic. She had flown Dolphin 224 swiftly over the stricken neighborhoods of West Seattle on a straight line to the shore. She had crossed the central hill of the West Seattle peninsula and swept down to Alki Beach over houses and apartment buildings, every third one of which showed major structural damage. Her eyes were open wide in mixed hope and fear. But as she and her crew searched the devastated shoreline with no sign of her family, her anxiety transitioned to pure terror.

In several sweeps of Alki Beach, they witnessed a vast number of tragedies—bodies floating amid wreckage offshore, corpses washed up on the streets, crushed cars, smashed houses, dazed survivors wandering aimlessly. But nowhere did they spot the familiar forms of her family among the living—or the dead.

Eventually, her panicky breathing slowed, and her heart palpitations diminished, to be replaced by a leaden feeling in her chest. Her mind grew numb. Then she had a flash of realization. "Tide pools!"

Ramon glanced around. "No tide pools here. It's all flat beach."

"That's just it! Ryan mentioned a place he went as a kid. It has tide pools!"

"Not here."

"Exactly!" She steered Dolphin 224 hard around and flew to the south side of Alki Point. There, she spotted something that dashed her hopes and renewed her terror. The family station wagon sat at the brink of the seawall with two of its four doors open and signs of having been flooded. *It was empty.*

Electric bolts of fear rippled through her. "They're… gone!" she cried. "They're gone!"

The crew kept a hushed silence as she overflew the car, then made a short loop over the turbid waters of the Sound looking for what she feared most. Then she circled back to examine the car again.

"They're not here!" she sobbed.

"No, they're not!" Ramon suddenly cried. "They're *there!*" He indicated a small blue house near the station wagon. On its porch stood a little old man and three people who were waving frantically. Ryan and the girls, wrapped to the waist in towels, wore grins Jane could see a hundred yards away. Caylie was so excited she was jumping up and down.

"They look fine!" Ramon said.

"They sure do!" Jane blinked away tears.

On the porch, Ryan and the girls shouted happy greetings at the helicopter, which hovered so low that its rotor-wash flattened the choppy surface of the Sound. Both girls waved joyously, crying in unison, "Mommy! Mommy!"

Inside the helicopter, they could see two helmeted, goggled, smiling faces. And the one in the pilot's seat was—

"Mommy!" Caylie cried again.

They watched her adjust the helmet microphone at the corner of her mouth and heard her voice come over the loudspeaker. "You guys gave me a terrible fright. Is everyone okay?"

The three had no means to communicate over the roar of the rotor blades, but Ryan held out an arm and gave a vigorous thumbs-up gesture. Old Joe gave a thumbs-up, too.

"Good," Jane sighed. There was a long pause while they all grinned at each other and the girls continued to wave. Then Jane said, "I'd… I'd love to come down there and kiss you all and take you home with me. But… I've got work to do. We're in a rescue situation now and people need us to do our job."

"Aw," both girls groaned. Caylie burst into tears. "I want to go with Mommy!"

"No dear," Ryan held her hand as she wailed. "Mommy's going to be very busy, and we're okay, now."

After a moment, the helicopter began to rise. "Goodbye for now," Jane said. "I love you, girls. I love you, Ryan."

Both girls shouted, "I love you too, Mommy!" They waved after the helicopter as it shrank with distance above them, until it turned and headed in the direction of Seattle.

"Come," Joe sympathized. "Some hot cocoa will cheer you up."

"Hello!" Matt called to the firemen gathered around Engine 9 as he and Grace walked into the engine bay. Driver Torrey Vega had been cranking the motor, but it was uncooperative. Flood water still dripped from the big rig's bumper and fenders.

"We need some help," Matt called up to Vega.

"A lot of people need some help." Vega's voice betrayed his frustration with the engine.

"What can we do for you?" asked Bob Jensen, who was among the other firemen watching Vega's efforts.

"Our friend is trapped in the Space Needle Restaurant," Grace explained. "He's bleeding awful badly!"

Jensen put his hands on his hips and gazed over their heads at the Space Needle, which loomed over the neighborhood. He thought a moment, glancing from the Needle to Grace's anxious face, to Engine 9, which Vega was cranking again but which still refused to start.

Matt added, "He'll die if we can't get someone to help him."

"Well, you're talking to the right guy, but…" Perplexation creased Jensen's brow. "We've got two vehicles stuck in here." He gestured down the line of engine bays to where a second crew struggled to manually raise the jammed door in front of the aid car. "And there might be a number of urgent cases between here and there that we can't neglect."

Hope that had arisen on Grace's face faded. "So, you're saying you can't help us?"

"I didn't say that." Jensen turned and walked toward the staircase, motioning for them to follow. "Come with me. I just might be able to arrange something."

Jane Hewitt steered Dolphin 224 on a course back to Seattle, flying over the beach north of Alki Point. She guessed that the downtown waterfront would be the place most in need of their rescue capabilities. Below her stretched a shoreline devastated by the tsunami. Whole houses had been flattened and tall condominium units had been stripped of their facades up to the third or fourth floor. Offshore lay a miles-long logjam of uprooted trees, splintered housing materials—and floating bodies.

"Look there!" sharp-eyed Ramon called out. Jane saw instantly what he was pointing at. In the midst of the floating wreckage, a man clinging to a log had raised one arm to wave at them frantically.

"I see him." Jane slowed the helicopter to hover over the man. "Tyrell!" she called through her helmet mic. "Get suited up."

"Already am," Collins replied.

She turned and shot a glance behind her, where Collins sat, belted into his seat on the flight deck wearing his red wet suit and black snorkel, mask, gloves, and fins. His ebony face was agrin. "I did a quick change while you were busy with other things."

She gave him a smile and a thumbs-up. Then she turned eyes-front and quickly brought the Dolphin down toward the survivor. Unavoidably, the rotor-wash stirred up the jostling tangle of wreckage around him.

"Do you think you can extract him from all that junk, Tyrell?" She turned to glance at him again. This time it was he who gave the thumbs-up gesture. He rolled the side door open and stood with his flippers over the brink, ready to go.

Gingerly, Hewitt brought the Dolphin down until its landing skids were inches above the water and debris. Jason Chow, at the winch controls, lowered a red, looped harness into the water near the survivor on a line of sufficient length that Tyrell could pull it to the man with relative ease. When Tyrell jumped, heels first, into the water, Hewitt adjusted for the upward lurch of the Dolphin and steadied the aircraft just above the two men. In seconds, Tyrell had the man cinched tight inside the harness. Next, he clipped himself to the line, chest-to-chest with the survivor. He raised a gloved hand, index finger up, and made a circular motion indicating that he and the man were ready to be lifted.

Gingerly, Hewitt steered the helicopter straight up until the rope line tightened and began to lift the men free of the water. At that moment, she was surprised to see Tyrell grab a small dog that was swimming nearby, lifting the poor thing by a red-white-and-blue bandana on its neck and taking it with them into the air.

Hewitt took the Dolphin to fifty feet. It was then a simple matter to fly the hundred or so yards to shore with the two men and the dog suspended twenty feet below. She guided them in for a soft touchdown on the wet sidewalk above the seawall on Alki Avenue. She did her job so deftly that both men alighted on their feet. Tyrell quickly unhitched them from the line. She watched as Tyrell looked the man over and apparently decided he had come through with little or no injury. There were no signs of blood on him, and he stood straight—gratefully shaking Tyrell's hand. The dog was fine too, jumping its forepaws up on Tyrell's leg to get a pat on the head.

"If he's okay," she said over the loudspeaker, "we'd better leave him and push on. There'll be a lot more people in need..."

Tyrell put the sling around his own torso and then circled his finger to indicate he was ready to be lifted. Moments later, Dolphin 224 was a hundred feet above the beach and Chow was reeling in Collins to bring him aboard.

Ramon Valenzuela had kept busy on the helicopter's radio, trying vainly to contact local and regional authorities on a variety of frequencies. So far, his search had been in vain. "Maybe a little more altitude would help," he suggested.

"Roger that." Hewitt rocketed the Dolphin straight up into the sky once Collins was aboard. In seconds the altimeter registered over a thousand feet and rising. A scratchy noise came over the headphones.

"That's Joint Base Lewis-McChord's frequency!" Ramon punched a key on the console. "Come in, JBLM?" he called excitedly. "Come in?"

"This is JBLM." The reply came back in clipped military tones. "Please identify yourself and your location."

"Oh, uh, yeah," Valenzuela sputtered, surprised to hear anyone at all. "This is USCG Dolphin 224, located over West Seattle."

There was a pause. Then the voice came back. "What is your status, Dolphin 224?"

Hewitt switched the comm-link to her mic. "We are nominal and have just performed a rescue. Ready for more assignments."

"Roger that. Give us a minute. We are working on a great many situations and communications are pretty bad right now. Keep the lines open, and we'll get back to you. Meantime move in the direction of Seattle. So far as we know, you are the only evac-capable aircraft operating in the area. We have no major damage here at JBLM. We are scrambling plenty more aircraft, but they'll take time to get there. Until then, you're all we've got."

Chapter 24

Aboard the fireboat *Leschi*, the crew was all business. Never mind that they had gone airborne off the first tsunami. Never mind that they had spent terrifying minutes tossed on the chaotic peaks and troughs of crisscrossed waves. Never mind that they had weathered yet another, larger tsunami coming north from Harbor Island. The waters of Elliott Bay, although still swirling and heavily laden with debris, had settled sufficiently to allow Captain Dale Klimchak to bring the firefighting juggernaut to bear on tasks she was designed to do. No assignment had come from Central Dispatch—that channel had gone silent with the quake and might be out of service for some time. Klimchak assumed the quake had killed city power and the Center's backup generator as well. He could only hope that it hadn't also killed some of his friends and coworkers there. Neither had there been any calls for assistance from other fire or police vehicles.

For a brief time, the radio channels had all been abuzz with voices of frantic firefighters and police patrolmen. The cacophony of exclamations and shouts for assistance had then devolved into loud static as the entire 800-kilohertz system crashed under a communications overload. It was anyone's guess how long it would be before the radio frequencies returned to a semblance of normal. In the meantime, Klimchak had reconnoitered the waterfront and picked his own choice of emergencies to respond to.

The waterfront as a whole presented a mixed picture, with some pier buildings spared by wave valleys, while other buildings had been demolished by wave peaks. One building in particular presented an undeniably urgent situation. The four-story peak-roofed structure of Pier 57 had been spared by the waves but was afflicted by a much worse problem. A fire had broken out, perhaps from a ruptured kitchen gas line in one of the restaurants clustered at the end of the pier. Black smoke and orange flames billowed out of the building, imperiling dozens of people.

The Great Ferris Wheel at the end of the pier had miraculously withstood the quake and the waves without collapsing. However, people riding the tourist attraction were trapped, eight-to-a-car, in forty-two glass-encased gondolas that hung from the wheel. When the power had failed, the gondolas had been marooned at various heights above the pier, the top-most being a prodigious 175 feet aloft.

Now, heavy black smoke encircled the gondolas as flames from the pier grew into a roaring inferno. Heat made the wheel a rotisserie, threatening to slowly cook the life out of the trapped sightseers. Some in the lower gondolas had broken out windows and jumped to their fates. Some had splashed into the Sound, where they clung to debris or floated lifeless. Others had landed in heaps on the pier surface. Most, however, were unwilling to jump from such great heights. These unfortunate souls remained stranded as smoke and flames billowed around them.

The *Leschi* wasted little time reaching the scene. In a few minutes, she stood just off the end of the pier, attacking the fire with streams of salt water blasting from three of her five guns. Under this heavy barrage, the flames diminished quickly, and vanished entirely within several minutes. Dense black smoke turned to gray and then to white steam. Still, the *Leschi* kept the torrents of water coming, making certain the flames were doused for good.

While the fire was being suppressed, Captain Klimchak did much more than watch water stream from the deck guns. He assigned Rita O'Rourke to launch the *Leschi's* rigid-hulled inflatable boat off the stern. In it, he sent her to fetch four firemen and a medical technician who made their way from Station 5 to a nearby pier on foot. Once the additional crew were retrieved, he dispatched Rita and her launch with two firemen aboard to collect floating survivors. Meanwhile, he kept the *Leschi* in place and the fire at bay.

One of Klimchak's new shipmates took the ladder's controls and extended it toward the wheel, with a fireman at its end, to begin transferring trapped tourists down to the *Leschi's* decks. This urgent and dangerous task was fraught with risk as Chip Sandoval grappled with steering controls, keeping the boat on station against cross-currents while the transfers took place.

The launch was soon alongside again, and its crewmen were assisting rescuees aboard. These people were triaged by the med tech into those who required immediate medical attention, those who could wait, and those who were lucky enough to only need a place to sit and a warm cup of coffee or cocoa. The med tech efficiently ran the ship's emergency treatment room, tending to a succession of life-threatening bleeding cases or people in shock from internal injuries.

The wheelhouse crew ran the vessel capably, but the *Leschi* was still short-handed for such a major event. She lacked the additional teams of communications specialists and departmental authorities who could have shipped aboard her if anyone had known such a catastrophe were coming. The mobile command center just below the bridge was fully equipped to provide satellite and multi-channel radio communications, even ship-to-shore Internet and ship-to-ship navigation capacity. Given the superlative capabilities of the *Leschi*, Klimchak and his crew had always expected their vessel to play a primary role in rescue and recovery operations—and now the day had come. With large stores of potable water aboard, a galley serving the needs of rescuees, and even showers for anyone coated with oil or muck, the *Leschi* had become a self-sustaining disaster response center afloat on Elliott Bay.

Fire Chief Bob Jensen had introduced Matt and Grace to Mari Novado, the radio dispatcher in Station 2's Emergency Command Center, before he hurried back to Engine 9. He had encouraged Mari to help them if she could but had explained that he was needed where more people were in jeopardy. He had also explained that, under the circumstances, sending a team to climb the Space Needle stairs was simply too time-consuming to prioritize. Disheartened, Matt and Grace listened while Novado attempted to contact police patrol cars in the field, ambulance dispatch units, and fire stations near and far, but to no avail. In every case there was only static in response, or someone reporting they were too tied up with urgent cases or too distant or too damaged to help anytime soon.

As the effort dragged on, Grace turned to Matt and leaned her forehead on his chest. He wrapped his arms around her, and they listened somberly, losing hope by slow, agonizing increments.

Then a new voice came over the radio. It was a sharp, clear, masculine voice. "Seattle Fire Station Two, this is Camp Murray Emergency Operations Center. Do you copy?"

"Roger, Camp Murray. We copy."

"Just calling to confirm we now have an air-rescue asset over your area. Do you have any requests for air evac?"

Mari shot Matt and Grace a glance of surprise and delight. Their faces lit too when Mari drawled, "Ah-roger Camp Murray. Affirmative. We do have a case in need of air rescue. Over?"

The diesel motor of Fire Engine 9 thundered to life just as Bob Jensen came down the stairs. He hurried to his red Fire-Chief SUV, BC2, which was parked on a side street near the station and had been dowsed by the flood up to her wheel wells. He climbed in just as Torrey Vega eased the big rig out of the engine bay. The aide car pulled out of the Bay 3 at the same time. Neither rig sounded its siren. There was no need, with no automobile traffic to be seen. To the south, however, a huge pall of dust drifted skyward where the Emerald Tower once stood. Several other skyscrapers billowed black smoke. By prearrangement, the aide car turned north to seek people in need of medical attention in the immediate neighborhood, while Vega turned E9 south and began slowly following debris-strewn Fourth Avenue toward the downtown district. This direction would have been against traffic, had there been any. Jensen steered BC2 around the corner and fell in behind E9.

"God only knows what we're gonna find down there," he muttered.

While the *Leschi* kept station at Pier 57, making sure every last occupant of the Ferris wheel came down the ladder safely, Rita O'Rourke ranged up and down the waterfront in the launch, fishing out survivors. A Coast Guard motor launch, complete with a 50-caliber machine gun on her bows, had been out on Homeland Security training maneuvers on Elliott Bay when the quake and waves struck. Now it pulled up alongside the *Leschi* and its captain shouted to Klimchak asking permission to drop off a load of survivors in order to go and search for more.

Klimchak shouted back, "Absolutely!"

He left the helm in Chip Sandoval's hands and went down to the main deck to help the Coast Guard rescuees get aboard, more than a dozen in all. The launch's officer called over to Klimchak. "These last six people?" He indicated a group of three men and three women, all drenched but otherwise unharmed. "They've got an interesting tale to tell."

"Welcome aboard," Klimchak said as the six clambered across a gangway from the launch to the Leschi's decks. "So, what's your story?"

One of the women said, "We were eating at Ivar's Restaurant at Pier 54."

"Outside, at the end of the pier," said another woman.

"We got through the quake okay," said a man who Klimchak guessed was the second woman's husband. "But we were kinda dumb. We didn't think about a tidal wave. So we stayed where we were. When the wave came, we were washed right off the pier, table and all."

"That table saved our lives," said the third woman. "We held onto it and floated until the Coast Guard boat came along."

"Sounds awful," Klimchak replied.

"It was."

Klimchak gestured to a door that led inside. "Please go in and find a place to get settled. Get a cup of coffee to warm you up. We've got a lot more people to help here, and then we'll put you ashore somewhere safe."

The group went inside and Klimchak was about to return to

the bridge, when the launch officer called to him again. "We've got one more here—a kinda special case."

"Yes?" Klimchak went to the gunwale and learned his elbows on it, looking down at the boat.

The officer moved to a form lying on the deck wrapped in a yellow tarp. He lifted the head end of the tarp to let Klimchak have a look.

Klimchak gasped. The naked male body looked much more than just dead. It looked mummified. The launch officer asked, "What do you make of him? He's stiff as a board. I've never seen anything like it."

"Well, I have." Klimchak smiled, recognizing the body. "That's Sylvester, the mummified cowboy from Ye Olde Curiosity Shoppe. Better bring him aboard too. Somebody'll want to claim him."

Chapter 25

In the Space Needle Restaurant, Carrie, DeWayne, and Monica tended to Earl. They kept him as comfortable as they could but watched in dismay as life slowly drained from him along with his blood.

"Am I gonna lose my leg?" Earl sounded dopey and weak. "I can't feel my foot."

DeWayne leaned near him. "I can't risk loosening the tourniquet again, man. You've lost too much blood."

Carrie pleaded, "Can't you let just a little down to his foot?"

DeWayne shook his head, pointing at the enlarging crimson pool around Earl's leg. "I don't think the blood will even make it to his foot."

"Am I going to die?" Earl's voice was alarmingly faint. His head lolled to the side. His gaze fixated on nothing.

DeWayne paused before answering, and that pause made Carrie burst into tears. But the sound of her weeping was drowned out by a new sound—the heavy thumping of helicopter rotor blades. Dolphin 224 rose into view just outside the shattered windows, and the wind from her rotor wash whipped wildly around the restaurant.

Carrie screamed. It was a scream of surprise—and of hope.

The helicopter hovered at their level while two helmeted crew members sized up the situation inside the restaurant. Then it rose out of sight, though its thumping continued. After what seemed an eternity but may have been only a minute or two, a man came running down the stairs from the observation deck. Dressed unexpectedly in a bright red wet suit with a red helmet and black gloves and boots, he hurried directly to Earl.

"Tyrell Collins, US Coast Guard," he introduced himself automatically to the others as he began examining Earl. "Is his bleeding under control?"

"Not too well," said DeWayne.

Tyrell examined Earl's leg and checked the tightness of the tourniquet. Satisfied, he glanced around the chaos of overturned tables and spilled dishes. "Get me one of your longest table-cloths!"

Monica went to an overturned table and pulled off the white cloth, about eight feet in length.

"That's good!" Tyrell took it and laid it out on the carpet beside Earl. "All right!" he commanded, looking intently into each of the three anxious faces. "We're going to work together as a team and get him on this tablecloth and use it as a sling to get him out of here. Are you ready?"

"Yes, sir!" DeWayne snapped back with military sharpness.

Earl had fainted away completely.

"One on each corner," Tyrell ordered. "I'll be at the head."

As soon as they arranged themselves, Tyrell called out, "Grab an arm or a leg, and on my four-count we'll lift him. Ready?" They grabbed limbs as instructed. "And, one, two, three… lift!" They raised Earl and, following Tyrell's move-ments, laid him on the white tablecloth, which immediately was white no more, but stained with deep red blood.

"Now," Tyrell called, "each one lifts a corner of the cloth!" They grabbed corners, Tyrell counted again, and they smoothly raised Earl off the floor.

"Upstairs! Upstairs!" Tyrell backed toward the staircase with the others following his lead. Carrie was on his left at the head end, and DeWayne and Monica held Earl's legs in a hammock-like stretcher of white-but-steadily-reddening cloth. They went up the stairs carefully and then moved onto the observation deck. The rotor of the Dolphin hovering overhead whipped up a furious wind and the whine of her turbine engines made a near-deafening sound. This did not deter the team from reaching a stretcher-shaped wire mesh rescue basket the helicopter had lowered to the observation deck. They quickly laid Earl in it, tablecloth and all.

Working swiftly, Tyrell cinched two straps across Earl and then backed away several steps. Raising a hand high, he made a twirling motion with an upraised index finger. Jason Chow in the helicopter's open side door worked control levers that pulled the line tight and lifted the basket and Earl into the air.

Once the basket had risen to the level of the bay, the Chow and Ramon Valenzuela pulled Earl inside and gingerly transferred him to a stretcher waiting on the flight-deck floor. As Valenzuela strapped Earl in place, Chow lowered the basket again. When the basket touched down, Tyrell leapt aboard it and sat at one end. He turned and looked at the three.

"Anyone family, here?" he hollered.

"I…" Carrie began, though it wasn't strictly true. "I am!"

Tyrell clasped one of the upright bars over the rescue basket and held out a black-gloved hand. "Come on then! We'll take you with us."

Carrie blanched but took the hand and stepped inside the basket. Tyrell guided her down to sit between his knees in the stretcher, then buckled a safety belt around her. Then he raised a hand and made his finger-twirling gesture. Swiftly, the winch lifted the basket and its two occupants skyward. Once they were well clear of the deck, Jane Hewitt steered the helicopter up and away from its dangerous proximity to the Space Needle's Indian-hat-shaped roof.

DeWayne and Monica waved farewell from below. Carrie, though petrified by the crazy carnival ride she was experiencing, managed a small wave in return.

Within moments, the basket was pulled in and fastened to the deck of Dolphin 224. Carrie was belted into a passenger seat by Collins and Chow. Jane Hewitt turned and gave a thumbs-up. "Welcome aboard! We are cleared to deliver you to the helipad at Harborview hospital. They've got emergency power there and doctors waiting to help him." Both Jane and Carrie looked with concern at Earl, who lay strapped in his stretcher, unconscious, unmoving, and apparently near death.

Matt and Grace had stood outside the fire station watching the helicopter make its dramatic maneuvers at the Space Needle.

"Wow!" Matt exclaimed as the aircraft turned and sped away. "That was incredible!"

"It was," Grace agreed. "But I've got to know if Earl will be okay. How do we get to where they're taking him?"

"Harborview hospital, is what Mari said."

"Do you have any idea where that is?"

"I think so." He turned and began walking southbound on Fourth Avenue, and she accompanied him. A man who had come out of the command center to watch the helicopter, a civilian in a plaid shirt and blue jeans with a Red Cross arm band, called after them. "I think Harborview is pretty far from here. At least a mile. There's going to be a lot of wrecked buildings and burst water mains and downed power lines between here and there. You could get yourselves killed."

"What else can we do?" Grace asked.

"You could stay here until morning. Our volunteers—people from the neighborhood—are going to set up a relief center. A few people from our team are already here. They'll set up cots for people to sleep on, sanitary facilities, and start providing food."

"I hadn't thought of food."

"You will by morning, believe me. Setting up food distribution is a high priority for us."

Matt said, "We'll find food where we're going."

"I hope you're right. I suppose I'd go too, if it was my friend. Stay safe, okay?"

"We'll try."

While Jane Hewitt was flying Dolphin 224 over downtown Seattle on the way to Harborview Hospital on First Hill, Camp Murray Control came on the radio. "Dolphin 224, please describe the scene. We still have limited data on conditions in Seattle. Are there fires?"

"Affirmative."

"How many fires?"

"Three skyscrapers obviously burning pretty good—or bad, I guess. And the glass is out of most windows in most towers.

Some others have limited smoke coming out in places, some high, some low."

"Other buildings? Apartment buildings?"

"Some are off their foundations. A few are flattened, but not too many."

"And on fire?"

"Some, here and there. But again, not too many."

"That's better than what we've been imagining, Dolphin 224. Thanks for that. If every structure had a gas leak, the whole city might be in flames."

"Negative, we see only sporadic fires."

"That suggests a main pipeline has ruptured somewhere, so no gas to fuel the flames."

"Roger, Murray. That's probably it. I see a possible gas main fire south of our position. A very large wall of flame rising out of Boren Avenue. Right out of the street. The flames are going—oh—maybe fifty feet in the air. Black smoke. No buildings involved."

"One blown-out gas main is a lot better than having a lotta buildings on fire."

"Roger."

"What else do you see? How are the freeways?"

"Mostly intact. But the tall southbound on-ramp spanning I-5 at Columbian Way—"

"Roger?"

"It's down. Blocking all lanes, north and south."

"That's bad news."

"Affirmative. Complete blockage. Looks like the bluff above the freeway on Beacon Hill collapsed in a landslide that took out the ramp. Traffic on the freeway is backed up both ways."

"Copy that. We'll plan our relief efforts with that in mind. Thanks, Dolphin 224."

"There's more."

"Go ahead."

"I-90 has a problem too. The tunnel openings at 23rd Street are partially collapsed. Rubble on both east and westbound lanes. Traffic is stuck there too."

"That's bad news. How's the bridge?"

"Still floating."

"That's something anyway. But we will advise our relief coordinators to plan for limited access."

"Roger, JBLM. I wish we had better news."

"Anything else major to report?"

"Yes, one more thing. That new skyscraper, Devine's Emerald Tower. It's—gone."

"Say again?"

"It has disappeared. Collapsed on itself in a giant hole in the ground."

"Is it burning?"

"Negative. There are traces of smoke and dust, but the hole is filled with water from the tidal wave. Could be a lot of casualties."

"Ah, negative, Dolphin 224. We show it as unoccupied."

"Let's hope that's true. Anything else we can report?"

"Do you see fire trucks, aid cars, police?"

She scanned the city again, this time seeing things she had neglected due to the large-scale impact of shattered buildings, flames, and rising smoke columns.

"Affirmative, JBLM. I see quite a few first-responder vehicles. Fire trucks with lights flashing, aid cars, police in a number of locations."

"That's encouraging."

"But I see something else now. There are piles of rubble from tall buildings, and streets are cracked open all over the place. That must be hampering ground operations."

"Roger, Dolphin 224. All the more reason we need air assets like yours. We've got more air support on the way from McChord and other bases. But arrival times are still minutes to hours."

As they spoke, Dolphin 224 reached the airspace above the hospital. "We are on station above Harborview," Hewitt said. "They appear to be in fairly good shape. Some brickwork down, but staff are waiting for us at the helipad."

"Roger Dolphin 224, we'll let you tend to business. Thanks for the report."

"You're welcome, Murray. Dolphin 224 over and out."

Chapter 26

"A lot of good *that's* gonna do us," Bob Jensen grumbled. Engine 9 stood at the intersection of Fourth Avenue and Cherry Street. Two crewmen had just used a hefty fireplug wrench to reef open the outlet bolt on a green street hydrant in front of the Columbia Center Tower. Instead of the hoped-for torrent, the hydrant poured out a thin, unpressurized trickle of water.

Jensen had watched his crew lay out empty fire hoses on the glass-strewn ground beside Engine 9 in the hope that they would soon be solidly pressurized with water. He muttered to a fireman standing nearby, "There's more than seven miles of standpipes and sprinklers in this building, with God knows how many leaks after what just happened. We can't *begin* to charge them with high-pressure water from that trickle."

The fireman nodded. "What are we gonna do?"

Jensen shrugged. "Hell if I know."

Firemen had already connected a hose to the one of the building's external standpipe fittings, but with no water to pump into it, their efforts so far were wasted.

Moments before, E9 had slid to a halt, rather than stopped, on a three-foot deep layer of greenish window glass that had fallen from Columbia Center's façade. Above, thick billows of black smoke issued from the thirteenth floor and another floor much higher up and still unidentified. Jensen had ordered two five-man teams to move inside, find the fires, and report their exact sizes and locations via walkie-talkie. So far, they had not reached their targets and Jensen could do little but wait.

While listening to his 800-megahertz unit crackle with static, he glanced down through layer upon layer of glass shards and saw an odd shape. It had the rough form of a body wearing a light blue coat and dark pants. One arm looked like it had been completely detached by glass that had sliced into the man. Deep red blood had spread under the glass and pooled around the body. There was no reason to dig him out in the hope that he might still be alive. He wasn't. And elsewhere in the sea of glass that covered the street, other red-encircled forms could be seen. Jensen's mind boggled trying to imagine the sight and sound of the glass torrent that had descended on the street—*how long ago?* Just a little more than an hour.

Suddenly, a scratchy voice came over the walkie-talkie. "This is Smithers on floor forty-five!"

"Roger, Smithers. What have you got?"

"The fire here is hot, but so far limited to one office suite. We are hitting it with handheld extinguishers, but not making much progress. How are you coming on standpipe water?"

"Negative on that," Jensen replied bitterly. "No hydrant pressure."

Smithers fell silent. Then he said, "Ah, Roger, Chief. I don't think we can suppress this without a lot more help."

Jensen felt deep frustration. "Just do what you can with local equipment. There ought to be multiple handheld extinguishers on every level."

"Roger. We are using them already."

"Go find more. I'll radio as soon as we get hydrant pressure."

"If we get hydrant pressure," the fireman beside Jensen muttered.

Jensen didn't pass the thought along to Smithers. "Just see what you can do," he said into the walkie-talkie.

"Roger," Smithers replied.

Dolphin 224 descended onto the bull's-eye target marking the helipad atop the parking garage at Harborview. A team of three white-uniformed hospital staff quickly transferred Earl to a gurney and raced him away toward the Emergency Room. Surging electrical lights made it clear that the hospital had its emergency power going, if only just barely. Carrie followed Earl.

"You brought us our first airborne delivery!" a hospital staff member called to Jane Hewitt over the whine of the helicopter's still-running turbine.

"First of many, I'm sure."

"I'm sure you're right." The man saluted her as he backpedaled a safe distance away. "All clear!" he shouted, extending his arms straight out to his sides and sweeping his hands upwards several times, the universal signal for liftoff. Jane pressed the thrust lever forward and Dolphin 224 rose into the air.

"What next?" Ramon asked.

"Let's go up a thousand feet and contact Camp Murray for more orders."

As they rose, Jane thought aloud. "I can't help worrying about Ryan and the girls. I'd go check on them again, if there wasn't so much to do."

"Yeah." Ramon nodded his helmeted head. "Way too much to do." He pointed across Elliott Bay to where the cruise ship *Alaskan Queen* sat stationary off West Point. "You think she needs help? She looks dead in the water."

"At least she's upright after two tidal waves. She has some lifeboats in the water, probably rescuing people who went overboard. Looks like they're handling things okay."

"And look there! A fireboat with a couple of motor launches picking up people in the water."

"What are those small boats farther out?" Jane wondered.

"Canoes! What are *they* doing there?"

As the surface of Elliott Bay had calmed, the canoe flotilla had gathered and conferred by shouts. Given that their destination, Pier 62, lay dead ahead, the consensus was to press on and learn the fate of friends and loved ones awaiting them on the shore.

As they resumed paddling, Johnny Steele spotted something pink moving in the water ahead and to the right. As they approached the object, he realized it was a woman waving an arm wrapped in a long pink-and-black sleeve. He alerted Kenny Helm and the skipper guided them near. The young woman floated on a splintered length of roof timber that was scarcely large enough to bear her weight. She appeared sluggish from hypothermia and seemed barely able to hang on. As they pulled up to her, a small bow ripple from the *Tatoosh* was sufficient to roll the timber. She went over with it. She made a few floundering motions, but her face went under.

People in the canoe gasped in sympathy but Johnny, who was nearest to her, didn't hesitate. He tossed aside his paddle, stood, and launched himself in a long dive that brought him quickly to the woman. He took her in his arms and went over backward in a rescue stroke, bearing her on his chest, so she could breathe. She was limp, but small choking exhalations proved she was alive.

Many hands helped pull her aboard, followed by Johnny. It appeared from her outfit of hot-pink and black form-fitting clothes, and her reflectorized running shoes, that she had been jogging along the waterfront when the quake and wave overtook her.

"She's got hypothermia," Ginny Musselshell said. "She'll die if we don't get her warm."

The plank seat in the bow where Arnie and Ginny sat was triangular. With the help of several others, they arranged the girl between them and hugged her from both sides. Someone fetched a gold-foil space blanket to wrap around all three, and Ginny spread her dancing shawl over that.

Kenny Helm called from the stern, and Johnny and the other pullers fell into their cadence, paddling for Pier 62.

When Ryan and the girls had arrived at old Joe's house, Caylie's teeth had been chattering. Her shivering stopped as she and Emily sipped hot chocolate in the warm sun, seated at Joe's side-yard picnic table with their legs wrapped in beach towels. Their pants were drying on a clothesline.

"I'm lucky!" Joe smiled as he watched them sip. "My house is hardly damaged. It kept going up and up, instead of shaking side-to-side. Some of my windows cracked, and the chimney fell down, but it can be repaired. And look now. I have a better view, higher up from the water."

"You're lucky all right," Ryan admitted.

Joe put his hands on the table and prepared to rise. "How about a beer?" he asked Ryan.

"No, thanks."

"Why not? The fridge is out. The beer will just get warm."

"Okay, then, a beer would be nice."

PART FIVE: END TIMES

Chapter 27

Matt and Grace had gone only a few blocks south on Fourth Avenue when they came to a scene that stopped them in their tracks. A five-story apartment building was partially collapsed, tilting at an alarming angle out over the street. Bricks shed from its façade covered the sidewalk and curb-parked automobiles. The first and second floors were buckled into the basement, so that the third floor was at street level in front but still third level in the rear. A crowd had gathered around a stone staircase that once led to the vanished front entrance. They were offering expressions of sympathy to a woman who crouched on hands and knees before the steps.

"My five-year-old!" she wailed. "He's in there!" She pointed into a narrow gap beside the staircase.

From somewhere in the black depths a tiny voice called out, "Mommy!"

"Please, someone," the woman cried. "Help my baby!"

The crowd stood around helplessly. Most were covered in gray dust, like the woman. Some were bleeding. All looked shocked and confused.

"He's going to die!" the mother screamed. "And I can't do a thing about it!" She held a trembling fist in front of her mouth and wept unrestrainedly. Bloody scrapes covered her forehead, her neck, and her shins, but most alarming was the condition of her left forearm. Just above the wrist it took a right-angle turn and the hand hung limp, the fingers palsied from shock and nerve damage. "I can't get down there to help him!"

Grace glanced at the crowd, especially the men. Their dull eyes and dusty, bloodied condition told her they would be no help. She knelt in front of the opening and peered down into its blackness. The gap, no more than a foot high, led under the stacked rubble of the first two stories, which had been crushed to a narrow remnant.

The woman, who identified herself as Ida Jacobs, touched her on the shoulder. "My son… Alex… and me… We live on the second story. Now it's… gone! The floor opened up and Alex fell. I tried to grab him—but he was gone before I could reach him. The floor closed on my hand." She cradled her left hand with her right, too much in shock to react to the pain the hand must have given her.

"I understand." Grace put a gentle hand on her shoulder.

From deep underground, the faint voice pleaded, "I'm scared, Mommy. I'm cold. There's water here."

Grace stared into the Stygian gap with a feeling like cold water running in her guts. For just a moment, gazing into that blackness, she remembered the desperate appeal in the eyes of the youth in Kathmandu. The memory shook her so badly that she sat back on her heels and wrapped her arms around her knees to fight off the terror.

"Help me!" the tiny voice sobbed.

Grace closed her eyes. Her head spun with vertigo. Then a thought crept into her mind. "No," she whispered. "This is not going to be another Kathmandu."

"What's that?" Matt leaned near.

"I said—" She paused to calm her racing heart, recalling how life had drained from that other face. Her pulse pounded in her head. "I said, I'm going down there."

"What?" Matt stared hard at her. "It's too dangerous!"

As if to bear him out, the rattle of falling debris came from the darkness.

"I'll take my chances."

"This is a bad idea!"

"Funny. It seems like a good idea to me." She sat and swung her legs over the concrete brink. She searched downward with her feet but found no foothold in the black spaces below. She took her cell phone from a small handbag she carried on a shoulder strap and shone its flashlight into the darkness. It was no help. She put it away and began cautiously sliding herself over the edge, but Matt caught her by an arm.

"Let me go first. I'm taller than you."

"I can't ask you to…"

"You don't have to."

She moved over, so he could join her at the brink. "Be careful."

"There's nothing careful about this whole idea. By the time we get to him, he'll probably be—"

"Don't even *think* that!" she hissed.

Matt glanced at Ida's panic-stricken face once more. Then, shaking his head, he slid over the edge, turned onto his belly, and gingerly began to lower himself into the inky space.

"Please hurry!" Ida begged.

Five feet below him, Matt's toes touched a ledge-like projection of torn flooring. Gingerly, he lowered himself onto it and let his weight settle until he knew the footing was solid. Reaching to his right, he grasped a twisted piece of iron pipe and tugged. It seemed to be anchored solidly enough in the concrete wall to bear his weight as he descended.

He peered into the dim spaces below. Fallen piles of bricks were scattered over the concrete floor of what had been a parking garage. Shattered wooden support beams pointed at odd angles. The air was a pall of dust. Torn streamers of insulating material hung from what had once been a ceiling but was now the roof of a sepulchral, claustrophobic space. Ten feet farther down, a second narrow opening penetrated to a deeper garage level. From that gap, the small voice moaned, "Mommy!"

"I'm not so sure about this," he told Grace, who was leaning into the gap above him.

"I'm sure," Grace replied.

"Then let me do it alone. It looks hella dangerous."

"If you're willing to risk it, I'm coming with you." She swung her legs over the edge and began to descend.

"My life isn't going so well these days!" he growled. "You've still got plenty going for you."

"I'm coming with you!" she repeated. "Maybe I care more for you than you care for yourself." She turned onto her belly as he had done and slid down to reach the floor ledge beside him.

"God bless you both!" Ida Jacobs cried.

"Which way do we go next?" Grace asked.

Matt looked around in the dim light. "I wish I knew. No way looks safe."

When Dolphin 224 reached a thousand feet, Ramon Diaz established radio contact with Camp Murray, and Hewitt took the comm link. "Our hospital run was successful. We are awaiting our next assignment."

"Roger that, Dolphin 224. Ah—we are still working on your next assignment. Downtown is too heavily damaged to get a good assessment of needs on the ground. Responders are blocked by wreckage, but we're working on it."

"Roger, Camp Murray. Let me advise we will soon be running low on fuel."

"Roger, Dolphin 224. Suggest you proceed to Boeing Field. They have an intact fuel supply, and emergency power is on. We will be establishing a forward base of operations there. Not much there yet, but soon. Meanwhile, you should be able to fuel up."

"Roger that. By the way, JBLM, is there any way I can get the status of my crew's families? They're probably safe in Port Angeles, but we have no way of contacting them."

"We'll check into it. Communications are better up that way. No significant quake damage reported there."

Ramon breathed a sigh of relief. He and Chow and Collins, listening over their headsets, exchanged smiles and thumbs-up signs.

Bob Jensen stood beside Engine 9, frustrated by the lack of resources keeping him from adequately attacking the two fires billowing smoke from the Columbia Center Tower. His shoulder walkie-talkie crackled, and then Smithers' voice came through clearly. "Happy to report the fire on the forty-fifth floor has been extinguished! Handheld units did the trick!"

A cheer went up from several firemen standing around Jensen as he congratulated Smithers and his team.

"Lotta men are blue in the face up here," Smithers replied. "Running up all those stairs and fighting a fire wasn't easy, but they got the job done."

"I need your team to hustle down to floor thirteen and assist the crew working there."

"The other fire is not contained?"

"So far, not so good on thirteen. They've got fire in the ceiling and extinguishers aren't putting it out completely. If it gets any hotter and gets away from them, it could burn all the way up through the building."

"Roger, Chief. We are on our way!"

"When you get close, scrounge some handheld extinguishers from the floors above. Everything on the eleventh, twelfth, and thirteen floors has already been used."

"We'll do that. Smithers out."

Jensen scowled at the trickle coming from the hydrant. "We need some God-damned water!"

Matt and Grace descended through two partially collapsed levels of the garage to reach Alex Jacobs. They wriggled through a narrow gap in the split-open concrete of the garage floor. Then they lowered themselves into the almost complete darkness of the sub-basement, which had accordioned down to a claustrophobic four-foot-tall recess.

Groping through extremely dim light, they found the boy laying on his back, pinned down by a large sheet of drywall with two-by-four studs still attached. He lay in several inches of water flowing from a burst water main somewhere above their level. Matt tried to lift the drywall but couldn't manage it. Grace joined him and, working together, they raised it off the boy and pushed it aside.

"See, Matt? I knew you'd need me down here." She picked up little Alex and pressed him to her. "He's wet, and cold, and he's shivering."

"I want Mommy," the boy moaned.

Grace pressed her cheek to his water-soaked head, which felt deathly cold. She fetched out her cell phone and used its light to inspect Alex closely. "No serious injuries," she told Matt.

"None that we can see."

"He's a brave boy, and he's gonna be okay," Grace soothed the child. "We'll get you to your mom—"

She was cut off by a jolt that pitched them all sideways.

"Aftershock!" Matt cried, though a loud rumble made it obvious what was happening. The surrounding wreckage came alive, moving and rattling with the violence of the fresh temblor. Alex screamed, and Grace hugged him close, protecting him with her body. Matt leaned over them both, covering his head and neck with his hands. Bricks and chunks of concrete clattered down and splashed into the water around them. A fist-sized chunk struck Matt on one hand, forcing a grunt of pain from him. Falling two-by-fours bonked on the concrete layer overhead. Ominous scraping noises of huge cement blocks, and groans of straining timbers came from above. A shower of smaller debris rained down, pummeling them with stones and choking them with dust.

Chapter 28

"That was a big-ass aftershock," Rutledge said into the microphone, temporarily adopting Kyle Stevens' argot. "Magnitude four, at least. But you're still better off staying right where you are, folks." By now, the crowd had settled down considerably, so the new tremor brought only a few to their feet. It was as if they were getting used to the rattling and shaking—and beginning to put their trust in Rutledge.

As the aftershock tapered off with no significant damage, a man came to Rutledge and gave him a handwritten note. He glanced it over and then read it aloud. "T-Mobile Park security personnel are in the process of inspecting the stadium and surrounding area. So far, we can report that the exits of all three major parking garages are blocked by wreckage and debris. All street-level parking in the area has been flooded and vehicles swept away. Ground-level exits from the stadium are also blocked. Furthermore, the area surrounding the stadium has many hazards, including downed power lines, sink-holes of soft mud, and broken glass. There is also the risk of another tsunami if a big aftershock occurs.

"Under the circumstances, we suggest you stay where you are. However, the sky bridges to the main garage are intact, and the right-field gate, which is elevated, is open as well. Those wishing to leave the area on foot may do so, but please keep to the elevated roads until you reach higher ground. For those who wish to remain with us awhile longer, there's good news: stadium personnel are re-opening some of the concessions. They are preparing hot food and cold drinks, which will be given out free."

The statement was greeted with ripples of applause.

Craig Palmer and the boys were already in line at a concession stand that was handing out steaming hot dogs and cold drinks.

"Can we go home?" Liam asked after the announcement.

"Not quite yet," Craig replied. "It sounds like our car is trapped inside the garage. Let's wait and see if they can help us get out."

"Let me go!" Ida Jacobs wailed. "Let me go!" She swatted away helpful hands trying to lift her from where she lay prostrate in front of the now-vanished gap into which her son's would-be rescuers descended many minutes before. The aftershock had caused the building to settle and the gap to vanish before her eyes. "I'm staying right here until I die!"

"It's going to be night soon," a man said sympathetically. He leaned near, but Ida swiped a clawed hand at his face, driving him back.

There had been no hopeful sounds from the spaces under the building for some time. The only noises were frightful ones—the cracking of overstressed beams, the clattering of falling masses of brick and stone, the hissing of small avalanches of fine grit. But the hoped-for sound of human voices had not come.

Ida rested her cheek on her uninjured forearm and wept softly.

Almost imperceptible, interspersed with the building's death rattles, a scraping sound became audible. Ida Jacobs raised her head and stared at the wreckage dully, her wellsprings of hope all but dry. A louder rumble—the sound of a large block of stone slipping into space—was followed by a tremendous crash when it hit pavement on the level below.

Its fall opened a new gap in the rubble, where a man's face appeared. Ida screamed as if seeing a ghost, and then clutched her way to the gap and reached out her good hand.

With a smile cracking dust caked around his mouth, Matt Balen handed out that which Mrs. Jacobs had lost all hope of seeing again.

"Ale-e-e-ex!" Ida shrieked, taking the boy from Matt and wrapping him in a one-armed embrace. He clutched her and cried weakly, "Mommy!" She sat back on folded knees and rocked him, bawling for joy.

Matt clambered out of the hole and turned to help Grace out. The crowd gathered around to slap them on the back and shake their hands, despite their own dusty and haggard condition.

"Bless you! Bless you both!" Ida Jacobs got to her feet with renewed energy, clutching her son one-armed like she would never to let him go.

"That's a nasty looking broken wrist," Grace told her. "You'd better go to the fire station and get it looked at."

Ida raised her maimed arm and stared at it as if seeing it for the first time.

"Come on, Ida," a neighbor lady put an arm around her shoulders. "We'll help you get there."

"Alex will be all right," Matt called as she walked away surrounded by the crowd. "He's a tough little kid. Aren't you Alex?"

"Umm-hmm." The boy made a small wave at them over his mother's shoulder. Then, with an exhausted sigh, he nestled his dusty cheek against her neck.

In moments, Matt and Grace were left alone.

"That was interesting." Matt let a wry grin crack more of the dust around his mouth.

"To say the least." Grace brushed dust and muck from her clothes.

"We'd better get moving." He slapped dust from his own pants. "The sun's gonna go down soon." He started to walk, but Grace stayed still, looking at him peculiarly.

"What?" he asked. "I guess I look pretty messed up." He stroked dust out of his long hair with his fingers.

"No, you don't look messed up." She gazed at him with a proud smile. "You look gorgeous."

He grinned. "So do you."

They embraced and held each other tightly, sharing a dust-flavored kiss. Then they started on their way, arm in arm.

As the canoers approached Pier 62, they were amazed to see that it had been generally spared by a low-water portion of the seiche.

Even so, it had been washed over multiple times and was strewn with flotsam. The big canvas pow-wow tents were missing, as was much of the expected paraphernalia of hawkers' booths, display kiosks, and steel-barrel barbecues. A few people moved here and there on the pier, but the expected crowd was missing. There was a small knot of people at the railing on the end of the pier, among them an old man pounding a buckskin hand drum. This was Henry George, accompanied by Franky Squalco and a few other Duwamish Tribe members. They sang a greeting chant as the canoes assembled into a floating line abreast.

As in the original greeting plan, George paused the drumming and called out in Lushootseed, "Wiaats!" He mustered a smile despite the circumstances. "Glad to see you pulled through. Did everyone make it okay?"

"All present and accounted for," Kenny Helm shouted back.

"I'm here to greet you like we planned," George replied. "Even after all that's happened."

Helm took things in stride. He stood at the stern of the *Tatoosh* and began his canoe-captain oratorio. "We have come far!" he hollered at George. "Really far, this time. We have suffered many dangers. Real bad dangers this time. And we really need food and shelter. We hope you will welcome us ashore."

"We are happy to welcome you to our shores," George proclaimed. "In fact, we're pretty damn happy to be here ourselves! Sorry we don't have much hospitality to share. Our tents and our barbecue grills got wrecked. All the food we brought got washed away. So we can't offer you much this time. Just our sympathy for what you've been through, and our praise for how well you came through it."

"That will be plenty!" Helm replied.

George responded by pounding a staccato on his drum and raising a cry that others joined, "Woo-hoo-oo-oo!"

"But where are all the people?" Helm called up with concern in his voice. "We expected a couple hundred here to greet us. Friends. Families."

"Oh, you shouldn't worry too much about *them.*"

"Why not? My sister and her kids are supposed to be here."

"Soon as the ground quit shaking, I yelled to everyone, 'Get to higher ground 'cause A'yahos will send a wave!' Everyone started running. We ran across the street to the Pike Place Hill-Climb." He pointed a thumb over his shoulder and laughed. "You never seen so many people run that fast. And a buncha people came out of the Seattle Aquarium and ran with us too. I guess somebody told 'em to head for high ground."

"Are you sure everybody got away?"

George chuckled. "I'm pretty old and pretty slow, so most everybody ran faster than me. And here I am to tell the tale."

"So where is everybody?"

"Oh, most of 'em are still up in the Pike Place Market at the top of the steps. Things got pretty shook up, up there too, but most everything is still standing. So, I think they're afraid to come back down here not knowing what to expect. I only came 'cause I knew you'd be here and somebody ought to greet you."

"What do you suppose we should do now?"

"Way I see it, you probably oughta paddle back to Suquamish and hope that town's in better shape than this here one. A cop told us the roads around here are all closed, so I'd say your best way home is the way you came. Paddle back to Suquamish or your home waters, whichever's easiest. My cell phone ain't good for much right now, but at least it tells me you've got eight hours before it gets dark. So you can get to Suquamish, or maybe some of you can get up to Tulalip, or some down to Puyallup. We don't even have Sani-cans to offer you here. They're out floating in the Salish Sea somewhere. So, if you gotta go—" he chuckled, "you better just hang it over the side of the canoe like they did in the old days."

"Before you leave," Franky Squalco, who stood beside George, piped up, "we want to give you something."

"What's that?"

"It's a gift from the Salmon People. There must be a big run going by, 'cause we've got a good three dozen salmon washed up on the pier. Big ones. Fresh ones. Some of 'em's still flopping a bit. So let us give you one for each canoe. A good-sized one ought to feed a whole canoe's worth of people."

"If you can't find a decent way to cook 'em," George added, "you'll just have to eat sushi!"

"There's a floating dock at the side of the pier," Franky said. "Pull up there and some of us will bring the fish to you."

"I guess we've got some hospitality for you after all," said George, "thanks to the Salmon People sending a feast."

The canoes moved to the south side of the pier where a long floating dock, connected by a long gangway, paralleled it. People from the pier began coming down the ramp carrying huge king salmon in their arms and placing them aboard one canoe after another. Henry George, Franky Squalco, and their group came to watch over the proceedings from above.

"One more thing," Ginny Musselshell called up to George. "We've got someone we need to put ashore." She pulled back her dancing shawl and the space blanket to reveal the girl Johnny had fished from the water. She was recovering quickly. Her cheeks had gone from blue to pink. Her eyes, dull and half-shut before, were open and focused. "Her name's Jenny Harbau—"

Ginny was interrupted by a scream from the group above as if someone were seeing a ghost.

"Jenny!" a young woman shrieked, literally jumping for joy. "Jenny Harbaugh! I've been looking everywhere for you. I thought you were—"

"I'm alive," Jenny smiled. "Thanks to these folks."

"Oh my God, Jenny!" the woman danced giddily. "I'm so happy!"

Jenny was still a little disoriented. She glanced at the buildings across the street. "How's our apartment?"

"It's fine! Nothing important got broken. Water came up to the second story, but we're on the third."

"Help her get out," Ginny Musselshell told Johnny.

He rose and stepped onto the floating dock, then helped Jenny debark the canoe safely. Once her feet were solidly on the dock, she turned to him and said, shyly, "Thanks."

Johnny gazed at her, dumbstruck by how beautiful her face

looked now that she had some color back. She stepped near and, taking his face in both hands, laid a long, soulful kiss on his lips.

"Woooooo!" the crowd reacted in unison.

Johnny stood, gobsmacked and grinning, as Jenny's friend escorted her away, keeping an arm around her waist to steady her still-wobbly legs. On her way up the ramp, Jenny turned and called back to Johnny, "I work at Starbucks Number One in Pike Place Market. Look me up sometime!"

"I will," Johnny promised.

One by one, the canoes back-paddled from the dock to begin their journeys home.

Kenny Helm shouted up to the pier, "What about you, Henry George? Want a lift somewhere?"

George waved him off. "Oh, no thanks. Franky's got his pickup in the Pike Place Garage. All's we gotta do is figure out a way to drive home. The cops say head north, but we live south."

"Don't worry," Franky said. "I'll figure it out."

After the passage of the second wave, the *Issaquah* had been adrift for some time. Without maneuvering power, they were at the mercy of the currents, which remained chaotic, but settled with time. Repeatedly, black smoke belched from her stacks as the crew kept at the task of reigniting her engines. At last, the massive cylinders rumbled to life. After a few minutes, the sound of a microphone being cleared was followed by the captain's voice.

"As you may have noticed, folks, we've got our engines running again. We should be able to get underway in a minute or two. We can't disembark you here, because Colman Dock is damaged and there's no power. On the other hand, we've been in touch with Winslow Terminal on the ship-to-shore radio. They say they've got power over on Bainbridge Island, and a spare slip we can tie up to. I can also tell you we've checked the ship from stem to stern, and she's sound. We'll go across slowly just to be safe. So, prepare yourselves for a long ride. There's cell phone coverage over there, so you'll be able to contact family members to come and pick you up."

"I'll bet your stepmom's worried sick about us," Dave said. "I'll give her a call as soon as we're in range."

Zack was distractedly staring to the south. "Look at Harbor Island. It's like, totally disintegrated."

Where the island had been, there now was a new southward extension of Elliott Bay. The surface of the island had slid off and sunk below the Sound. In its place was an inlet extending nearly to the West Seattle Bridge, whose columns stood on a remnant of the southernmost tip of the island. In what had been twin channels bounding the island on the east and west, two huge cargo ships lay half-sunken on their sides. Other ships had ringed the island, but they were simply gone, capsized and dragged to the bottom of Elliott Bay with the landslide.

"Man!" Zack exclaimed. "What an insane ferryboat ride this turned out to be!"

The *Issaquah* blew her horn three times and began to move. The captain picked his way cautiously, steering a zigzag course among half-sunken cargo containers, capsized yachts, and other wreckage.

Bob Jensen stared at the trickle coming from the opened hydrant, feeling disheartened and frustrated. He looked up at the Columbia Center Tower and worry lines creased his forehead. The smoke from the forty-fifth floor was all but cleared. Smoke from the thirteenth floor, on the other hand, was rolling out in dense black billows. The thought crossed his mind to abandon his useless command position at the rear hatch of BC2 and go inside to assist the crew manually combating the fire. But he knew better than to do that. He held his position. Suddenly, and unexpectedly, the radio in the SUV came alive with a strong, clear voice.

"This is Fireship *Leschi.* Fire Unit Niner, what is your status?"

Jensen pressed the talk button on his shoulder radio. "This is Engine Nine. We are responding to a major fire at Columbia

Center Tower. Over."

"Roger Unit Niner. We've got visual on that. Do you have water?"

"Negative *Leschi.* Hydrants are not flowing."

"Copy, Niner. We may be able to assist you."

Jensen's heart leapt with hope. "Copy, *Leschi!* But how—?"

"We are tied up at Station Five, directly below you on the waterfront. We are preparing to pump salt water into the downtown area in a hose line. We got word you might need some."

"Affirmative. In a hurry, please!"

"Roger that."

Within minutes, Jensen rushed downhill in his SUV to rendezvous with *Leschi's* shore crew, who attached a length of firehose to BC2's trailer hitch. He then made a long drive back uphill on steep slopes with copious glass on the pavement. After much skidding, sliding and tire-squealing, Jensen finally stopped on the debris-strewn intersection of Fourth Avenue and Cherry Street. Firemen below had been coupling hoses together in a line that now stretched nearly a quarter of a mile, originating at the *Leschi's* huge water manifolds. Within a few minutes, *Leschi* sent word that she was ready to start pumping.

Jensen saw to it that members of his crew quickly connected the hose to Engine 9's own pump manifold, with a hose-link to the building's standpipes. "*Leschi,*" he called into his microphone, "we are linked up and ready for water."

"Stand by, Number Nine," Captain Klimchak replied. "We are about to start pumping."

Moments later, Jensen could see evidence of the water coming uphill in how the slack hose stretched tight and thin sprays jetted out from the brass couplings. A firefighter at the pump control panel on the side of E9 yelled, "We've got pressure! Opening valves to the building standpipe."

"Excellent!" Jensen glanced up at the smoke billowing from the thirteenth floor. "Let's hope there are no broken pipes between here and there!"

Leschi was anchored just off her normal berth at Fire Station 5. The dock was wrecked, but the station itself was intact, though wet and minus a few windows, as was Ivar's Restaurant on the adjacent Pier 54. The area had been another low spot in the seiche.

Captain Klimchak allowed himself a little smile of satisfaction despite the rigors of the situation. All was well with the jury-rigged system sending salt water to Columbia Tower. He stepped in through the hatch doorway that led to the Emergency Command Center, where Rita O'Rourke and two newly arrived firemen now constituted an effective Emergency Response Communications Team.

"I know you've got your hands full," he told Rita, who was dried off and wearing a headset at a desk with radio equipment and a computer screen jammed with information. "But can I get a quick update?"

"Sure. Communications are still pretty bad. The 800-megahertz channels keep going in and out of service. Water lines are out almost everywhere in Seattle. Some engines are pumping from Volunteer Park reservoir and a few other sources around town. An engine at South Lake Union is pumping lake water to supply the two fire-response teams. Another has just arrived and should be able to double the flow pretty soon. There's an apartment building and three residences burning there, but hopefully they'll contain them. Two more units are getting into position to pump from sites along the Duwamish River. Some industrial sites are burning there. More units are *en route* from communities that were not hit so hard by the quake. Everett, Tacoma, Bellingham, and Olympia have teams on their way as we speak."

"Can they get through to Seattle?"

"From the north and east, yes, thanks to all those years of earthquake-hardening projects on the freeways and overpasses."

"Thank heavens for a little foresight. What about south?"

"Not good. A fallen freeway overpass blocking all lanes on I-5."

"What about Columbia Tower?"

"Let's check. Come in Unit Niner? Can you give us an update?"

Jensen's voice came back immediately. "Roger, *Leschi.* We have water in the standpipes and hoses on the fire now. Water is coming through with strong pressure all the way up to where it's needed."

"Any casualties in need of help?"

"Not too many. There are some fatalities that we'll have to leave in place for now. Otherwise, just a few small injuries from broken glass and falling objects."

"Send them down to us, if they are ambulatory. We've got a full emergency medical unit aboard, and more space inside the station. Is Columbia Tower evacuated?"

"Affirmative. Staircase evacuations worked fine. A few hundred people took the long walk down. Most of them are dispersed now, though I couldn't say where."

"Any other issues?"

"None that we know of. We've got a survey team working its way up through the building. We'll let you know if anything else turns up."

Klimchak leaned near the desk microphone. "What's the status of Devine's Tower? We can't see it from here."

"From what I can tell, looking downhill," Jensen replied, "total annihilation."

"Say again?"

"It's disappeared into a hole in the ground. Complete collapse. We're leaving it alone for now. I don't think there's anyone we can help there, nor is it a threat to nearby structures. It's just gone."

Chapter 29

Within several hours following the catastrophe, there began a mass movement of people leaving the central downtown area. Although the population in business towers was relatively low on the weekend, the opposite was true for apartment towers, shopping centers, movie theaters and other public attractions. These now disgorged tens of thousands of shocked, bewildered—and in some cases injured—people onto the ravaged streets.

People emerged from stricken apartment buildings, having descended staircases often many stories tall. They added themselves to a growing flow of humanity on the damaged and rubble-strewn streets. Some seemed at a loss as to where to go. Others moved determinedly in one direction or another, intent on reaching homes, loved ones, or friends in one suburb or another by nightfall, on foot if necessary.

Those with cars in parking garages, and who could get them out, began making their way tortuously through streets half-blocked by debris. Inevitably, many vehicles became disabled when tires were punctured by debris and glass, and their occupants were forced to join the exodus moving on foot. Power was out throughout the city with no indication it would be restored soon. Stoplights were dark, though there was little traffic for them to regulate given the near impossibility of negotiating the shattered and cluttered pavements. The notion that trains or buses would carry people away was beyond thinking. There were none.

Despite the substantial movement of people in the streets, there was also a significant trend of people staying put. From many an apartment-building balcony, dazed residents surveyed the chaotic world around them without any desire to descend and join the migration. Although need for food or medical attention might force many to come down eventually, exactly when was uncertain.

Along the waterfront and around the stadiums, there was minimal foot traffic, and no vehicle traffic at all. The low areas were still draining water brought in by the tsunamis. That drainage moved slowly over and through a layer of muck, several feet deep, that was shot through with splintered wood, tangled electrical wires, twisted metal, glass shards, and God knew what else. The few intrepid souls who waded in soon found themselves mired in nearly impassable dark glop to their knees in which they tripped, stumbled, and sometimes fell. Under the circumstances, a sizable portion of the crowd in T-Mobile Park chose to remain in the relative safety of their seats.

In the announcer booth, Ronald Rutledge was relieved of his duty as voice of the stadium when Brett Stertzel reappeared, telling a tale of a near-miss with death. He had considered joining the crowds fleeing outside, only to be turned back by Rutledge's admonitions. After a handshake and a heartfelt thank-you, he took the headset and began to comfort and inform the crowd.

As Rutledge pondered how he would find his own way home, the set director came and shook his hand. "Thanks, Professor. I'm sure you saved a lot of lives."

"I did what I could, but I've seen too much death for any self-congratulations. How long has it been, anyway?"

"Since the quake? It hit at first pitch. That was one-ten. It's almost five now, so nearly four hours."

"I'm exhausted," Rutledge said. "I think I'll take the long walk home."

Aron Carter, who had been listening nearby, said, "I'll go out with you."

"Good luck to you both, gentlemen."

They made their way down to the main concourse and went to the right-field gate. A small crowd had gathered there, surrounding a man who was gamely signing his autograph on programs, baseball hats, and even a few bare arms.

As they passed the group, Aron smiled and called, "Some things never change, eh Eddy?"

"Wait! I'll join you!" Shredder used the moment to gracefully disengage from the fans and jogged to catch them as they went out the exit ramp. "Where are you guys going?"

"Home."

"On foot? Mind if I join you?"

They used the elevated roadway of Atlantic Avenue to reach the freeway interchange of I-5 and I-90. The highways were intact and all but free of traffic, offering thoroughfares north, south, or eastbound, over which a slow stream of fans and other people had begun to trek. It so happened that each of the three men would take a separate path, Carter to an estate in the Mount Baker District to the south, Shredder to a place on Capitol Hill to the east, while Rutledge faced the longest walk, north to the U District and beyond to his home in Laurelhurst. As they were saying their farewells, the thumping sound of rotor blades drew their attention to a Coast Guard helicopter descending into the stadium past the star-spangled banner that Shredder had saluted so eloquently a few hours before.

That helicopter, Dolphin 224, came to a hovering attitude over the place where the pitcher's mound lay submerged under a layer of muck. The crowd hushed as if awaiting a pitch to a full count with bases loaded at the bottom of the ninth and the score tied.

The helicopter couldn't land on the swamped field, so it held station just above the ground while four-person medical teams brought injured fans onto the field in stretchers. Wading and stumbling in knee-deep debris-laden muck, they managed to wrangle their patients aboard the aircraft through its open side door. Simultaneously, a human chain of stadium security and first-aid personnel passed boxes of medical supplies and other needed items back to the stands.

Seated in those stands, Craig Palmer and his boys watched the spectacle. Craig had tried to call home on his cell phone but got a NO SERVICE warning. To keep its power from draining, he switched it off.

"Wow!" Willy sang out. "A real helicopter right inside the stadium!"

"I thought they were just going to fly over!" Liam added.

Craig put his arms around the boys, who sat one on either side of him. He smiled at their youthful enthusiasm and ability to shake off the horror. "Looks like their plans got changed, too," he said.

Aboard Dolphin 224, Jane Hewitt's crew worked swiftly, taking on seven stretchers bearing critically injured patients while coordinating the transfer of a heavy load of medical supplies and blankets to the chain gang on the ground. As soon as the supplies were offloaded, the crew arranged the stretchers one above another in racks on the flight deck.

While they worked, Brett Stertzel's voice came over the PA system. "They are picking up some of our most seriously injured fans for a short flight to Harborview hospital. Join me in wishing them well. And let's also give a hand to the brave rescue team in that helicopter."

A roar went up from the crowd that could be heard through the crew's helmet headphones. It was easily as thunderous as if that ninth-inning pitch had been a game-winning strike.

Jane glanced around at the cheering crowd and felt a blush of humility warm her face under her helmet and visor. She glanced at Ramon, who gave her a thumbs-up and a grin.

"Just doin' our job," he quipped in massive understatement. "Just doin' our job."

Meanwhile, Jason and Tyrell got all seven patients strapped into their on-board stretchers. As they shut the side door and ground personnel scrambled a safe distance away, Jane said, "All right. Let's get these folks to Harborview, then get back here for another load." She pushed the thrust lever forward and Dolphin 224 rose, bringing another roar from the crowd that she could easily hear over the whine of the turbine engine.

"Look at that sunset!" Ryan Hewitt held up his partially finished glass of beer in a salute to the Olympic Mountains. The serene and distant peaks had turned deep purple as the sun dropped behind them. They were silhouetted by a pastel-pink sky blending to gold and then turquoise above. Rippled lines of clouds blazed in bright coral and fiery orange. "How can such beauty come at the end of such a horrible day?"

"It's God's way of saying things will get better," Joe replied.

"Hah!" Ryan laughed involuntarily. "Things couldn't be much worse right now."

"I have a better view of sunsets now."

"That's something, I suppose."

"Why don't you stay here tonight and enjoy the view with me?"

"Thank you so much, but no. You've been a godsend, but we should go."

"How *can* you go? Your car is trapped until the road gets fixed. And then you still don't know if you can get home. All the roads might be this bad." He nodded at the buckled surface of Beach Drive.

"You've got a point."

"Please stay. My daughter's bedroom is empty now she's married and living in Portland. There's a big bed and a couch in there. It's room enough for three."

"That's awfully nice of you."

"Can't Mommy give us a ride?" Caylie wheedled. "I wanna go home."

"That would be great," Ryan said. "But I think Mommy's going to be very busy for a few days. She wouldn't be able to stay home even if she took us there."

He turned to Joe. "It's a deal then. I don't know what we'd do without your hospitality."

"No problem. Any time there's an earthquake, you're all welcome to stop by."

They all laughed. Then Caylie pouted, "That's really not very funny."

"I guess you're right," Joe agreed. "How about, stop by any time you want?"

"That's better," Emily said. "And we will, for sure. You make the best hot chocolate!"

A thumping sound over the water grew to a roar that made everyone look up. A flight of six Blackhawk helicopters passed over them northbound in a tight formation.

"More help for Seattle," Joe remarked.

"Probably from McChord Air Base," Ryan said.

"Anyone getting hungry for dinner?" Joe winked at the girls.

"I am!" they replied in unison.

"I have frozen hamburger patties in the freezer and French fries too! They'll go bad if we don't eat them now. After dinner, I've got vanilla ice cream with Chukar Cherry topping."

"Yum!" Caylie smiled.

"Look at the sunset on the mountain!" Ginny Musselshell gushed, pointing at Mount Rainier, which was bathed in pink alpenglow against the purple wedge of sundown. She and Arnie and Johnny Steele sat on cedar-round chairs outside the House of Awakened Culture in Suquamish, eating platefuls of the salmon they were given in Seattle, now freshly cooked on the outdoor grill.

"After what we've been through," Arnie remarked between bites, "that old mountain looks prettier than it ever did before."

"It's a sign that everything's gonna be all right," Ginny smiled.

"Not everything." Johnny nodded at the Seattle skyline. "Devine's tower is gone."

Johnny's older sister Tleena joined them. "I think she meant, everything that's *important* will be all right."

Tleena, who was to drive them home to Neah Bay, had stayed with friends in nearby Indianola and had experienced the earthquake there. She had waited through the afternoon, terrified that something awful had happened to Johnny. Tears of joy had run freely when a dozen canoes rounded the point and headed for shore. The wave had come ashore here too, but it had shrunk with distance from Seattle. Scarcely overtopping the thirty-foot bank, it had done little more than strew the lawn with seaweed and driftwood. The First People of Suquamish had chosen this site well, perhaps through knowledge of past tidal waves.

Chapter 30

The Blackhawk helicopters were indeed inbound from Joint Base Lewis-McChord, dispatched by the Emergency Response Center at Camp Murray. By early the next morning, they formed part of a much larger relief operation in full swing. With the arrival at Boeing Field of the first National Guard truck convoys filled with food, fuel, and bedding, those helicopters, as well as Jane Hewitt's, were pressed into the delivery service, shuttling needed supplies to areas cut off by collapsed roads and evacuating injured people to hospitals. Fuel was the most limiting resource due to pipeline breaks, some of which were still burning and stopping the flow of natural gas and gasoline. But the supply of aviation fuel at Boeing Field was never-ending, due to constant comings and goings of tanker trucks from supply sources farther south.

Sometime before dawn, a long stream of camouflage-green National Guard trucks began to arrive at the airstrip, delivering supplies sent from areas less hard-hit. Highway travel was swift for the convoys until they got to within a few miles of the epicenter in West Seattle. More severe damage there meant detours and even one crossing of the Duwamish River on a hastily assembled pontoon bridge. But the route had been opened with remarkable speed in the dark of night.

Although rescuing trapped or injured people was necessarily of the highest priority, the process of clearing critical routes accelerated as the National Guard delivered bulldozers, backhoes, and other heavy equipment. Their all-night efforts began to allow a counter-flow of vehicles filled with people escaping the privations of downtown and heading for surrounding communities where basic services were more intact.

Within the core of Seattle and West Seattle, damage was extensive. Any notion of people moving in or out by land-based vehicles was still more a dream than reality. Debris-laden streets with cracked and gaping pavement, and slumped hillsides assured that it would be many days before most parked or garaged cars could make their way out. Streets were generally deserted or used only occasionally by groups of people trudging for miles to reach services and safety located in less damaged suburbs.

One convoy of military trucks had reached Harborview in the middle of the night. The trucks brought medical supplies, food, and additional personnel to bolster the growing medical relief facilities within and outside the buildings of the hospital complex. A dozen barracks-sized, camouflage-colored tents were pitched near the hospital garage and helipad during the night, even as helicopters bearing severely injured people came and went. Inside the tents were several hundred cots for use by staff and people who accompanied the injured, as well as some of the injured whose wounds had been tended to.

Earl had the good fortune to be billeted in a small multi-occupant room, owing to the gravity of his wound and his early arrival at the hospital. Carrie had passed the night in a chair beside him. Matt and Grace were shooed away by a nurse and went to claim adjacent cots in one of the tents a little past midnight. Exhausted, they had quickly passed into deep sleep.

In the night, Grace had wakened briefly, disturbed by the noise of a helicopter coming and going. She had turned to Matt, whose regular breathing indicated the helicopter's roar hadn't been sufficient to wake him. In the dim glow from the heliport lights, she had propped herself on an elbow and gazed at his peaceful, slumbering face, noting the lines of his lips, the fine details of his mustache and beard, and a little scar within one eyebrow.

Suddenly, his eyes opened and looked directly into hers, sending a jolt of surprise through her.

"What?" he asked groggily.

"Oh, nothing." She lay back on her pillow and stared up at the tent roof, watching it ruffle in a calm breeze. After a moment, she asked, "Do you think two people could fall in love under these circumstances?"

"I don't know," Matt mumbled. "Why do you ask?"

"Never mind."

Moments later, they had both fallen asleep again.

They arose this morning much refreshed and went through a Red Cross food-service line outside their tent. They loaded paper plates with pancakes, scrambled eggs, and sausage, and got small paper cups of orange juice. Sitting at an army camp table nearby, they ate heartily with white plastic utensils. Matt glanced at Grace with an amused smile.

"What?" She crooked an eyebrow.

"That was some first date yesterday, wasn't it?"

"You call almost getting killed a dozen times a first date?"

"We got to know each other pretty well. That's what people are supposed to do on a first date, isn't it?"

Grace saw the humor in it. "I've got to admit, you sure know how to show a girl a good time."

Matt watched her face carefully. "I hope it won't be our last date."

She smiled at him. "I'm sure it won't be."

After cleaning up in a National Guard field-tent shower, they went inside Harborview and entered Earl's room to find him lying propped up with his stitched-up leg elevated. Carrie sat in her chair by his side. Both were eating breakfast from porcelain plates with real silverware. After Grace inquired about Earl's health and Carrie's comfort—or lack thereof—she said in the course of conversation, "We'll see you guys again real soon."

"What do you mean by that?" Carrie glanced at her sharply. "Where are you going?"

"To my shop in SoDo," Matt replied. "It's a two-mile hike from here. If it hasn't collapsed or burnt down, I can get one of my power systems and make some electricity for folks who need it."

"Good luck," Earl said between bites. "I hope it works the way you want it to."

"Oh, it will," Matt nodded confidently. "A Red Cross lady told me there's an evacuation center being set up at Starbucks' headquarters. That's just a few blocks from my shop. Grace and I will take a unit over and see if they can use it."

"One thing before you go," Earl said. "I didn't get a chance to thank you two. For… you know… saving my life."

Grace smiled. "You'd have done the same for us."

"I suppose. Or maybe died trying. Anyway, you both have my undying gratitude."

"We'll keep in touch by cell phone," Grace said. "Once the service comes back on."

"If you can keep your phones charged," Carrie said.

Matt grinned. "I think my power system can handle a couple of cell phones."

At T-Mobile Park, Craig Palmer and his boys had spent the night in their car, which was trapped in the garage along with hundreds of other vehicles. Given the alternative of a long hike to an uncertain destination, and continued provision of food and drink by stadium concessionaires, Palmer chose to stay. In the evening, they ate Ivar's fish and chips while watching helicopters bring supplies and take away injured people. As the evening chill descended, they went to the SUV to make the best of things. Craig arranged a comfortable nest in the back using helicopter-delivered emergency blankets and some coats. The boys stretched out and drifted off to sleep.

Craig had sat up awhile in the front seat. The SUV was nosed in on the west side of the garage, giving him a grandstand view of an awesome spectacle at the Seattle Public Utilities Massachusetts Substation, two blocks west on Utah Avenue. The substation, which normally provided half the power to Seattle's downtown area, had misguidedly been built well within the tsunami hazard zone, and had been inundated by both waves. The combination of salt water and superlatively huge electrical equipment had resulted in vast arcs and fountains of sparks jetting into the sky. This short circuit on a colossal scale assured complete blackness in the area, punctuated by repeated flashing arcs and zapping, crackling noises that persisted for hours. Finally, blackness and silence had fallen throughout downtown and SoDo, with the exception of the stadium, which glowed with its own emergency lighting.

Sometime past two a.m., Palmer's cell phone had beeped when service was restored briefly. He called his wife, at home in Burien and frantic to know their fate and whereabouts. He reassured her she would see them all safe and sound as quickly as he and the boys could cover the twelve-mile journey home. Then he had placed a similar call to Liam's parents. After that, the service had failed again, and he grabbed a few hours of sleep in his seat.

Silence was interrupted around four a.m. by immense rumbling and scraping sounds. Huge Army vehicles—bulldozers and tracked tow-trucks capable of moving tanks—rolled into the area, illuminating it with glaring headlights. They alternately towed or bulldozed vehicles and tangled wreckage to the sides of First Avenue. This in turn opened a thoroughfare from south to north toward downtown, a group of tall black silhouettes against a starry sky. Craig slept fitfully in the driver's seat, keeping one eye on happenings below, until dawn suffused the hills to the east.

He shook Willy lightly by a shoulder.

"Hmmmph?" the boy mumbled.

"I'm going to get some coffee in the stadium, and maybe bring back some breakfast if there are still places to get food. You boys stay put till I get back."

"Um-hmm," Willy replied drowsily, then turned his head and fell back to sleep.

Craig got out, locked the door, and made his way to the pedestrian overpass above Edgar Martinez Drive. Glancing down as he crossed, he noted small groups of people leaving the stadium. It was now nearly sixteen hours after the quake. Larger crowds of people were moving southbound in the cleared center of First Avenue. The flow of people—no doubt evacuees from high-rises and apartment buildings—seemed to be swelling as he watched, although he had no inkling where they might hope to go.

Fuel brought to Boeing Field by convoys had been adequate to keep rescue helicopters flying constantly, including Jane Hewitt's Dolphin 224. She and her crew were nearing exhaustion after non-stop missions all night, including more trips to Harborview with injured baseball fans, and deliveries of supplies to T-Mobile Park.

After a long night's work, they had started again in the predawn light without pause. Their first morning task was delivering medical supplies to Starbucks Headquarters in the SoDo District. The parking lot there had been transformed into a displaced-persons marshaling area with a tent field hospital for minor trauma cases—of which there were many. In addition to the injured in need of treatment, an awe-inspiring mass of people had gathered in and around the parking lot. Nearly 10,000 downtown residents and baseball fans had been directed by cops on bullhorns and stadium speakers to walk south to where military personnel could provide transport out of the area. Arrangements were made to get them to home neighborhoods in the south, or to transfer areas where they could board buses for more distant destinations.

Starbucks was the logical choice for handling this exodus because its parking lot, a city-block wide, had been spared tsunami inundation by a matter of a few blocks. National Guard members set up sawhorse barricades to funnel the flow of pedestrians into a line four abreast, that folded back on itself like a giant airport security maze. This line eventually passed by the front entrance of Starbucks Center to reach the north curb of Lander Street. There, soldiers directed people to board vehicles designated for different evacuation destinations. These vehicles were a hodgepodge of troop transports, military supply trucks, Humvees towing trailers, and civilian vehicles ranging from parcel-delivery vans to private automobiles.

Unfortunately, the much more capacious city buses could not be used. Their long, low chassis were incapable of crossing buckled roadways or negotiating tightly twisted lanes past fallen trees and shattered building façades.

Jane Hewitt and her crew sat in their idling helicopter in a marked-off landing area in the center of the parking lot while their manifest of supplies was unloaded. The ground operations crew brought them hot coffee drinks freshly made inside the Starbucks Headquarters Building. Starbucks employees had volunteered to help in the way they knew best—providing caffeine to fuel the first-responders' tired brains and bodies. As Hewitt and crew sipped their more-than-welcome cups of java, a uniformed police officer came to Dolphin 224's side window.

"Hello! Are you Captain Hewitt?"

"Yes sir. How can I help you?"

He smiled. "You mean, how can *I* help *you*. I got a radio call from Officer Smith over in West Seattle. Said he had a message from your husband and kids."

Hewitt caught her breath, nearly spilling hot coffee in her lap. Her heart pounded. Before she could ask what the message might be, the officer went on.

"They're fine. They stayed the night with a nice old man named Joe. They'll try to get their car out of there after breakfast and find a way home. They send their love."

Hewitt blinked back tears. "Thanks."

The cop pulled a folded piece of paper from a pocket and glanced at it. "Another thing. Tell your crew members I have word that their wives checked in, too."

"And they're okay?" Valenzuela asked anxiously.

"Roger that." The officer glanced at the names on his list. "Mrs. Valenzuela, Collins, and Chow are all okay. Kids too."

"We've been so worried about them," Valenzuela sighed.

"But you kept doing your jobs," the officer noted. "That's commendable."

"Didn't stop us from being scared all night and all morning," Hewitt said. "Thanks for finding out."

"It's the least we can do. Keep up the good work."

"Roger that!"

There was no shortage of work waiting. As the last of the supplies were unloaded, medics appeared from the biggest of the tents with two stretchers. One of the medics called to Hewitt. "We've got a couple of cases here we can't treat adequately. Can you take them to Harborview?"

"We sure can. Load 'em aboard."

Matt and Grace followed a tortuous path from Harborview to reach his workshop on Third Avenue South in SoDo. Along the way, they crossed under the I-5 freeway at James Street. The elevated roadway had shed many tons of concrete fragments onto the streets below. Nevertheless, its circular pillars, reinforced against earth tremors with steel sheathing, had weathered the shaking well. The twin spans of north and southbound lanes were carrying traffic, albeit only slow-moving military supply vehicles intermingled with a few police and aid cars with lights flashing. The highway was devoid of private vehicles and commercial trucks. No doubt the authorities weren't allowing such traffic into the disaster zone.

Matt and Grace skirted the main downtown streets, which they could see from a distance were piled deep in glass and debris shed from tall buildings. Instead, they paralleled the freeway's southbound lanes on an access road to reach SoDo, where buildings were much shorter and consequently the debris less extensive.

Here and there, they passed people picking through rubble on unknown quests, or teams of police and medical responders dealing with injured people. Eventually they arrived at a two-story commercial building on Third Avenue just off Holgate. The place had been shaken by the quake and wetted to the two-foot level by the tsunamis, but it was basically intact. Although Solaris Corporation had technically been evicted and Matt's equipment confiscated against rent in arrears, the landlord had been lax. Matt's key still opened the lock. His workshop on the upper level was as he had left it. His prototypes were still neatly boxed on shelves.

Matt pulled a cardboard tube, three feet long by six inches wide, off a shelf. He took it to a long workbench in the center of the facility. Twisting off the top cover, he unloaded a cylinder that looked like a large roll of black plastic wrap.

"DayLite," he launched into a familiar presentation, "is a system so portable it can go anywhere a truck or helicopter can go, or a four-man team can hike. It's intended to serve the smallest needs, like providing decentralized power for third-world villages. It's also intended for temporary use during emergencies like hurricanes, earthquakes, and tsunamis."

"How prophetic!" Grace marveled.

"This is the key to the DayLite system." He placed the roll at one end of the bench and gestured with an open hand. "Each roll is a yard wide and eight yards long." He walked beside the bench, unrolling the sheet of dark film. "When you get to your destination, you unroll them on the ground or hang them on lines or lay them on top of tents. Then you connect them to the power unit. The sheets are Mylar, one of the toughest, thinnest plastics known. That's what's in those gold emergency 'space blankets.' Only, instead of a reflective surface, Solaris developed a coating of Perovskite solar-absorbing mineral in a micron-thin layer."

When he had unrolled the full eight yards on the bench top, the core of the roll was revealed to be a yard-long plastic rod integrally attached to the Mylar along one edge. "There are dozens of printed circuits on the underside of the Mylar that carry solar energy to the core. Inside the rod is a stack of capacitors that transfer electricity to the power unit via a cable." He pointed to a shelf where two blue boxes about the size of medium picnic coolers sat. "The one on the left is the storage battery; the one on the right is a power transformer that puts out AC current."

"Whew!" Grace breathed when he finished his exposition. "I'm not sure I understood your techno-babble, but I get the idea. It's light, it's flexible, you can carry it just about anywhere—and it's an act of sheer genius!"

He smiled modestly. "Thanks for the vote of confidence, but I won't be happy until I see it in a real-life situation."

"So, how do we make that happen?"

"The original idea," Matt said, lifting a corner of the battery unit and let it thump down on the shelf, "was to make this a two-part system so two men could carry it up a mountain in backpacks. Even so, the half-units still weigh about fifty pounds each."

Grace lifted a corner and let it drop as Matt had done. She gave him a worried look. "That feels like more than I can carry."

"Yeah," Matt acknowledged. "Gary and I imagined two strong soldiers hefting these—or one good-sized pack mule."

"So, what are *we* going to do?"

"No worries. There's a roller cart downstairs—if it didn't get washed away."

Within twenty minutes they wrangled four solar-array tubes and two power units down the stairs and loaded them onto the cart. Then they set off, maneuvering along cracked sidewalks in the direction of Starbucks Headquarters.

Chapter 31

Tim Carrington and Valerie Styles had passed the night in her apartment without running water or power, but at least in a familiar place of relative safety and calm.

The day before, they had made their way off the West Seattle bridge via the Delridge Way on-ramp. They had trudged two miles to her condominium, passing a mix of damaged as well as relatively intact houses, businesses, and apartment buildings. Valerie's own condo was in decent shape. Being a modern three-story structure built primarily of wood, it had flexed while other buildings fell, and was still livable, though perhaps in need of some repairs.

The food in her refrigerator was still cold, and they had made an evening meal of salad, leftover chicken, and white wine. When bedtime came, they had assumed they would fall asleep immediately in exhaustion. Instead, Valerie began to experience heart palpitations as her mind replayed the day's traumas. She had reached out to Tim for comfort. One thing led to another, until surprisingly powerful passions were ignited.

In the morning, they were sitting on the bedroom's balcony, sipping bottled iced tea, when they heard a patrol car loud-speaker moving slowly through the neighborhood. The cop was repeating a message: "You can obtain food, water, and other supplies at the shopping center at Delridge and Sylvan Way. The National Guard is establishing a distribution center there. Those with less than one-eighth tank of gas can get four gallons at the gas station. Expect long lines. We urge everyone to leave the area and find shelter outside the city limits where damage is less severe. The low-rise bridges at Spokane Street and First Avenue South are available for evacuation, but the West Seattle high-rise is out of service indefinitely."

"Don't we know it," Valerie sighed.

Bob Jensen and Torrey Vega stood at the brink of the block-wide hole where Eldon Devine's once-imposing Emerald Tower now lay collapsed upon itself. At the request of Mariah Rey, they had left the crew buttoning up Engine 9 after its night of successful firefighting to come and look for survivors in the wreckage. There were none. The edifice had smashed down well below ground level, about two stories lower than where they stood at the brink. The last wisps of steam rose from what had been an inferno judging by the char on the sides of the pit. Tsunami water ponded between piles of rubble had put out most fires raging in the wreckage, but a few embers still glowed among heaps of twisted metal and pulverized concrete.

"We're not gonna find any survivors down there," Vega asserted.

Jensen shrugged wearily. "When the boss says come and take a look, you come and take a look. She's getting a lot of heat from Devine's family. His last known location was here. So, I said okay, we'll search for one particular man in a city where thousands need help, if it will make your political situation better. So here we are, looking for one special billionaire whose life isn't worth a penny more than anyone else's as far as I'm concerned." He stared down into a pool of brown, murky water still bubbling steam. "It looks like the tenth level of Dante's Inferno. I can't think of a better place for him."

"My thoughts exactly," a man who came to join them interjected.

Jensen glanced at the newcomer. "You look familiar. Where have we met?"

The man nodded down into the pit. "There. When it was standing."

"Oh, yeah. You're the building contractor."

"Torgelson." The man shook Jensen's hand. "You came by on a fire-safety inspection just last week. You asked me lots of questions about whether the building was up to earthquake codes."

"And you answered me honestly," Jensen recalled. "I'm glad

to see you made it out okay."

"I employed one hundred and eighty-two workers in there. You know how many survived?"

Jensen's expression darkened. "I don't think I want to hear."

"All of them!" Torgelson laughed. "We all went out on strike Friday, thanks to that pig, Devine, refusing to pay his bills. Not one of my people was in there when…" He paused to look over the brink.

Vega glanced from Jensen to Torgelson with a mystified expression. Noting his reaction, Jensen explained. "You'd know what we're saying if you had ever *talked* to the man. I got a gut-full of his high-and-mighty attitude. More than once."

"He's not so high and mighty now," Torgelson crowed.

"Too bad he'll never pay what he owes you," Vega suggested.

"Oh, I'm not so sure. I already had a lawyer working on our claims against him. Now I suppose we'll be first in line when they settle his estate."

Jensen picked up a hunk of concrete and hurled it into the hole. "And good riddance," he muttered as the stone splashed into a muddy pond. Then he turned to Vega with a lighter expression. "You know what I think they should do with this place?"

"I don't know. Maybe build another tower?"

"Nah! Just gather up the rubble from the streets around here and dump it all in the hole. Then put in some topsoil and plant trees. Then forget there ever was a man named Eldon Devine or such a thing as his Emerald Tower. Make this into a park where ordinary citizens can enjoy some fresh air in the middle of downtown. And never mention that power-mad billionaire again."

"Amen." Torgelson smiled.

Three people had been approaching for some time, making their way around the pit from the City Hall Building on the far side. Two appeared to be a couple dressed in nice, but rumpled dinner attire. A second woman was dressed in a fashionable blue coat but with gray coveralls underneath, as if she had borrowed clothing from the building's janitorial staff lockers—which indeed was the case. As she neared, Jensen recognized her.

"Hi, Mariah. Came to see for yourself, did you?"

"Yeah. I've been up all night at the Emergency Operations Center. Mayor Jimmy Dunkin and I have a skeleton crew at City Hall coordinating the city's relief efforts—including these two." She gestured at her companions.

"Dan Federly, right?" Jensen pointed at the man in recognition.

"And my wife, Alisha."

"They're helping us plan for building damage assessment—not that we're in shape to do very much just yet. I thought we'd come over and say hello."

"And get an eyeful," Torgelson added.

"Oh, I had quite an eyeful yesterday. A ringside seat when this monstrosity came down."

"Us too," Alisha said.

"I bet you never expected it would come to this," Jensen said to Rey.

"Truth is, I *did* expect it. I fought Devine every step of the way. Now look what's become of all his vainglory."

Jensen nodded. "And what's become of *him*."

Grace watched disappointment grow on Matt's face as National Guard Colonel James Dixon, in charge of operations at Starbucks Headquarters said, "I'm sorry, son. We've got matters well in hand here. I don't think we'll need a small unit like yours anytime soon. Thanks for bringing it by, though. I'm sure if you keep looking..."

A young soldier approached at a trot, stopped, and saluted. "Sir, we've got a problem."

"Another one, Corporal Morton? What is it?"

"Generator Bravo just gave out."

"How long till it's fixed?"

"Unknown, sir. Sergeant says he thinks the rear main seal is blown. He says he thinks we should get a replacement unit."

Colonel Dixon scowled. "That could take some time." He turned to Matt. "Will that rig of yours power a medical field clinic?"

Grace watched Matt's face light up. "That's exactly the sort of thing it was meant to do!"

The Colonel patted Matt on the shoulder, grinning. "Then I think I've got an assignment for you after all."

Craig Palmer got back in the car with a bag of breakfast sandwiches and a tray holding two hot cocoas and a coffee.

"I haven't thanked you boys yet," he said as he handed them their breakfasts.

"For what?" Liam began unwrapping a ham-egg-and-cheese muffin.

"For saving my life yesterday, when you told me to duck and cover. If I'd waited just a second longer—"

"We know," Willy said glumly. "You'd be dead."

"Or I might have gotten hurt pretty bad."

"That wouldn't be so terrible," Liam quipped brightly.

"What—!"

"You'd get a ride in that helicopter."

"That'd be cool!" Willy agreed. "Maybe we all would have."

Craig chuckled at their naiveté. He rubbed the back of his neck, pondering how narrowly he escaped a fracture and the evacuation the boys took so matter-of-factly.

"We haven't thanked you either," Liam said.

"For what?"

"For making us go back into the stadium. We'd have gotten drownded."

"By the tidal wave," Willy concluded.

"Hurry and eat your breakfasts," Craig said. "Then I'm going to find a way to get you guys home."

How he would accomplish that was uncertain. The car was intact and was the logical way to cover the twelve miles separating them from Burien. But the upper-level exit ramps of the stadium garage were crumpled. The street-level exit at the south end of the building was no better, sealed by mountains of wreckage washed there by the tsunamis. The only option was to abandon the SUV and go on foot, and that would be no easy task. The surrounding landscape was littered with thousands of vehicles, cargo containers, and wreckage the waves had deposited like vast arcs of driftwood on a beach. The flow front meandered from the International District in the northeast across First Avenue at Horton Street, arced through rail yards and across the ground-level segment of Highway 99. Then it continued to the south on a line winding near the Duwamish Waterway. The only open path was First Avenue, cleared by the National Guard the previous night.

Craig and the boys left the car and made their way down to join the flow of refugees on First Avenue. Falling in step with the others, many of whom carried bundles of valuables or had luggage in tow, the trio trudged the muddy pavement past irregular masses of heaped wreckage shoved aside by the military dozers the night before. At the intersection of Holgate and First, as they crossed the gap where the Army machines had broken through the wall of wrecked vehicles, Craig spotted something disturbing. "Come here, boys," he ordered, pressing them against his flanks as they walked and covering each of their faces with his fingers. "Just keep your eyes closed, boys. No peeking. I'll make sure you don't trip over anything."

"What is it, Dad?"

"Something I don't want you to see." Amid the wreckage, which was piled three vehicles tall at this point, bodies dangled out torn-open doors or hung through shattered windshields of the mud- and blood-soaked vehicles. The victims, Craig had no doubt, were people who ignored Rutledge's pleas to remain in the stadium. They had rushed to their vehicles only to find themselves stalled in traffic. The first wave swamped them, and the second overwhelmed them completely. Like the deaths on the field the previous day, Palmer knew these images would haunt his memory for a lifetime. He wanted no such thing for the boys. Not until they were well past the macabre wall of destruction, did he release them.

"Wow!" Willy exclaimed, pointing ahead of them. "Look at that!"

South of Holgate Street was a Krispy Kreme doughnut shop. Its shattered-out window glass was no surprise, but astonishingly thick billows of black smoke rose into the sky from giant vats of cooking oil that had caught fire and were still burning. The Fire Department had apparently decided to let the building burn itself out. Continuing several blocks south, they approached Starbucks Headquarters and were guided by police officers into the sawhorse-lined path that led to the evacuation vehicles. Moving slowly in the four-abreast column, they endured several hours in the growing heat of the day. Eventually the maze led them onto Utah Avenue, a brick paved plaza fronting Starbucks' headquarters building. They continued their stop-and-go trek under a long *allée* of shade trees where Starbucks maintained an outdoor bistro seating area. The benches, tables, and chairs allowed the boys and some elderly refugees to rest briefly, and all within sight of the transports loading at the south end of the lot.

Grace Toscano was there. She had helped Matt assemble his DayLite power cell beside the field hospital tent but had left him dealing with the intricacies of wiring it into the hospital's electrical circuits. Hoping to make herself more useful, she found her calling at the Starbucks coffee shop, which was fully operational with power supplied by a huge National Guard power trailer. The shop was, however, woefully understaffed, with an interminable line of hungry and thirsty refugees to serve. Though unversed in espresso-making, Grace was glad to serve as a runner, taking orders from people in the line and delivering free drinks and food to them.

"Who ordered two grande vanilla chocolate frozen frappuccinos?" She smiled, pretending she didn't know exactly who requested them.

"I did! I did!" Liam Beasley and Willy Palmer cried out in unison.

"Here you go!" She held out her drink carrier, so they could take their fraps and Craig could claim his venti iced mocha with whipped cream.

After a sip, he crooned, "You're an angel of mercy!"

Willy, munching one of three ham-and-swiss croissants she had brought, added, "We're going to ride in an Army truck!"

Grace smiled. "You boys have a safe trip home!" She moved on to the next people in line.

Chapter 32

Palmer and the boys didn't have long to wait before they were ushered aboard an Army troop transport. Within an hour they debarked at the Burien Transit Center, where Lindsey Palmer rushed to hug them both and wept through a joyous reunion. Within minutes, she delivered Liam to his parents and brought her loved ones home. The house had suffered minor damaged but was quite livable with power, water, and gas service restored.

Similar evacuations were carried out in other stricken parts of the city, including Ballard, Greenwood, and the U District in the north, and White Center, Georgetown, and Rainier Beach in the south. Emergency response units from armed services, law enforcement, fire, and disaster relief agencies streamed in from throughout the Northwest and the nation. Each established food and water distribution, medical services, evacuation support, temporary shelters, and other ways and means to respond to the emergency. FEMA began marshaling hundreds of temporary living quarters, although their shipment and arrival dates were days to weeks in the future.

The morning of the second day after the quake found Starbucks Center busier than the first. With the continued opening of streets and highways, it became possible for buses and other large transit vehicles to begin arriving in a steady stream from the south. They came northbound on First Avenue, then circled a block bounded by Forest Street, Utah Avenue, and Lander Street, to reach a loading area at the south curb of the Starbucks parking lot.

There, the head end of the long line of refugees waited under the shading roof of Amazon Fresh's grocery pick-up shelter. Ushered by polite-but-firm police and National Guardsmen, people boarded buses that departed southbound on First

Avenue for destinations in surrounding towns like Burien, Federal Way, Kent, and Auburn, or in some cases as far away as Tacoma and Olympia. In each municipality, school gymnasiums or tent camps were set up to house people for weeks or months —whatever was required to restore public utilities in neighborhoods hardest hit by what was now officially called the Great Seattle Earthquake.

The last fans from T-Mobile Park had long since departed Starbucks Center, but new throngs moved out of downtown and inner-city neighborhoods, goaded by hunger or in need of other help. People were remarkably orderly, even those heavily burdened with goods on their backs or in hand, including children and pets. Having weathered the terror of the original event and the privations of lost power and dwindling supplies, they were for the most part quiet and compliant, although tempers flared here and there. Violence, however, was entirely absent. People understood that following orders was the best way to reach safety, comfort, and shelter.

The military organizers had chosen well in establishing their Starbucks Center relief operation. The location possessed an abundance of food supplies on hand. Not only was the large Starbucks Reserve facility well stocked, but within the same large building were the vast refrigerated storerooms of Seattle's primary Amazon Fresh outlet. Nevertheless, it remained impossible to make hot food and coffee fast enough to meet the demands of the hungry, exhausted refugees.

Matt Balen and Grace Toscano provided the means to solve this problem. After spending the night on cots in a troop tent pitched in the parking lot, they rose before dawn and retrieved a second DayLite unit from the workshop. They hung its four solar collectors on the south-facing sides of two tents, ready to collect energy as soon as the sun came up. Within an hour, their electricity was powering a quartet of Starbucks espresso machines on folding tables, and a complete Red Cross kitchen providing substantial meals to people who hadn't eaten much in days. More-than-ample electricity from this second unit powered a pancake grill, two microwaves, and a refrigerator.

At mid-morning, Colonel Dixon came around with his field staff for fresh hot coffee. "I'm impressed," he remarked, looking over Matt's second DayLite unit and the many people it served. "I wish we had a couple hundred of these. We could carry twenty of 'em in a single truck. A dozen in a helicopter. And store some in every fire station and armory in the state. They would have come in handy, if we'd already had them in place."

"I'm sure I can make that happen," Matt responded, "if I get my shop going again."

"You'll find a way." Grace smiled with pride, twining her arm around Matt's.

The Colonel turned to a junior officer. "Make a note to write a recommendation for Matt Balen's portable power units. We'll send it straight to the top at the Department of Defense."

"Yes, sir."

They all glanced up at a small airplane approaching from the south.

The twin-engine Beechcraft had taken off thirty minutes before from Olympia Airport. It carried Governor Sheila Long and Federal Emergency Management Agency Region 10 Deputy Director Rudolph Jones, as well as other government officials, military personnel, and members of the press. They had flown over increasingly damaged towns on their way north but nothing in the still-functional municipalities of Tacoma, Federal Way, or Tukwila had prepared them for what they saw here.

"Hurricanes Katrina and Harvey were nothing compared to this," Jones remarked. A small man with gray hair and a high forehead, dressed in a blue suit, he spoke almost apologetically, as if FEMA had somehow neglected preparing for the disaster.

Governor Long was ten years his junior but today she looked older, as if her graying, shoulder-length hair had turned a shade whiter overnight. She shook her head slowly. "I can hardly believe all this happened on my watch. I hope FEMA is ready to help us get things straightened out."

"Our offices in Lake Forest Park were shaken pretty heavily, but they're basically intact. Our team is coordinating the nation-wide relief effort the President called for when he approved Mayor Jimmy Dunkin's disaster declaration. Help is definitely on the way."

"Look there!" National Guard General Darren Haywood, sitting across the aisle, barked. They gazed, open-mouthed, where he pointed. "The West Seattle bridge looks totaled. That's a huge gap in the center span."

Long murmured, "West Seattleites just went from having the best commute in the area to the worst."

"They've still got two other bridges," Jones pointed out. "I see the lower Duwamish River Bridge has a few cars on it right now, crossing to what's left of Harbor Island."

"Which isn't much."

"Who knows? Maybe the upper span won't be too hard to repair. The way it broke reminds me of what it looked like while they were building it—two opposing pieces reaching out toward each other. Patch the middle part and hopefully it will be good as new."

"I appreciate your optimism," the Governor told Jones. "But should we even rebuild it? If it's in such a quake-prone area…"

"Yes, we should. This was a once-in-a-thousand-year event. I think the replacement will stand for quite a while."

They stared wordlessly at the long wide inlet where Harbor Island had been, flanked by fallen cargo cranes and sunken container ships. No less breathtaking was the Coast Guard cutter, *Polar Star,* high and dry on Pier 46.

"Just ahead is our largest relief operation so far," General Haywood interrupted the silence, pointing at Starbucks Center. Military supply trucks were arriving and buses full of refugees were departing southbound, while thousands of displaced people poured in from city neighborhoods. "They've helped more than twelve thousand refugees already."

"Look at all those people!" the Governor murmured. "I feel so sorry for them."

"At least they're keeping calm," Haywood remarked.

"Other cities have had riots and looting when disaster struck. We've got a sharp eye out for it here."

"I don't know," the Governor replied thoughtfully. "There's something about the population of this state. They're naturally given to cooperating, not fighting. My sources tell me merchants at grocery stores, convenience stores, and hardware stores, are generally giving people whatever they need. And the police and my guardsmen are making sure it's an orderly process."

"Amen," Jones affirmed.

"Look at the wreckage!" Long agonized as they crossed the snaking path of tidal-wave outwash south of T-Mobile Park. Tears welled as she examined thousands of vehicles, shipping containers, and other spoil jumbled in heaps where the waves deposited them. Between or inside some cars were many un-recovered bodies. "I can hardly bear to look."

"It's awful," Jones agreed. "But look at the baseball stadium. It's pretty much intact. A lot of people came through okay there."

"Things could have been much worse. They were convinced to stay inside when the wave hit by some university professor. I'll want his name for a commendation."

"Holy Jesus!" Haywood suddenly blurted. "Look at the Highway 99 tunnel entrances! They're full of water!" Both the northbound entrance and the southbound exit were filled to street level with muddy water topped by iridescent slicks of fuel and lubricant oil that had risen from unseen vehicles below.

"There'll be a lot of bodies to recover." He shook his head.

"The poor people!" Long moaned. "If those entrances had walls around them—tsunami barriers ten feet tall, the water would have flowed around instead of going in."

"Hindsight is twenty-twenty," Haywood observed.

Jones nodded. "We've got to make sure those barriers get built, so this can never happen again. I'll make it a FEMA disaster-preparedness priority."

"And I'll speak to the State Legislature," Long added.

As the pilot steered north at five hundred feet, they got their first overall impression of the city itself. Dust still billowed. Thin columns of smoke still rose from a few recalcitrant fires. The great majority of buildings stood, although most were devoid of glass. Inside them could be seen floor-upon-floor of upended desks, fallen shelves, overturned couches, scattered chairs, and other signs of chaos.

"Thank God it happened on a Saturday when most offices were empty," Long reflected.

Jones pointed just southwest of the main downtown area. "Look at Pioneer Square!"

Long caught her breath. "So many buildings are just piles of rubble!"

The historic district—previously a warren of vintage three-to-five-story brick buildings—was now an undulating landscape of brick rubble and red dust. Here and there, it was punctuated by buildings that withstood the shock despite their seeming fragility.

"It seems the political debate of the last four decades has been settled," Jones asserted.

"You mean, whether to force building owners to retrofit their buildings against their will? I know that political football game too well. I've played it unsuccessfully every year since taking office. But the State Legislature has failed to enact a law with teeth in it. Special interests and lobbyists gathered like vultures, not to mention real-estate moguls like Eldon Devine. But why do you say the debate is settled?"

"Because the brick buildings that were reinforced are now the only ones left standing. So you've got one-hundred-percent compliance."

"It's a cruel irony, but I get what you're saying. And at what human cost? There must be hundreds of people buried under bricks and rubble down there."

"I hate to say anything harsh at a time like this, Governor, but the building owners had their chance to take the initiative. Now Nature has decided for them. Given the repeated warnings they ignored and disputed, I imagine the courts won't be too kind when negligence and wrongful death lawsuits are brought against them."

"They'll only be getting what they deserve. Still, the innocent people…"

Their route next took them for a close-up look at the main business district. Thin smoke rose from several skyscrapers and a few lower structures, but no large-scale conflagrations could be seen. On streets still strewn with megatons of glass and debris, scattered fire department vehicles fought small fires or attended to other problems.

"Compared to San Francisco in 1906, we're very lucky," Jones said. "Much of the destruction in San Francisco was caused by fires that got out of control and swept the city. Here, the structures are fire resistant and the Seattle Fire Department was able to put out any blazes that threatened to spread."

"How badly are these tall buildings damaged?"

"Most of them can be repaired. Some will need to be dismantled and another structure built in their place. By the way, see that huge hole in the ground right below us? That's what's left of Devine's Emerald Tower."

Long gasped. "That was going to be the tallest building in the Northwest."

"Not anymore."

The Governor stared down into the still-steaming pit. "Truth be told, I've hated that man for years. I hope he loses a lot of money. Is it wrong for me to feel that way?"

"Feel how you like. I don't think he cares about money anymore. He's listed among the missing. Last known location, his Emerald Tower."

"Pride comes before a fall," Long murmured. Then a thought struck her. "I want a thorough investigation of every person or agency that approved that building. I want to know how they justified it—and I want a criminal investigation of anyone who shows evidence of bribes or *quid pro quos* for their approvals. We'll get a good housecleaning out of this if nothing else. Eldon Devine and his sort have had their day."

They flew along the waterfront, looking at buildings and wharves, some shattered, some miraculously spared by the irregular action of the seiche and its wave patterns. It was easy to see where the water rose high or come ashore low. Ivar's Restaurant and totem-fronted Ye Olde Curiosity Shoppe had taken water damage but were still standing. Other wharf buildings were less fortunate. Several had walls buckled by water pressure. Others were reduced to splintered wreckage.

"This is the height of the tourist season," the Governor sighed. "There must have been thousands of people on the waterfront. The death toll…"

"Is remarkably low," Haywood interjected.

"How can that be?"

"One cop—one single individual—took it upon herself to make the difference."

"How much could just one person do?"

"She was on traffic duty outside T-Mobile Park. She'd been briefed about the professor's tsunami presentation. Realizing how many people were in danger, she drove her squad car up the full length of Alaskan Way. She got on her loudspeaker and told the crowds to get uphill as quickly as they could. And people did what she said—most of them, anyway."

"Amazing. I hope she got away safely, too."

"She did. She went all the way from the stadium to the north end of the waterfront, then turned up Broad Street just as the wave came in."

"She deserves a commendation, too. Do you have her name?"

"We'll be able to locate her without too much trouble. Her precinct is reporting to me, now."

"Good. She'll get some richly deserved praise—and a medal. We should install some early-warning loudspeakers to do what she did. Now, what's this up ahead?"

The solidly-built Seattle Aquarium was still standing, though flotsam on its roof suggested it had been washed over entirely by at least one huge wave.

Jones murmured, "I wonder if their fish swam away when the display tanks were submerged?"

"Not a high priority on my list," Long said. "They can get more fish. Come to think of it, they may have taken in more fish than they lost."

Next, they approached Pier 62 Park, where a white pow-wow tent was drawing a large crowd. Among people waving up at the plane, some were dressed in native dancing costumes.

"Looks like the tribes were the first to recover," Long remarked. "Look at those barbecues set up outside the tent. I think they're cooking fish for the crowd."

"You're right. They've got their own relief center going. Looks like they've got some mighty big salmon on those grills."

"At least *some* Seattleites will eat well tonight."

Farther north, the Space Needle stood tall with little damage in evidence.

"It was built earthquake-resistant," Jones explained. "Way back in 1962, for the World's Fair. Far beyond the standards of the times."

"Looks like it was worth the trouble."

"That's true of the new, modern business district of South Lake Union." Jones pointed beyond the Space Needle. "It looks like the offices of Amazon, the Fred Hutchinson Cancer Research Center, and other high-tech buildings withstood the shaking, minus a lot of window glass."

"Hopefully they'll help us get the city's economy back on its feet."

"Camp Murray to Governor's aircraft, over?" The voice came through the cabin sound system as well as the pilot's headset. "Maintain altitude at no more than five hundred feet and keep an eye overhead. You may see heavy aircraft arriving Boeing Field."

"There!" Haywood sang out, pointing high above Elliott Bay. A huge, gray, lumbering Air National Guard C-17 transport seemed to be moving in slow motion at several thousand feet, wing-flaps down and descending on a line for Boeing Field.

Long remarked, "I expected Boeing to be closed to large aircraft for a long time. Wasn't the flight-control tower knocked flat?"

"Yes, it was," the General admitted. "But our teams assembled a deployable flight-control tower there. Looks like they've got it working."

"That's a gigantic plane."

"The first of many, if things go as planned. Carrying everything from medical supplies to food, to bulldozers and backhoes, if needed."

"They're angels of mercy."

"That's their job. I'm sure they're glad to be of service."

The intent of the Governor's trip was to get eyes on the destruction to better guide the state's efforts to bring relief and start the recovery process. Because that process would be coordinated from offices in Olympia, the plane made a sweeping turn over Elliott Bay to begin the flight south to the capital. Doing so, it overflew the shoreline of West Seattle, which included the epicenter of the earthquake.

The majority of the apartment buildings on the inland side of Alki Avenue still stood, although most showed structural damage and a few had collapsed. Others were wave-washed as high as the fourth story. At Alki Beach proper, immense amounts of sand carried ashore by the tsunami formed long sandbars covering streets or heaped against buildings that still stood. As was true of the apartment buildings, the many single-family houses in the Alki neighborhood showed a range of effects from little to almost complete destruction, either by the earthquake or by the waves, or both.

"We are going to need a lot of temporary housing for the survivors," Long murmured.

"There is a huge flow of people out of Seattle," Jones replied. "FEMA will give them cash to pay for hotels, or pitch tent cities they can stay in, or eventually make trailers available in parks or on their own lots at no cost. But if recent hurricanes are any guide, many will want to stay in their own homes."

Haywood nodded. "They'll want to protect their property and their valuables. There's always a criminal element on the prowl. So, a lot of people are making tough choices right now. Living conditions are awful when you don't have water, power, or working sewers."

Long sighed. "Your National Guard units are doing incredible work, General."

"Along with police and fire services—and there are literally dozens of relief organizations like the Red Cross on the way or on the scene already. But it's taking time to get basic services organized—food and water, that sort of thing."

Jones added, "Some folks will need assistance for months, if not years."

The Governor sighed deeply, and the conversation trailed off.

As they flew farther south, Long suddenly cried, "Oh! My! God! What's going on there? The Alki Lighthouse used to be on the point. I remember visiting it. Now it's on a hill! And the point—"

"The point carries on a couple hundred yards farther west," Haywood completed her thought.

"I can't believe my eyes," Long moaned. "Alki will never be the same."

"Neither will Bainbridge Island, Governor. It looks like Restoration Point has added a couple hundred yards pointing in this direction. The fault must have broken all the way across Puget Sound."

"Attention folks," the pilot announced over the cabin speakers. "We'll continue south to Olympia—unless anyone would like to fly over another area."

"No thanks," Long murmured. "I've seen enough."

Chapter 33

Groups of people on Alki Beach looked up to watch the Governor's plane fly over. Most people were trekking one direction or another carrying bags or backpacks of belongings, seeking better accommodations or other aid.

However, one group of three had come specifically to visit the beach. Leon Curtis, Ann Butterfield, and Peyton McKean had just driven down Bonair Drive in McKean's Lexus sedan. After escaping the tsunami, Leon and Ann had descended their jumper-cable rope, and then hiked to McKean's house, a view home not far from the top of Bonair. There, they were welcomed to a house without power but minimally damaged. They stayed two nights with McKean, waiting for impassable streets to be cleared. When phone service returned, Leon's wife informed him that their home in Mill Creek sustained no damage that couldn't wait for attention. Ann's neighbors were happy to use a hidden key to inspect her apartment, and provide food and water for her cat, Silky.

Now, compelled by concern for their excavation, they had gotten McKean to drive them here. After descending debris-strewn Bonair, and passing Ann's red Blazer, still nestled in its tree, McKean had parked on Alki Avenue between two huge drifts of sand. They got out to look around.

"Where did so much sand come from?" Leon said, puzzled.

"There!" Ann indicated the beach—or what was left of it. The wave had swept tremendous quantities of sand from the shore and deposited it on the road. The entire surface of the beach had been lowered several feet by the excavating power of the wave, re-establishing the prehistoric level of the land's surface. And spread over that surface…

"A half-dozen longhouses, at least!" Leon gasped. Though the wood was blackened with age, rectangular arrays of house-post stubs marked longhouse outlines. Logs lying in chaotic jumbles appeared to be fallen roof beams.

"Just look at it all!" Ann exclaimed.

They hurried to the shore. Around them, a profusion of blackened cedar wall planks lay strewn over the area. "Bentwood boxes." Ann pointed at two bulky, squarish objects nearby. "Look at the gorgeous native carvings on them!"

"And about a zillion small artifacts!" Leon rejoiced. "Here are some carved wooden bowls, and there's a raven dancing mask! And canoe paddles! And harpoons! And coiled fiber ropes."

Ann and Leon clasped each other and danced up and down like giddy schoolchildren. Leon's wire rimmed glasses clouded with tears. "There must be a whole native village here!"

"An entire culture," Ann bubbled. "Covered in sand for centuries, just waiting for us."

After a moment, they settled down and their expressions sobered as the weight of the brutal event that revealed the trove returned with leaden effect.

"We've got one huge job ahead of us." Leon said thoughtfully. "An entire village worth of priceless artifacts to collect and catalog. We'll need a way to keep souvenir hunters out."

"I've got some red climbing ropes at home," McKean said. "You can use them to cordon off the area. I'll drive home and fetch the rope and some tools you'll need to do the job."

Leon stood with fists on hips, surveying the area. "We may be looking at the archeological find of the millennium, uncovered by a wave like the one that buried it in the first place."

"A tsunami tooketh away," Ann observed. "And a tsunami gaveth back."

Two people came along the sand-strewn sidewalk—a hefty, bearded man and a little woman. Both wore backpacks with sleeping bags strapped to them. The man carried two stuffed gym bags and the woman carried a heavily filled leather satchel slung on a strap over one shoulder.

Seeing Ann looking at them curiously, Zoey felt compelled to explain. "We've survived on canned goods and bottled water for two days and two nights, but we're running low. And our cell phones are dead, so we can't keep in touch with family and friends. We're going to search for some better living conditions."

"Besides," said Moe, "the National Guard brought in a flatbed truck, and they're piling it with body bags—full ones, I mean."

"It's too depressing to watch," said Zoe.

"The Admiral Way bridge at Schmitz Park is down, so we're looking for another way up the hill. We were told we should try Bonair."

"That's the right way to go," McKean agreed. "There is a tent camp set up at West Seattle High School. The school was earthquake-hardened, so it's in good shape. They've brought in a power trailer to run the school's kitchen, and they've got a tank-truck and hot water for showers."

"Mmmm," Zoey cooed. "A shower sounds good right about now."

Ann asked the two, "Didn't you have a shop in one of these buildings?" She pointed across Alki Avenue, where every other building was flattened but a fair number still stood.

"Yeah," Zoey nodded. "That square brick building, two blocks south. It got retrofitted just last year. It came through the shake pretty well, but the waves washed completely over it. So there's not much left inside."

"Everything in our marijuana dispensary floated away," Moe added morosely. "All our stock was in plastic bags and glass jars. I guess it just drifted out to sea." He made a wave-like motion with one hand.

"And our dog Rex, too!" Zoey burst into tears and threw her arms around Moe's stout chest. He put down his bags and patted her on the back. "The wave just swept him away!" she sobbed.

Leon said, "You know, there are a lot of dog tracks around here." He shaded his eyes and looked far along the beach. Then he pursed his lips and gave out a quick, shrill whistle. "Here poochie! Come on!" Everyone turned to follow his gaze.

Several hundred yards up the beach, a small dog—no doubt the maker of the tracks—pricked up its ears and then came dashing toward them. Simultaneously, Zoey let out a scream as if seeing a ghost.

"Rexxie!" She knelt and the animal rushed into her arms. "Oh, Rexxie!" The little mutt licked her face and wagged its tail so frantically it seemed about to fly off. Moe knelt with Zoey, and they swept up their wriggling, yapping pet and smothered him with hugs and kisses.

The reunion brought tears to the eyes of Leon and Ann, but analytical Peyton McKean observed it with detachment. "Many canine breeds are excellent swimmers. Apparently, Rex inherited the trait in one of his bloodlines."

The dog ate some kibbles Zoey retrieved from her satchel and then trotted off to sniff among the village ruins. McKean remarked, "Too bad you lost your overly buoyant stock. People could use some de-stressing psycho-pharmaceuticals under the circumstances."

"Er...yeah. Right on!" Moe agreed. "That would help a lot of uptight people chill out a bit. Including me."

Zoey nodded. "I missed my wake-and-bake session this morning."

"I'm sure you're not the only ones." McKean smiled.

"Yeah," Moe said. "Lotta people probably need to get baked about now."

"To blaze up," Zoey added.

"Rip a bong, Babe," Moe shot back.

"Put flame to flower."

"Four-twenty."

"Munch some medibles."

"Hit a bowl."

"Enjoy the psychodynamic effects of some trans-delta-nine-tetrahydrocannabinol," McKean interjected.

After a moment, Moe said, "Uh, yeah, Doc. That's it."

Leon and Ann turned back to the uncovered Indian village and began stepping off distances and discussing the area in need of a cordon line. Moe and Zoey sat on a sand dune to rest before ascending Bonair Drive. Rex trotted around the site as if he aspired to become an archeologist, too. McKean stood staring into space, long fingers stroking jawline, contemplating some intellectual challenge regarding lost villages, marijuana, or both.

"Hey, look!" Zoey called. "Rex wants to help you guys dig!" She nodded at where the dog had stopped his wanderings to scratch at a sand drift.

Rex yapped enthusiastically as he dug. Then he paused, sniffing at an object still half-buried. He cocked his head to one side, whined, and yapped several more times in Moe and Zoey's direction.

"What have you got there, boy?" Moe went over and picked up what the dog had sniffed out, holding it in front of his face with a look of wonderment. "Well, I'll be doggoned. If it isn't a jar of Himalayan Howdy-Doo. That's great stuff. Heavy on the indica. Real mellow. Good boy, Rexxie!" He patted the dog's head and Rex gave him a tongue-lolling pant of appreciation.

Zoey wasted no time in producing a small glass pipe and a lighter from her bag. They quickly loaded the pipe and lit up. They took deep drags, kept it in, and then blew out clear air. Zoey held the pipe out. "Anybody else want some of this?"

Ann and Leon waved her off and continued their pacing and calculations. Peyton McKean, on the other hand, turned to them with a smile. "Answer: yes! I'd like just a little, uh, rip."

She handed the pipe to him, and he took a deep draw.

Jane Hewitt guided Dolphin 224 onto a landing area just off the main runway at Boeing Field. A sense of completion was running through her over-stressed and exhausted nervous system. After more than two full days on rescue-and-recovery duty, she and her crew were finally granted a furlough for some much-needed rest and recovery of their own.

Airport personnel hurried to the helicopter, preparing to give Dolphin 224 sufficient fuel to reach home base in Port Angeles. While they tended to the needs of her aircraft, Hewitt took off her flight helmet. Leaving it in her seat, she got out to walk a short distance and take a look around. Everywhere, Boeing Field was alive with activity. Huge gray transport planes arrived and departed in an endless procession of landings, taxiing, debarking of payloads, more taxiing, and takeoffs to make room for arriving flights. She watched one of the big C-17s disgorge first a Humvee with Red Cross markings and then a good-sized army-green cargo truck with a heavy load, ready to transport needed materials to locations she couldn't guess at.

Across the runway she saw huge hangars capable of housing 747 jet aircraft, now stacked high with supplies. There were wooden pallets loaded with what appeared to be twenty-pound bags of rice, beans, and flour, as well as large cartons of other foods, medicines, and equipment. The efficient flow of materials to and from the airport seemed nothing short of miraculous.

All this she took in at a glance. While her crew mates chatted with maintenance personnel tending to Dolphin 224, she had other more urgent concerns. She searched this way and that, looking for three people who had contacted her via newly restored cell phone service just two hours before. Three people who, with the help of old Joe, had gotten their car moving through a maze of semi-passable streets trying to meet her here. She was just about to conclude that they hadn't made it—when she saw them.

Instantly, she raced toward Ryan and the girls, who were waiting in a grassy viewing area beside the old red-brick King County Airport building. As she ran, tears streamed down her cheeks. Emily and Caylie cried too, as they raced into her open arms. She knelt, swept them to her, kissed each profusely, and was kissed in return. Everyone blubbered attestations of love without concern for appearances. They hugged each other so tightly there was scarcely room to breathe.

When the girls finally relinquished Jane, she rose and embraced Ryan, sharing more kisses and tears. When the they came up for air at last, the girls joined in a four-way family hug.

"You look exhausted," Ryan said, gazing lovingly at her.

"I *am* exhausted. Two days with very little sleep. Day and

night assignments, almost nonstop. We're all so glad to get a furlough." She nodded at her crewmen who were busy overseeing refueling from a tank truck pulled alongside Dolphin 224. "They've given me forty-eight hours at home and I'm going to stay in bed the whole time."

"We'll bring you breakfast in bed!" Caylie cheered.

"And dinner!" said Emily.

"And I'll—bless the day I met you." Ryan hugged her more tightly.

"Oh!" She tried to get them all inside her embrace at once. "I love you guys so much!"

"Forty-eight hours," Ryan said when they had all hugged enough. "Then right back at it?"

Jane's expression darkened somewhat. "The rescues will be finished by then—most are done already. But there will be a lot more to do. Salvaging sunken boats, offshore wreckage to clear, and… bodies."

"Don't think about that now. Think of forty-eight hours at home with us. We're going to take real good care of you. Aren't we, girls?"

"Yes!" they cried in unison.

"You'll probably get home before we do. The local ferry terminals are out of commission. We'll have to drive around the Sound and cross the Tacoma Narrows Bridge. We'll get there as soon as we can."

"You'll know where to find me," she said. "If you get home quick, I'll be in my bubble bath. If it takes a while longer, then *do not disturb* me until morning."

"Aye, aye, Ma'am!" Ryan grinned.

"Aye, aye, Mom!" the girls echoed.

Grace Toscano stood with Matt Balen as he and Colonel Dixon discussed the ins and outs of solar-power collection. A convoy of camo-green trucks rolled up from the south and parked one after another along First Avenue. As they did so, one of them, a Humvee towing a tan trailer, pulled onto the lot. The driver, a sergeant, saluted the Colonel. "Got that replacement diesel power generator you ordered, Sir. Don't ask what I had to do to get it."

"I won't." Dixon smiled. "But I also know we don't need it anymore. Mr. Balen's units are handling the tasks. We'll send it on to another location that needs power."

As the Humvee and trailer rolled away, a car pulled onto the lot and a familiar male voice called, "Hey! There you guys are!"

Matt and Grace turned to see Earl in the passenger window of his BMW, with Carrie at the wheel. They went to the car and Matt lightly patted the fender. "I never thought I'd see this ride again. How'd you get it back?"

"Easy!" Carrie explained. "I took a long walk this morning and fetched it from the Seattle Center parking lot. It was just fine. Untouched. Then I picked up Earl at the hospital and, well, here we are. We're headed out of town, just like everybody else who can manage it. The Red Cross volunteers at the hospital booked us accommodations at a high school gymnasium in Tacoma."

"But I'm thinking I'd like to press on south," Earl said. "Maybe down to Portland if my leg can take it. Plenty of nice hotel rooms available there, including some real swanky ones. We swung by to see if you guys wanted to come with us."

Matt and Grace were silent, as if the thought of going anywhere hadn't occurred to them. They glanced at each other uncertainly for a moment, and then Matt told Earl, "Thanks, but no. I've got to stay here and help people."

"We understand," Carrie leaned across to look out Earl's window at them. "How about you, Grace?"

Grace put a hand through the crook of Matt's elbow and hugged his arm. "I'm staying with him."

"It might be quite a while before I leave this place," Matt cautioned her.

"Then it will be quite a while before I leave."

"Sleeping on a cot every night?"

"Sleeping on a cot."

Carrie said, "Sounds like you two have your minds made

up."

"We do." Grace gazed into Matt's eyes, and he smiled at her warmly.

Watching them, Carrie moaned poignantly. "We'll miss you guys. It's been… quite an adventure."

"That's an understatement," Earl gingerly patted his bandaged calf.

"I need a hug!" Carrie suddenly cried. She put the car in park and jumped out to squeeze Grace and Matt in turn.

'Scuse me if I stay seated," Earl apologized. "I don't get around too swift right now."

Matt went to the window and shook Earl's hand. "Thanks for letting me bum a ride from Yellowstone."

"Bum?" Earl grinned. "It has been my privilege having you along on this trip."

"And what a long strange trip it's been," Carrie added as she got back in.

Earl pointed at the nearest solar collector and the medical tent it was feeding. "Is that the prototype you were talking about?"

"Yep."

"Looks like it works as advertised."

"Yep."

"You know, when I get back to Massachusetts, I'm gonna have a chat with my father. Maybe his investment firm could scratch together some money to help get your company back on its feet."

"Any help would be appreciated."

"I'm not talking small beers, here. I'm talking millions, tens of millions. Do you think that might get your operation up and running?"

"I'm sure it would." Matt broke into a grin.

A police officer had been trying to get Carrie's attention for some time. Now he blew his whistle and emphatically waved his hand to indicate that she should drive off the lot and onto the street heading southbound. "Well," she said reluctantly, "I guess we'd better be going." She put the car in gear and began moving along as the officer directed. "Keep safe!" Earl shouted as they drove off.

"You too!" Grace called after them. Then she wove her arms around Matt and hugged him. He put his arms around her and kissed her lightly on the forehead as they watched the Beemer drive away.

"One chapter ends," he murmured.

"Another begins," she replied. "It seems to me your fortunes are looking distinctly up—and at the same time, the earthquake snuffed out your nemesis, Eldon Devine."

"Curious how life works out, isn't it?"

For a time, they watched the bustle of supply trucks coming and going, and refugees boarding transports.

"I've been thinking about your question," Matt said eventually.

"Which question?"

"Do I think two people could fall in love under these circumstances."

"And—?"

"I'm sure they could."

He took her in his arms, and they shared a long tender kiss.

His cell phone, which hadn't made a noise since the quake, rang. His mother was on the other end. In a few minutes of conversation, she inquired after Matt's wellbeing and explained that their home had weathered the quake with minimal damage. Matt passed the phone to Grace and let her introduce herself. When he got it back, his mother asked, "So, when will we see you?"

"I'll be there in a day or two. You can meet Grace, and we can help you straighten up the house. Then we'll be off to a certain Tillamook dairy farm. I've got some people to meet down there."

Grace smiled blissfully.

EPILOGUE

As Governor Long's flight approached Olympia, she and the other passengers watched a television screen at the front of the cabin. On it was a feed from the University of Washington where a press conference was about to begin. The podium was empty for the moment, and while waiting for Professor Rutledge to take the stage, the camera showed a static shot of the small auditorium.

"Not many people there," Rudy Jones said. "Looks like about a dozen in a room that could hold five times as many."

"Reporters probably have other urgent matters to cover," Long suggested.

"Or had a hard time getting there," General Haywood said. "Plenty of streets still need clearing."

Long pointed out a woman seated in the first row. "Laura Stern, the *Seattle Times* reporter. She pestered me many times on this subject. Now I only wish she had been more persistent. She might have goaded me into pushing harder on earthquake preparedness."

"What else could you have done?" Jones asked.

"I don't know. Start condemning structures that weren't up to codes?"

"That only would have gotten you into a thousand lawsuits."

"So now it's a new day. Most of the substandard buildings are heavily damaged or down completely. I'll get word out to building inspectors to be hard-nosed when they assess the habitability of damaged structures. I can tell them to red-tag the great majority and only issue occupancy permits after they're retrofitted to bring them up to codes. Not just patched up, but fully earthquake-hardened."

Jones nodded. "Then at least *some* good will come of this."

Though media attendance at the press conference was low, reporters from two local television stations were present as well as several from print and internet media. A large proportion of the crowd comprised university personnel, including Kyle Stevens and Lori McMillan. As they waited for Professor Rutledge to come from his office where he was making last-minute additions to his notes, they chatted softly.

"The Mariners flew out of Sea-Tac this morning on their way to Oakland," Kyle said. "Gonna replay that final game down there. I hope they win it."

Lori was preoccupied with another thought. "You really got me worried about that tidal wave reaching us. Were you just pranking me?"

"No way. I was like, 'Duh! It could happen!' But didn't you hear? It almost *did* happen."

"What?"

"One big-ass surge from Elliott Bay made it all the way to Lake Union, which is right at the base of the slope the UW sits on."

"Oh my God! Then, we *were* in danger!"

"Not too much. It still would have had a long uphill run to get to us. But it sure gave everybody living in a houseboat a crazy ride. Pulled some of them free of their moorings. They're still floating around the lake. Then it rolled into Lake Washington and made the Evergreen Point Floating Bridge look like a roller coaster—up five or six feet, then down again."

A University Public Relations woman stepped to the podium. "Okay folks. Let's get started. I'd like to introduce Professor Ronald Rutledge of the Northwest Seismographic Network, who is going to update us on some details about the earthquake. Professor Rutledge."

She moved aside, and Rutledge stepped to the podium and cleared his throat.

"Good afternoon. Although it is still too soon to give any precise calculations on the earthquake's exact magnitude, I'd say we are narrowing things down with some pretty good computer models. One thing is certain. This was a shallow quake. It was essentially right at the surface. It ruptured heavily along an east-west axis from the center of West Seattle entirely across the bottom of Puget Sound to the center of Bainbridge Island. Smaller movements occurred all along the fault from the Cascade foothills in the east to Bremerton in the west."

A slide appeared on a screen behind him, illustrating the crack in the earth he had just described. "This is a fault that is well-known to us, a main branch of the Seattle Fault complex. In relative terms, the land to the south of the fault rose up and over the land to the north. In several areas we have reports of forty to fifty feet of uplift. In my experience studying such things, that is a truly huge overthrust for such a small fault. Given that most of the uplift occurred underwater, it is not surprising that the initial tsunami was larger than predicted, as well. Of course, the first wave was followed by an even bigger tsunami from the collapse of Harbor Island."

Laura Stern put her hand up and Rutledge acknowledged her with a nod.

"Can you give us an approximate magnitude?"

"Our current estimate is around 7.8. We'll be refining that number as we add more data from seismographic stations around the region to sharpen our calculations. But the final answer will be close to that figure." He glanced around the room. "That's all I can tell you for certain at the moment. We'll release further information as we get more data."

Laura's hand went up again. "Do you have casualty figures?"

"No, I don't."

"Well then, let me share what I've learned so far. Seattle Police and Fire give figures of more than five hundred known dead and ten times that injured. And these are only very preliminary numbers, given how many people and bodies are still buried under rubble. Compared to other such emergencies, and looking at the extent of building damage, the Seattle Office of Emergency Management tells me we are likely to see five thousand deaths by the time all missing persons are accounted for. Maybe twice that, if their initial estimates are low. Do you have any comment on that?"

"I—" Rutledge stopped, flustered. "No, I don't."

"Let me ask you something more specific to your work. How much worse could this quake have been, both in terms of magnitude and deaths? There must be precedents for quakes like this in other countries."

Rutledge shook his head. "We never thought an earthquake this powerful could happen here."

"But the earthquake magnitude scale goes well beyond 7.8. Every single-digit increment—seven-to-eight, eight-to-nine—is ten times as bad as the one below it, right?"

"Right."

"And the largest ever recorded was 9.5, in Valdivia, Chile in 1960. It killed many thousands of people. It set off a volcanic eruption and sent a tsunami across the Pacific that killed people in Hawaii and Japan."

"You know your earthquakes," Rutledge acknowledged glumly. "But that event took place on a continental subduction zone. Subduction faults are easily ten times bigger than the Seattle Fault."

"So, something ten times worse couldn't happen here?"

"It's unlikely."

"But if 7.8 brought down one skyscraper, how much worse would it have to be to bring everything down?"

"I don't want to speculate—"

Stern was implacable. "I've seen reports of thirteen older schools in the area that were all but leveled, because they hadn't received earthquake retrofitting. Thank God it was Saturday and there were no students in them. We'd have a couple thousand more deaths to report, and it would be mostly kids."

Rutledge became visibly shaken. "I hate to think of it."

"People should have thought of it before. Politicians have debated earthquake retrofits for years. Lots of arguments about costs and disruptions, but precious little action."

As the exchange went on in the lecture hall, those aboard Governor Long's plane watched in numb silence. "That's Laura for you," the Governor said. "She never lets up. I'm appalled at how bad things are, and she's pointing out it could have been worse!"

As Leon Curtis and Ann Butterfield completed cordoning off the Alki village with McKean's red ropes and stakes fashioned from splintered lumber, a man called out to them.

"Hey, bone-diggers! Find anything interesting?"

"Yes!" Peyton McKean replied enthusiastically to two newcomers, Henry George and Franky Squalco. "An archeological site of the first magnitude!"

"I don't know about no magnitudes," George chuckled. "I just came to see the old village."

"Here it is in all its glory." Ann gestured at the dark waterlogged wood lying all around her.

"Hallelujah!" George replied. "This place almost looks familiar. It's in my family's legends, you know."

"How did you guys get here?" Leon interjected. "So many roads are still blocked."

George pointed a thumb at his companion. "Franky's got a four-wheel-drive pickup. A regular dune buggy, when it has to be."

Franky gestured at the old, rusted, blue Ford truck parked near McKean's Lexus. "She'll go just about anywhere."

"I'm glad to see you fellows are doing all right," McKean said.

"Sure, we are," said George. "Staying with Franky's aunt, Clara Seaweed. Best food I ever ate, earthquake or no."

"She's on a hill a ways up the Duwamish River," Franky explained. "Not too far from the Duwamish Longhouse. Power's still out, but she cooks in her back yard with split firewood, the old way. Big pots of Indian-style salmon soup with veggies from her garden.

"Dee-licious!" George rubbed his belly. "Franky nets a bunch of big salmon every day, and Clara cooks 'em. Between Franky and her, they're keeping the whole neighborhood fed."

"As long as the gas holds out for my dinghy."

"Even if it doesn't, Franky. There's plenty of young bucks

at the Duwamish Longhouse that'll take you out to your nets in one of their canoes."

"Earthquake didn't stop the salmon running," Franky said. "I think it might have brought more of 'em. Folks do the salmon dance at the Longhouse every evening. So, maybe Shuq Siab told the salmon people they should send more food."

"That's an amazing story," said Ann. "Considering the city as a whole is desperate for supplies."

"Indian people have their ways of getting by," George explained. "Always did. Salish Sea is our supermarket. It's our highway too. All them canoes that was on Elliott Bay, they all got home, even if the freeway was out. Paddled back to Suquamish, or Tulalip, or Nisqually, or wherever they came from. Ain't no bridges out when you got a canoe and a strong back."

George glanced at the remains of the village. "Hoo-wee! A lot of my people used to live here, looks like."

"A lot died here," Franky suggested.

"Some died, some lived." George let out a husky laugh. "Otherwise I wouldn't be here."

Franky mused, "I think A'yahos is telling us something. It was a bad time for Indian people when these longhouses got knocked down. Maybe it was a punishment for something. This time's different. These old houses are seeing the light of day again, and the skyscrapers are falling. Eldon Devine and his Emerald Tower, they're gone. But Clara Seaweed and her little one-story house are still here."

"Yeah!" George agreed. "That Devine guy, he was too high and mighty. Long time ago, Old Man House at Suquamish was the biggest house ever built by our people. It was prt'near eight hundred feet long—but it was only one story tall!"

"So, it would have been shaken badly by this earthquake," McKean suggested, "but it wouldn't have gone down."

"That's right! But Devine's tower was as tall as Old Man House was long. If a man's so proud he's gotta build a place that stretches all the way up to the clouds, then maybe that's too tall. Maybe when he got so far away from the earth, he lost his connection to the soil. He didn't keep his feet on the ground no more. So A'yahos knocked him and his building down."

"You're suggesting people need to stay in touch with the earth physically?"

"Yep! That's why my people used to go around barefoot—to keep in touch with Mother Earth. By the way, over at Suquamish, so I hear, the House of Awakened Culture came through the quake and the wave just fine. They set up a community shelter there for folks whose houses got wrecked. Don't matter if they're pahstud or native. Everybody's welcome."

"They're taking in the tired and the hungry," Ann said. "Just like in your canoe-greeting ceremony."

"Sure. And another thing. When pahstuds burnt Old Man House in the 1890s, they burnt away their own history, not just my people's history. They burnt away the traditions of how we lived on this land. Back then a house was a living thing. It had its stories and its traditions. Pahstuds thought they could burn it down and forget it. But you know what they say about history."

"Those who cannot remember the past," Ann said, "are condemned to repeat it."

"That's right. My people learned about earthquakes and tsunamis the hard way, when our villages were destroyed at Alki and West Points. But the pahstuds wouldn't listen to our old stories, so now they've learned the hard way too."

"Speaking of learning," McKean gazed over the sunken village. "I think I understand something that hadn't made sense until now."

"What's that?" George asked.

McKean raised a thin forefinger. "I believe I can explain the mystery of this village's impossibly low elevation."

"And the answer is—?" Leon prompted.

"Eleven hundred years ago, the land south of the point rose up and over the north side, just as it has done now. That threw the land out of equilibrium, so it settled down over centuries until the forces within the earth were in balance again."

"I see!" said Leon. "The village wasn't below sea level when the AD 900 quake struck. It was forced down afterwards."

"The ocean didn't rise so much," McKean explained, "as

the land sank and was filled with beach sand. I'm sure that's what will happen again over the next few decades. In fact, I'd wager there wouldn't be any sand on Alki Beach at all, if it weren't for quakes and subsidence of the land. This beach would be rocky, like the one on the south side of the point."

"If you say so, Doc." George laughed. "All I know is there's a lot uncovered here that people should pay attention to."

"For instance?"

"The way people used to make their homes low and humble and close to the ground. Didn't build nothing taller than a tree. Shuq Siab and the S'kellelaitu don't like people reaching for the sky. If you get your head in the clouds, then along comes A'yahos to shake the ground and knock your house down. But if you're humble and live near the earth, you'll be okay. That is, if you build your place up on a hill a little ways in case a wave comes. Then the forest will keep you safe and the sea will nourish you."

After a pause, Franky asked, "Any other questions, Peyton McKean, my friend?"

McKean shrugged. "For once, I'm all out of questions."

"That's good," said George. "Sometimes, Native wisdom gets the last word."

###

Please Write a Reader Review!

If you enjoyed this book, please write a reader review on the website of the bookseller from whom you obtained it. Reviews and star ratings help other readers find great books, and they help authors get the word out about their stories. Simply go to this web page: www.thomas-hopp.com/blog, where you will find a link to a page with all of Thomas P. Hopp's books listed in every format. Thanks!

ABOUT THE AUTHOR

Thomas Patrick Hopp routinely imagines the unimaginable. He writes science fiction and mystery thriller novels that draw on his background as a scientist and scholar of the natural world in all its glory and terror. His stories have won multiple literary awards and garnered him a worldwide following. He is a member of both the Mystery Writers of America and the Science Fiction and Fantasy Writers of America and has served for several years as President of the Northwest Chapter of MWA. Tom is also an internationally recognized molecular biologist. He discovered powerful immune-system hormones and helped found the multi-billion-dollar Seattle biotechnology company Immunex Corporation. He advised the team that created Immunex's blockbuster arthritis drug Enbrel. He developed the first commercially successful nanotechnology device, a molecular handle for manipulating proteins at the atomic level, which is used by medical researchers around the world to study human cells and every major microbe known to science.

Tom's NORTHWEST TALES are thrillers set against backdrops of disaster, whether natural or man-made. Earthquakes, eruptions, and asteroid impacts are grist for these gripping adventures. Tom's mystery stories follow Dr. Peyton McKean, a super-intelligent sleuth known as "The Greatest Mind Since Sherlock Holmes." Viruses, microbes, and evil geniuses form the core of his opposition. Tom's DINOSAUR WARS science fiction stories read like "Star Wars meets Jurassic Park." Featuring laser-blasting space invaders and huge beasts from the past, they follow Yellowstone Park naturalist Chase Armstrong and Montana rancher's daughter Kit Daniels, who struggle to survive in a world where dinosaurs live again. Most of Tom's tumultuous adventures are suitable for readers young and old.

JOIN TOM'S EMAILING LIST

If you would like to receive email alerts whenever Tom publishes a new story or attends an author event, go to this web page: www.thomas-hopp.com/blog, where you will find a link to a sign-up form.

ACKNOWLEDGMENTS

Let me preface the following thank-yous with a simple statement. *None* of these experts in any way encouraged me to write such a dramatic, worst-case scenario. The magnitude of events described here are one-hundred-ten percent my own choice. Most experts advised caution in predicting how severe an event might be. But on cross-examination, most allowed that there might be worse possibilities than they had been talking about—or training for. As my research progressed, I realized that even experts can find it hard to admit just how bad things could get.

That said, my thanks go especially to *Seattle Times* reporter Sandi Doughton, whose recent book on earthquake risks in the Pacific Northwest, *Full-Rip 9.0*, served as a major inspiration for my tale. Furthermore, her in-depth reporting in a series of "Seismic Neglect" articles in the Seattle Times heightened my awareness of risks Northwesterners face. She's a reporter who looks hard facts squarely in the eye. I would also like to acknowledge invaluable help given by Bill Steele, outreach Director at the Pacific Northwest Seismic Network, who provided copious information on Seattle-area earthquakes, faults, and seismology. Vasily Titov of NOAA's Center for Tsunami Research provided a time-lapse film model of a tidal wave striking Seattle after a quake. My thanks also go to University of Washington Applied Mathematics Professor Randy LeVeque, who shared further models of tsunamis that might strike Seattle. Other major sources of information and assistance were Captain Gene Davis of the Coast Guard Museum NW, Colonel Randolph Petgrave III, JAG, Joint Base Lewis-McChord, Kristin Tinsley, Public Information Officer of the Seattle Fire Department, Lieutenant Robert Kerns, Captain of the Fireboat Leschi, and Captain Cody Scriver, SFD Emergency Preparedness Officer. Numerous people have described their personal experience with earthquakes, and I myself have lived through the terrifying events of the Seattle Earthquake of 1965 and the Nisqually Earthquake of 2001. Cecile Hansen and Ken Workman, descendants of Chief

Seattle, generously shared Duwamish Tribal lore about earthquakes and natural disasters of the past.

I made frequent reference to public documents including the Seattle Disaster Readiness and Response Plan of November 13, 2012, issued by the Seattle Office of Emergency Management; the King County Comprehensive Emergency Management Plan of December 2013; the information websites of the King County Emergency Coordination Center and State Emergency Operations Center; and the Safeco Field Emergency Response Plan of 2016. I also studied National Oceanic and Atmospheric Administration publications regarding models of earthquakes and tsunamis on the Seattle Fault (NOAA Technical Memoranda OAR PMEL-124 and -132).

I am indebted to all these people and agencies for information used to put this story together. Any discrepancies are my own responsibility and in no way should be attributed to my sources. Lastly, I'd like to thank Jim Thomsen for his excellent editorial eye.

BOOKS BY THOMAS P. HOPP

Available in ebook and paperback versions

The NORTHWEST TALES Series

Rainier Erupts!
The Great Seattle Earthquake

The DINOSAUR WARS Series

Earthfall
Counterattack
Blood On The Moon
Dinosaur Tales

Peyton McKean Mysteries

The Smallpox Incident
The Neah Virus

Short Stories

The Treasure of Purgatory Crater
A Dangerous Breed
Blood Tide
The Ghost Trees
The Re-Election Plot

Made in the USA
Las Vegas, NV
21 October 2022

57848437R00159